Catfish in Paradise

LOVE, LIES, AND CATFISH
BOOK TWO

JOI JACKSON

Catfish in Paradise

A Love, Lies, and Catfish Novel

JOI JACKSON

First published by Purple Peacock Press 2024

Cover Designer: 100Covers.com

Editor: Aubrey Spivey

First edition

Paperback ISBN: 978-1-960485-15-1

EBook ISBN: *978-1-960485-04-5*

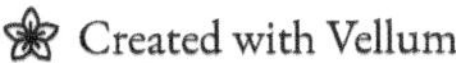 Created with Vellum

Catfish Defined

A catfish is someone who creates a false online identity. Catfishing is common on social networking and online dating sites. Sometimes a catfish's sole purpose is to engage in a fantasy. Sometimes, however, the catfish's intent is to defraud a victim, seek revenge, or commit identity theft.

-From whatis.com

CHAPTER 1

Aja

"Hi Mrs. Schmidt, this is Aja Lewis from Exposé returning your call." Aja pushed her earbud deeper into her ear, straining to hear the woman speaking.

"Yes, ma'am, we look into dating and internet scams. Do you believe someone is trying to scam you or a loved one?"

Aja, late for work and irritated, strode into the elevator headed toward the suite of her firm, Exposé, trying to smile her way into a better mood. She was speaking to a potential client and struggling to not sigh heavily. Maybe it was time to cave in and get an assistant to handle calls like these.

"Oh, you're looking for a date for an event?" She lifted a brow while pressing the button for her floor. She was not running an escort service. "No, ma'am, unfortunately, we don't provide dating services. We investigate online dating mates."

She wanted to rub her temples but that would have to wait. This wasn't the first call they'd received about matchmaking services lately. She had recently done a session at a lifetime learning center for seniors on romance scams, where con artists targeted people online seeking relationships and convinced their victims to send them money or gift cards. Aja had provided her contact info during the session and now she was fielding tons of strange requests like the one from Mrs. Schmidt.

Aja glanced at the time on her smartwatch. "No, Mrs. Schmidt, I don't recommend finding a date for your event on gregslist.com," she scanned her memory of the event. "You came to the session with your girlfriends, right? Those two women that were sitting with you?" She remembered them because they were the main ones asking about the best dating apps for women their age. "What if you made a girls' night out of it and took them? You might meet someone there."

Mrs. Schmidt declared her a genius and promised to call her girlfriends. Aja wished her well and reminded her again not to seek love on a free-for-all website. She sighed, tapping in the door code for her suite.

As soon as she entered, one of the maintenance men strode over to her. "Ms. Lewis, we're gonna need to turn the water off in the building in a few minutes. I'm giving everyone a heads-up."

"Turn the water off?" Aja replied, her eyebrows knitting together in a frown. "For how long?"

The maintenance man shrugged, a sheepish grin on his face, "Not sure, ma'am. Could be a few hours. The main line's got some issues."

Aja pressed her lips together, fighting back a groan. She had several important meetings lined up today, and the thought of a waterless office was far from appealing.

She should probably send everyone home to work. "How long do we have before it goes off?"

The man glanced around. "Until I get back downstairs and inform the crew, so about fifteen minutes."

"Thank you," she managed to say before the man wandered off to deliver the news to the next office.

Aja made a beeline to her cousin London's office. She would have London send out an email to everyone.

London was in charge of onboarding clients and Aja trusted London to make sure each client was taken care of once they signed up for Exposé's services. She'd hired London last year after her cousin had moved back to Atlanta from DC.

"London, I swear, it's always something in this fucking building," she huffed. "Now the water in the building is going off in about ten minutes. Can you..." The words died off as Aja stopped short in the doorway of London's office, staring at London's wide-eyed panic and faux smile plastered to her face. London's head tilted slightly, communicating they were not alone.

Aja stepped cautiously into London's office. There was a huge man seated across from London, his long fingers supporting his chin. His deep brown eyes met hers as she scanned her brain frantically. Had she scheduled an appointment with a potential client this early? Was he an applicant for one of the two contractor positions they needed to fill?

Breaking eye contact, she took in the man's attire. He was dressed in business casual wear: a button-down shirt and dark jeans. Too formal to be a developer looking for his next gig and too casual to be interviewing for a permanent job. She crossed job applicant off her mental list.

Pushing her glasses up on her face, Aja frowned. Did she know this man? She couldn't see his facial features very clearly.

She normally wore contact lenses to correct her astigmatism, but she had ripped a lens and had to resort to wearing her glasses while she waited for replacements. The lenses were thick; she could barely see her hand in front of her face with uncorrected vision. She swore she'd get her damn eyeglass prescription updated as soon as she could get an appointment with her eye doctor. This was ridiculous.

London stood, clearing her throat, interrupting Aja's thoughts. "Aja, good morning," she said brightly. "This is Del... Del Parris?" She looked at the man, who stood up quickly.

London motioned at Aja. "Del, this is my cousin Aja Lewis. She's the one you're looking for."

"Did we have an appointment, Mr. Parris?" Aja asked slowly, mentally reviewing her calendar for the morning.

"No. I was hoping to get a few moments of your time before you started your day." He shoved his hands in his pockets.

She blinked, distracted by the rhythmic flow of his voice. He was from somewhere in the Caribbean, she guessed, and spoke deliberately with an accent that sounded like he should be doing voiceovers for an island resort. She could see him charming unsuspecting women with that velvety deep voice.

Aja's frown deepened. If this man were selling something, she did not care what, she would point him to the door immediately. But he didn't give off the vibe of a salesperson. "Okay, I normally don't take walk-ins. And we don't allow solicitations in this building."

London's eyes got wide again, and Aja got the impression she had said the wrong thing.

Del nodded. "Right."

He turned to her, impatience in his eyes and stance. She considered him to be taller than the average man and a bit arrogant, if she were being honest. "Ms. Lewis, might I speak to you in private?"

Something about his tone had her on high alert. "What's this about?" she asked, feeling her hackles rise.

Del's eyes slid to London. "Your mother," he said, turning back to Aja.

Aja put a hand on her chest. "My mother? Do you mean my former stepmother?" She glanced at London for clarification. Maybe they had talked before she came in. But London looked as puzzled as she was.

"Diana Lewis is your birth mother, correct?"

Aja nodded slowly. "Yes, but I haven't seen her since she took off when I was five. What about her?"

Again, Del eyed London. "It would be better if we spoke in private, Ms. Lewis."

Whatever this man had to say, Aja figured she might need a

witness. Aja sighed, turned, and closed the door to London's office. "My mother is London's aunt, so whatever this is about, my cousin can hear it too. She stays."

Del regarded Aja and after a beat, motioned toward the empty seat next to him. "Please take a seat."

Aja started to protest; this was her company, and some smooth voiced stranger was not going to direct her to sit if she didn't want to sit. But something in his demeanor made her comply. He sounded grave and she sensed she would not like what he had to say. She smoothed her knee length pencil skirt and sat, crossing her legs at the ankles.

Del took his seat again. "I apologize if I'm intruding," he said, looking at both women in turn.

"What about my mother? What's this about?" Aja asked, her patience running thin. She didn't have time for small talk. She needed to give everyone in the office a heads-up about the water.

He let out a breath. "Your mother was living as an expat in Barbados. I'm sorry to inform you that she passed away last week. You are listed as the sole beneficiary in her will."

London gasped, raising a hand to her mouth.

Aja froze. She wasn't sure how she was supposed to react to hearing this news. She blinked, realizing her heart was still beating rapidly. What did this mean? Her mother was gone?

"How did she die?" Aja asked, slipping into investigator mode.

"From what I've been told, she was out on her boat and it capsized and she drowned."

Aja nodded. "Is that where you're from, Barbados?"

He bowed his head. "Originally, but I live here in Atlanta now."

That explained the accent but not why he was here telling her about her mother. Aja adjusted her glasses so she could see him clearly. Her mother was living in Barbados and had a boat. And she had left everything to Aja. She could not wrap her head around the concept of her mother's life in another country. She would put a pin in that for the moment. "And you were what exactly to my mother?"

She waited for his response and resisted the urge to tap her foot impatiently.

Del sighed. "Your mother named me the executor of her will." He paused for a beat. "I was also her life coach."

Aja arched an eyebrow then looked at London, who sat in rapt attention, taking everything in.

Her mother had to be close to this man if she had designated him to handle her affairs. But how close were they?

"Her life coach?" London asked before Aja jumped in. "But she lived in Barbados?"

Del nodded. "She did. Most of my clients are here but she convinced me to take her on during the pandemic. She'd met my aunt Felicity, who introduced us."

He smiled as he said this, and Aja's radar went off. That smile was intimate, indicating there was more than a business relationship there. She had been in business for over four years and she'd yet to smile about any of her clients like that.

Aja sat back with her arms crossed. "Okay, you're her coach and the executor of her will. As I said, I haven't seen her in about thirty years. I didn't even know she was alive, let alone that she had a life in another country." She eyed him. "Did you know she had a family she left behind?"

His nod was reluctant. "Yes, we talked about it, and I urged her to reach out to you, but she resisted, saying it was too late."

Aja snorted. "It was. Way too late."

Del's eyes held an undeniable sympathy. "I understand that this is a lot to take in," he said, breaking the silence that had fallen over the office. "Diana talked about you often. She was very proud of you."

"Do you know if she had any other family?" Aja asked. Surely there was someone else that would want her mother's assets, whatever they were.

"She wasn't married and you are her only child."

"And I've inherited what exactly?" she asked, back to the business at hand.

"Your mother had a house in Holetown, Barbados as well as a glass studio there. Plus, her bank accounts." He paused. "And the boat."

Del sat back, watching Aja.

She blinked back at him, fully assessing him for the first time since she'd realized he was looking for her. His head was bald, and he sported a closely trimmed beard, his skin the color of rich mahogany wood, reminded her of a boy she'd liked in middle school who told her she was dark and ugly. She narrowed her eyes at Del. He did look a lot like that jerk. But that boy was from East Point. Not the same person at all.

"I don't want anything to do with my mother's assets," she said finally. "She wanted nothing to do with my father and me so..." she let the words trail.

Del looked taken aback, but quickly recovered. "I understand that this situation is challenging for you, but your decision shouldn't be rushed."

Aja leaned forward in her chair, her arms folded. "Why are you here? What's in it for you?" Her voice rose with each word.

Del lifted his hands in a placating gesture. "I am just trying to fulfill my duty as the executor of your mother's will. She wanted you to have her possessions," he said, shifting uncomfortably under Aja's intense gaze.

Aja sighed. She didn't have time to think about any of this. She had a business to run, and she needed to get a new set of contact lenses as soon as humanly possible.

She stood. "Thank you for letting me know in person about my mother, Mr. Parris. If you have a business card, I'll take that and pass it along to my legal counsel so they can coordinate the estate matters."

He remained seated.

Aja frowned, looking over at London, who, taking the hint, stood as well.

Del didn't budge. "I understand this is a lot to process, but I would prefer if we could discuss this further before involving lawyers."

Aja was polite but firm. "I'm sorry, but I have a business to run, and I really don't want to waste any more time discussing this with you."

Del sighed and finally stood up. He towered over Aja's petite frame, but she held her ground, refusing to look up at him.

Finally, she gave up, curiosity getting the best of her. She watched as Del's lips pursed ever so slightly, like he was struggling to hold his tongue. "I'll let you get back to your work."

He reached into his laptop bag and fished out a business card for Aja, then one for London. Aja read the card. Delford Parris, Certified Life and Spiritual Coach.

She smirked. Not only was he a coach but he was a spiritual coach as well? That saying about a sucker being born every minute had to keep him in business.

She held up his card. "So, what exactly does a certified spiritual coach do, Delford?"

"It's Del. I help people figure out their spiritual health. That doesn't mean that people become religious fanatics after working with me. I help them understand the role spirituality plays in their lives."

Aja could not help but roll her eyes.

"By the look on your face, Ms. Lewis, it doesn't appear that you are a believer."

"I don't believe in any of that," Aja said. "You do palm readings and tarot cards and all that, right?"

"No, none of that." Del shook his head, amused. Aja got the distinct impression that he was laughing at her.

She nodded, placing the card he'd given her in her pocket. "Well, good luck."

Del looked like he had something to say but thought better of it. He looked toward the door.

She wanted to sigh in relief. Finally.

Aja moved quickly, ready to open it and shove the man out.

"It would behoove you, Ms. Lewis, to come to Barbados yourself as soon as you can to protect your mother's interests."

"Do you have a copy of her will or any other documentation proving what you say?" she challenged.

Del reached into his bag and pulled out a folder. He handed a stapled stack of papers to her.

"This is a copy of the application I filed for the Grant of Probate," he explained. "It will probably take about three months for it to be approved, but in the meantime, we should ensure the house and her other assets are secure."

Aja took the papers begrudgingly, giving them a cursory glance. They were filled with legal jargon and property details that made her head spin.

She didn't like his use of the word 'we.' She had no plans to go to Barbados.

"I hear it's about eighty degrees year-round there," London said wistfully. "Aja, you should go."

Aja glanced out the window at the cold, dreary February day. Eighty-degree weather sounded like heaven right then.

But she shook her head, handing the papers back to Del. "My plate is already full. Honestly, it's overflowing right now."

Del put the papers back in their folder and regarded her for a moment, a knowing smile on his face. "You're only given as much as you can handle, Aja."

He was using her first name now, she noted. The words struck a nerve, and she clenched her fists by her side. She did not need spiritual platitudes right now. She needed practical solutions.

"I can't. I've got to get more contractors in so that we can finalize our app. And as you probably noticed, we've run out of space and I need to find a bigger office location," she threw a frustrated arm up. "There's no way I can just drop everything and deal with my mother's estate."

Del stuck a finger on his lips in contemplation, drawing Aja's attention to them. They were full, the top lip darker than the bottom and for a split second, Aja was mesmerized by them, picturing him running his tongue over his bottom lip in anticipation.

"Give it some thought." He bowed slightly as he left the office. "I'll be in touch."

Pushing her glasses up, Aja watched his confident gait as he left the office. He struck her as a man used to getting his way.

Well, she wasn't going to fall for any of his spiritual nonsense. And she wasn't going to Barbados.

CHAPTER 2

Del

The weekend after he'd made that unsuccessful trip to Aja Lewis's office, Del glanced in the full-length mirror outside his closet door. He was dressed in a sharp black tuxedo, crisp white dress shirt, and a black satin bow tie. Tugging at his lapels, he had to admit he looked good.

Del moved around his house, gathering the necessary items for the night. His black patent leather shoes clicked softly against the hardwood floor. He collected his keys, wallet, and phone, stowing them away in the inner pockets of his jacket. His eyes swept over the well-kept space, rich brown leather furniture contrasting starkly against the clean white walls. Picking up a black silk handkerchief from the coffee table, he neatly folded it into his breast pocket.

But if he had his way, he'd rather be at home tonight, reclining in his favorite chair, reading and listening to good music. He glanced outside. Tonight the skies were clear but there was a bite in the air and the temperature would dip down into the low twenties. Even though Del had lived in Atlanta since he was a teen, he still hadn't quite acclimated to the cold weather. He loathed the cold.

As he checked his watch, Del realized it was already seven-thirty and he was running late. He quickly grabbed his black wool coat and scarf then stepped out into the cold February night.

The chill immediately hit him, causing him to shiver. He pulled his coat tighter around himself and wrapped the scarf around his neck.

His phone rang as he pulled out of his driveway. Hitting the phone icon to answer, Del said "Yes, Andre, I've left the house. I'll be there shortly."

"I'm just checking to make sure you're still going. I know it's cold outside and all."

"I told Mia I'd attend and I'm going," Del replied.

He could hear the smile in her voice as she responded. "You're nothing if not a man of your word, Del. I'll be waiting."

He navigated the evening traffic with ease borne of years living in Atlanta's pulsing sprawl.

"You'll be outside?" he asked, knowing the answer.

Andre gave a little snort. "Please. It's too cold out and this dress I'm wearing leaves little to the imagination. Just call me when you pull up and I'll sprint out."

"Ah, so you're on the prowl tonight?"

"Yes, sir. You know Operation Rich Husband is in full swing. I figure since your client is a reality star, she should know plenty of eligible bachelors."

Del laughed, a deep rumbling sound that conveyed both his amusement and skepticism. "Good luck with that. Just don't let the hunt distract you from having fun."

"I never forget to have fun, darling," Andre assured him, her voice teasing through the phone's speaker. "We are going to turn heads tonight, you and I."

"I'm sure you will. I'm there to show my support. That's it."

"You're such a Debbie Downer! You'll have a great time, I promise, and if not, we'll cut out early and hit the Varsity."

Del snorted. "What are you, twenty? Hard no for me, I can't eat like that late at night anymore."

"Oh Grampa...lighten up!" Andre laughed. "Anyway, I gotta finish getting dressed. See you in a few."

Del could picture her now at her apartment: dressed to kill, makeup flawlessly applied, and an eager sparkle in her eye. It was all part of the game, and nobody played it better than Andre.

He swung his car around the familiar streets near where Andre lived, passing the street art that turned everyday buildings into canvases.

Pulling up by Andre's building, he dialed her number as promised, announcing his arrival with a curt, "I'm outside."

"You're my knight with heated leather seats," she teased before hanging up.

He shook his head, smiling despite himself. Within moments she emerged from the building's entrance, a blur of confidence and curves in a short, dazzling emerald green dress that skimmed her thighs.

The dress hugged her figure in all the right places and Del felt sorry for the men in Andre's sights. With a mane of chocolate curls tumbling over her shoulders and a deep red lipstick that accentuated her full lips, Andre could've graced the cover of any magazine that crossed Del's coffee table.

He stepped out to open the door for her.

"You look stunning," he said, as Andre slid into the passenger seat with grace.

She flashed him an appreciative smile, one that held both warmth and mischief. "And you, Del, look like you've stolen this tuxedo from a Bond movie set. I approve."

Andre wasted no time in adjusting the mirror to check her appearance, tucking a stray lock of hair behind her ear with a practiced motion. "What's Mia Germaine like in real life? I've only seen her on TV."

"Mia's...intense. But nothing like her TV persona. She's so driven to succeed on her own terms and she has a big heart but doesn't want anyone to know it," Del said thoughtfully. "I think you'll like her."

"So she's not a back-stabbing bitch?"

Del shook his head. "Not even close."

The party was being held at a mansion in Buckhead, one of Atlanta's wealthiest neighborhoods. Even though he'd attended plenty of parties like this one before, he always marveled at the massive displays of wealth in the city.

They pulled into the circular driveway and a valet hurried to Del's side. Del handed the man his keys,.

Andre linked her arm with Del's as they approached the grand entrance, her heels clicking on the stone pathway like a metronome dictating their pace. The air held an electric buzz, mingled with the scent of expensive perfume and anticipation. Before them, the mansion loomed large, its windows spilling warm light against the night.

"You ready?" she whispered, her breath visible in the cold air.

"As I'll ever be," Del replied, squeezing her arm reassuringly.

They were greeted at the door by a hostess draped in black satin, her smile practiced but not reaching her eyes. She ticked their names off on her list and handed them each a flute of champagne from a passing waiter's silver tray.

As Del and Andre made their way through the foyer and into the living room, Del took in the opulence of the mansion. The walls were adorned with original artwork and Del immediately thought of Diana, his former client. She would have appreciated the bold art that made the space come alive. He couldn't believe Diana was gone.

When he'd learned from his aunt that she'd died and he was named as executor of her will, he was shocked.

It was a tragedy that she had passed away, especially since she was so young. He thought about her often and how much he'd enjoyed their sessions. Since she was living in Barbados, they did video calls and Diana always had a funny story to share when he greeted her. She had been one of his favorite clients, and he had helped her through some tough times.

Andre nudged him, breaking him out of his musings. "You

know any of these people?" Del scanned the room. The guests were a mix of older Atlanta socialites and younger, trendier types.

Del eyed Andre. "I know a few faces. But looks like you've got plenty potential victims to choose from."

She swatted his arm. "Ha ha. I might need you to get lost for a bit."

Del spotted his client, Mia Germaine, in the corner of the room surrounded by a group of admirers. She was radiant in a brushed gold strapless jumpsuit, her neck and wrists glittering with diamonds. Her blonde highlighted hair was swept up on top of her head in a sculpted mass of curls.

"Delford! I'm so glad you made it! I know you don't like the cold." She air kissed his cheeks.

"Happy Birthday, Mia," Del said then turned to Andre. "This is my good friend Andre. This is Mia Germaine."

"Oh, aren't you stunning! Del, where have you been hiding her?" Mia sized the other woman up.

"We're friends, it's not like that," he held up a card and a small wrapped gift. "Where should I put this?"

"Ah, thank you but you didn't have to get me anything," she chided, taking the items. "Make yourselves at home. But stay put for a sec, I have someone I want you to meet who needs your services."

Before Del could stop her, Mia was off.

Del watched Mia disappear into the throng of party-goers, leaving him and Andre to take stock of their surroundings. Most of the crowd had broken off into smaller groups, drinking and chatting amongst themselves.

Andre took a sip of her champagne. "Quite the spectacle, isn't it?" she mused, her eyes dancing with reflected light.

"It's Mia's style," Del said. "Showy, but not without substance."

Del sipped his champagne and took in the opulence of the mansion. The polished marble floors, the crystal chandeliers, and the intricate moldings on the ceiling. The place was decorated in gold, pink and black with the number forty on the tablescapes. It was clear that Mia had spared no expense for her milestone birthday.

He had to look no further than the woman being dragged over to him by Mia.

"Del, this is Aja Lewis, Aja, this is my life coach, Delford Parris! He has worked miracles in my life! You must hire him."

Del watched as Aja sized Andre up then their eyes met. Aja smirked. "Actually, Mia, we know each other." She turned to him. "Hello, Del."

"Hello again. Aja, this is my friend Andre." Del said, turning toward Aja.

Andre shot Del a look then extended her hand to Aja. "Nice meeting you."

Aja looked good, Del had to admit. The glasses and scowl were gone and she seemed at ease with herself. Aja wore a fitted sequined cocktail dress in a ravishing navy blue. The dress hit just above the knee and hit her curves in all the right places. His gaze traveled back up to her berry colored lips, lingering for a beat.

"Aja, it's good to see you again," he said, offering his hand to shake hers.

As soon as his hand made contact with Aja's skin there was that spark - subtle, almost imperceptible, but undeniably there. The brief contact sent an unexpected shiver through him, and he could tell by the quick rise of her eyebrows that she felt it too. But as quickly as it came, it was gone, replaced by her cool facade.

"Likewise," Aja replied smoothly, her voice betrayed none of the electricity that had just passed between them.

Mia clapped her hands together, oblivious to the awkward tension between Del and Aja. "Well, we'll skip all the small talk since you two know each other. Aja, Del. Is. Amazing. Sis, I tell you what, he's helped me in so many ways, you have no idea."

Aja raised an eyebrow. "Oh really? What ways are those, Mia?"

"He helped me see that pivoting my career was what I needed to do to get to the next level! Reality TV has opened up a ton of doors for me." She looped her arm through Del's. "All thanks to this man right here."

Del stroked his beard, trying not to fidget. He wasn't entirely comfortable with all of the praise Mia heaped upon him.

Aja nodded slowly. "Interesting."

"More than interesting," Mia patted his arm. "He's changed my whole outlook on life. And I have no doubt he can do the same for you."

Tilting her head, Aja studied Del for a moment before speaking again. "I'm glad it's working out for you but I'm good on the coaching thing right now. I prefer to deal in reality, not trust the universe."

Del couldn't say whether it was the dismissive tone or her words that offended him but something in him snapped.

"Oh yeah? Based on the controlled chaos I saw at your office, you have some limiting beliefs holding your business back." The words shot out before he could reign them in.

Andre's eyes widened, and even Mia seemed taken aback by the blunt assessment. Andre gave Del's arm a subtle, cautionary squeeze, but he ignored it, his eyes on Aja.

Aja's lips parted slightly as her composed facade wavered for a fraction of a second before slipping firmly back into place.

"I see," Aja said coolly, taking a step closer into Del's personal space. "And you gathered all this from one visit?"

Del straightened up, meeting her intensity. "I don't need long to identify patterns. It's what I do."

Mia looked between them, seeming to sense the tension. "Is this a party or what? You two can discuss business on Monday. Have more champagne and mingle," she grabbed two more flutes from a passing server and shoved them at Del and Aja. Del hadn't finished his first glass.

Aja took the flute with a thin smile. "Thank you, Mia," Aja said, though her attention was clearly focused on Del, who accepted the extra glass with a nod.

"Maybe I'll take that under advisement," she said, lifting the flute in a mock salute before sipping.

Del watched Aja, wondering what thoughts were ticking behind those sharp eyes. Andre leaned in, her voice low. "Play nice...we don't want to be the talk of the party."

But Del couldn't help himself. He was always pushing, always digging deeper to uncover what lay beneath the surface. The truth was, he found Aja intriguing–a puzzle that beckoned. Her defensive walls were high and well-maintained, but he had seen something in her, a flicker of something more during their brief connection.

"I'll remember that," Del replied to Andre, without taking his eyes off Aja.

Mia's voice broke the intense standoff as she motioned at one of the passing photographers. "Let's get a group photo, everyone! Del, Aja, you're in this!"

Before he could protest, Del was being nudged into position by Mia's strong arms. Andre stood on his other side, her presence a comforting buffer between him and Aja, who was positioned awkwardly close to him for the photo op.

"Say 'Forty is fabulous!'" Mia chirped, raising her glass in celebration as the photographer readied the camera.

Aja leaned slightly toward Del for the photo, her perfume mingling with the air between them. The moment was fleeting, but again that spark flickered, sending another jolt through him. He managed to put on a polite smile just as the camera flashed.

The jazz band ended their set and a DJ cranked up a mash-up of hip-hop songs from the nineties. Mia screeched, raising her hand. "Yassss...y'all come dance with me! It's my birthday!" She beckoned to no one in particular. Grabbing the arm closest to her, she pulled Andre toward the DJ tables and a makeshift dance floor.

Andre shrugged at Del and let Mia lead her away.

Del watched the pair with a smirk on his face. Mia, giddy from too much champagne, was tottering on her heels.

He turned to Aja. "Hey, I shouldn't have come at you like that. I hope you'll accept my apology."

She lifted an arched eyebrow at him. "No harm done. People have said worse about my business."

They stood there silently watching the dance floor.

Del couldn't help himself. "Wanna dance?"

An expression he couldn't read crossed her face. "No thanks."

Del's smirk faltered but didn't disappear. "Suit yourself," he said with a shrug that was a little too casual to be genuine. He lingered for a moment, watching as Aja took another sip of her champagne, her gaze drifting off toward the dance floor where Mia and Andre were already losing themselves in the music.

He studied her profile. If he didn't know better, he'd swear that was longing on her face. But that didn't make sense. Not with the way she held herself with such determination and self-assurance. Aja seemed the type to go after what she wanted without hesitation. Yet, here she was, watching others find joy in abandonment while she maintained her professional air.

The uncomfortable silence lingered and Del struggled to find a neutral topic. "So, how do you know Mia? Hopefully not as a client."

Aja turned toward him. "I wouldn't tell you if she was, but no, she used to live in our neighborhood and our dads know each other."

Del nodded, taking another sip of his champagne. "Small world."

"Too small," Aja agreed.

The conversation stalled after that. Del sipped his champagne as he studied her. Diana talked about her only child constantly but as she hadn't been around Aja in so long, she hadn't known any other particulars about Aja's life. Del had assumed she'd be more like Diana, outgoing and quick to laugh but Aja was more reserved. He could tell she didn't let people in easily.

"I'm sorry about your mother, Aja. She was a wonderful woman," he said softly.

"I'll have to take your word for it but thank you." She twisted the strap of the evening purse on her shoulder, clearly uncomfortable with the topic.

The silence between them felt heavy and awkward but Del didn't know how to break it. He was usually skilled at charming women but Aja seemed immune to him.

"I can't drop everything and go to Barbados," she blurted.

He heard the frustration and resentment in her voice, knew she was dealing with the weight of her responsibilities.

"I understand that, but it may help you get closure."

Aja frowned, taking a small sip from her own champagne flute. Del noticed the way her eyes lingered on the bubbles before she spoke again.

"I don't think closure is something I can ever really have. Not when it comes to my mother," she said, her voice firm.

"Why not? I know she regretted leaving her family behind but I think the trip will do you some good. And it's a beautiful place. I know I'm biased, but," he shrugged. "I can't help it."

Aja scoffed, rolling her eyes. "Of course you're biased. You're from there."

"Hey, don't knock it until you try it," Del said with a grin. "But seriously, Aja, it'll give you a chance to see where she lived, her studio where she created her art. And it'll give you a chance to say goodbye, properly."

Aja sighed heavily. "I don't know, Del. It's a lot to think about."

"I'm not saying you have to make the decision right now. Just think about it, okay?" Del finished off his champagne and set the glass on a nearby table.

Aja nodded, still deep in thought. Del took the opportunity to study her again. She looked like her mother and when she made certain facial expressions, he swore it was exactly the same as Diana would have made. There was something about her that he found intriguing. He couldn't quite put his finger on it, but he wanted to get to know her better.

Not that he was going to do anything about that. He didn't need any complications in his life right now.

She seemed to sense him pulling away because she told him she was going to the ladies room and he knew it was her polite way of extricating herself from his company.

Del maneuvered his way toward the bar for a refill when he felt a tap on his shoulder. He turned to find Andre flashing him a grin and tugging at his hand. "Let's dance!"

He let her lead him to the center of the floor as the DJ dropped a medley of Outkast hits. Andre turned so her back was to him and started moving in rhythm with the bass line, her movements fluid and full of life. Del found himself feeling the infectious energy of the crowd, the music, and Andre's unapologetic dancing pulling him out of his thoughts about Aja. He matched Andre's enthusiasm, letting go and enjoying the moment.

Then a slow jam came on, changing the vibe of the dance floor. Couples paired up naturally and Andre leaned in close enough for her voice to tickle his ear. "I'm gonna grab another drink." She patted his chest. "You want anything?"

"Actually, I'll come with you," he said, his eyes scanning the room for Aja.

She was nowhere to be seen, likely still in the ladies' room, or maybe she had decided to leave early. Either way, he felt a strange twinge of disappointment as he followed Andre to the bar.

The bartender was a guy in his mid-twenties with a tattoo sleeve and a friendly smile. He nodded at them as they approached. "What can I get for you two?"

"Whiskey on the rocks for me," Andre said, her voice raised slightly over the music.

"Coke with extra ice," Del added, scanning the crowd once more just in case.

The bartender set to work, and as they waited for their drinks, Andre leaned against the bar and looked up at Del with curious eyes. "So, what's up with you and Aja?" she asked bluntly.

He stalled. "Me and Aja? What are you talking about? I just met her a few days ago."

Andre rolled her eyes. "Delford Parris. How long have I known you?"

"Since the hourly wage days at Office Depot," he sighed.

"And since then, you have dated countless women and they all fall into a type...headstrong Type A badasses."

She glanced toward the balcony, where Aja happened to be talking to an older man.

"You gonna stand there and tell me she's not your type?"

"It hasn't exactly worked out for me, has it?" Del pursed his lips. "Besides, I'm not in the market."

Andre snorted, a playful, knowing look in her eyes. "Negro please! You've been watching her like she stole something the whole night." She received her whiskey from the bartender and took a slow sip. "And she sized me up like I was competition when Mia brought her over."

Del accepted his Coke with extra ice and decided to deflect. "Regardless, I'm not acting on it. I have too much going on right now."

"You always have too much going on," Andre pointed out, nudging him gently with her elbow. "It's your go-to excuse. But you just need to find someone that needs you to be that missing piece in her life."

CHAPTER 3

Aja

Aja sat at her desk, surrounded by a stack of resumes and file folders that she was ignoring for the moment. Instead, she'd pulled up Del's YouTube channel and was intently watching his sessions. After the party Saturday night, she couldn't get his words out of her head.

Limiting beliefs.

She'd turned the term round and round, refusing to give it any weight but finding it inching its way into her thoughts at the most inopportune times. Like now when she should be working. It was like a virus, slow-moving but insidious, infecting her with the idea that perhaps she was standing in her own way.

Aja's fingers paused over the keyboard, her eyes fixed on Del as he spoke about personal empowerment and overcoming mental obstacles. His voice was hypnotic, the Bajan accent growing thicker the more passionate he became and she felt herself being pulled in despite her skepticism. She frowned, she'd always thought this woo-woo stuff was a scam. But something about him compelled her to keep watching. She'd watched almost an hour's worth of videos already.

"Is this why you haven't responded to my texts, you've been sucked into a social media rabbit hole?" Zaria Laurent, Aja's best friend and sales manager, quipped from behind her, making Aja jump then swear. She hadn't even heard her approach.

Zaria leaned in. "Hey, I met him. His name is Del something, right? Sexy as sin from Barbados?"

Aja paused the video. "Del Parris," she tried to keep her voice neutral. "When did you meet?"

She waited, assuming Zaria would say that she and Del had dated, or even worse, slept together at some point.

Zaria continued to study the image of Del on the screen.

Aja tried to make light. "Seriously, though, are there any men in Atlanta that you *don't* know?"

Zaria crossed her arms. "Put your claws away. We have a mutual client. Remember Rochelle, the film producer that asked us to check out her billionaire boyfriend?" Aja nodded and Zaria went on. "She's Del's client and she swears by him. She introduced us at one of her release parties. That's how I know him."

Pursing her lips, Aja debated on asking for more dirt on Del, but Zaria would immediately want to know why she was asking.

"You hear that accent? It will curl your toes but I hear he doesn't mess with American women. He was there with some Black Barbie looking woman from Nairobi."

"Hmm...when was this?" Aja feigned casualness.

"Uh, maybe a year or so ago?"

An image of the woman draped over Del at the party popped into Aja's head. "Was her name Andre? Tall, slender, long curly hair?"

Zaria snapped her fingers. "Yes! I remember because it's an unusual name for a woman." She peered at Aja. "Wait, how do you know them?"

"Well, you know as soon as you leave town for any length of time, there's drama. Monday, I had the worst morning ever which started with me waking up late, ruining my last contact lens, my glasses suck, by the way. I don't think I've gotten a new prescription in at least two years, so I couldn't half see anything.

Then, I find out my mother, who apparently lived in Barbados, died and left me everything." Aja folded her hands in front of her laptop.

Zaria blinked. "I was only gone five days! That's...a lot. Why didn't you call me? How did you find out? Aja, you should have called me." She stared at Aja. "Are you...how are you doing?"

Normally, Aja would wave the sentiments away, assuring everyone that she was fine. She wasn't exactly fine but she also wasn't sure how she was supposed to feel about the news. "I'm... still processing, I guess."

Her father and grandmother had served as her parents after her mother left so she would know how to feel then. Beyond some vague memories she held of her mother taking her to run errands, they spent a lot of time at Target, she recalled, Aja's mother was a complete stranger to her.

Zaria sat up in her seat. "When are you heading to Barbados? I assume the service will be there? Or do we need to plan something here?"

Aja was shaking her head as Zaria spoke. "I'm not going anywhere. I'm trying to get an estate lawyer to handle her affairs and sell the property, I guess."

Aja sat back in her chair, defensiveness rising in her. She could tell by Zaria's stare that her friend didn't agree with her decision to leave everything to the lawyers, but she was standing firm.

"I know you don't want to hear this, and I'm saying this because I love you, but I think you should go. It will give you some closure on your relationship with your mother. Maybe you can start to forgive her," Zaria said gently.

"There's nothing to say or do. I've already released her," she said, knowing the words weren't true. Part of her was still that angry, confused little girl who longed for her mother.

Sighing, Zaria raised her hand. "Okay, okay, I'm not trying to pry open any wounds. All I'll say is don't make a decision now. Think about it some more. This trip could be beneficial to you."

Aja crossed her arms.

Zaria nodded, indicating the subject was closed. "I'm here if you need me." She pointed at Aja's laptop. "Now, what does all that have to do with Del Parris?"

Aja relaxed. She knew she needed to deal with her mother but she wouldn't do it right then. "I was getting to that. When I got in, I saw that London was in her office so I stepped in to vent and I was pissed and in full potty mouth mode and there's this man sitting there, apparently waiting for me. I wanted to melt into the carpet."

"What did you say?" Zaria leaned in.

"I wasn't my best self, we'll put it that way."

Zaria hooted then covered her mouth. "Oh wow... so he wasn't a client, I take it?"

"No, it was Del. He was my mother's 'life coach'," Aja put up air quotes. "And he was the one to tell me she passed away," she dropped her arms, still mortified by the whole experience.

"God, Atlanta is small."

"Oh it gets smaller," Aja said, rubbing her arms. "I went to Mia Germaine's fortieth birthday party on Saturday and guess who I ran into?"

Zaria rubbed her hands together. "Let me guess...Del and Andre?"

Aja nodded. "Of course."

Smirking, Zaria crossed one leg over the other. "Funny how DaMia Hogan, the original mean girl we knew from the block, is now Mia Germaine, reality star extraordinaire."

"Right? I'll admit, she's nicer now and Del is her coach. Maybe he can work miracles..."

Zaria's eyes sparkled with interest, a bit of tension from the previous topic easing. "Right? Then what happened?"

Aja paused, recalling the shock of energy she felt when she'd shaken Del's hand and the flicker of disappointment that crossed his face when she turned his offer of a dance down. After she'd returned to the party from the powder room, the DJ switched to a soca mix, sending the dancers into a frenzy of winding and hip grinding. She watched them, her focus on Del and Andre and the fluidity of their movements together. It was almost as if they were having a silent conversation with their bodies. Del moved with confidence and swagger and Andre looked like she'd been born to dance. Aja had felt an unexpected twinge of something akin to envy, though she couldn't fathom why.

That was a lie.

She could never move like Del and Andre. She wasn't going to dance in public and be made fun of.

"Nothing happened," Aja said, pulling herself back to the present and wriggling her shoulders as though she could shake off the memory. "Mia's party was fun. She had a DJ playing old school hip-hop and R&B most of the night. I people watched and drank too much champagne."

Zaria cocked her head to the side. "You spent the night people watching? By yourself?"

"I talked to a few people and of course Mia and her wife. But once the DJ started, that was kind of it for me," Aja replied, a half-smile playing on her lips despite the lurch she felt in her stomach.

Zaria's expression softened. "Aja, you know you're just as amazing as anyone else at that party. And besides, who cares about dancing? You have other talents."

Aja chuckled dryly. "Yeah, like making spreadsheets for everything and creating data models."

"Yes ma'am!" Zaria held up a finger. "And don't forget it. Speaking of data models, you're still coming with me to Black Women LIT, right?"

"Of course. We said we're leaving from here?"

"Yep, it's at the Microsoft office. I'll drive and that'll give you more time to do whatever this is," Zaria motioned at the stacks of folders.

"We need a couple more developers to help Lavender out," she explained. "I like to print the resumes out so I can make notes and have them handy when I do interviews."

Zaria sighed. "Lavender is brilliant and I'm sure she can

handle this, you know? You should just be doing the final review before you make an offer."

Aja nodded, knowing Zaria was right about Lavender's capabilities. Still, she couldn't help but hover and micromanage everything that came her way. It was her company, after all, and every new hire felt like a gamble on its future.

"I know," she pushed the stack of resumes aside. "I just want to make sure we're bringing in the right people. The last two people I brought in were a disaster."

Zaria leaned forward, resting her elbows on Aja's desk. "Look, I get it, but you also need to trust your team. We've got a great thing going here, Aja. And think about it, we might find some potential new hires at this event."

Taking out her phone, Zaria sent out a quick text then motioned at the resumes on Aja's desk. "These are all developers, right? Can I see them?"

Aja scowled. "They aren't going to make sense to you. There's a lot of technical jargon-"

"Trust me please." Zaria cut her off and stuck out her hand.

Aja exhaled and gathered the resumes in a neat stack then handed them to Zaria. "I've made notes already on the first few."

Lavender Vaughn strode in, her expression a mix of concern and curiosity. "You wanted to see me?" The former hacker turned software engineer was a recent Atlanta transplant from the UK.

Aja sat back in her chair. She had to trust her team. "Yep, have a seat."

Lavender nodded, folding her tall, slender frame awkwardly into the low white chair opposite Aja's desk.

"Zaria was just suggesting that I ease off on being so hands-on with the recruiting process," Aja began, shooting her friend a brief glare as she did so.

Zaria held out the stack of resumes. "As you know, we desperately need to get you more help. I think you know best on what we're looking for, so would you mind reviewing these and giving Aja your top picks?"

Lavender's brow arched ever so slightly—a movement that Aja had learned to read as Lavender's curiosity piqued. "And you're okay with that?" she asked Aja coolly, crossing one leg over the other as she settled into the chair beside Zaria.

Aja pursed her lips. Maybe Zaria had a point. "I think it's time we give our current team more responsibility in shaping who joins us next."

Zaria nodded at Aja's words, a triumphant smile spreading across her face. "Yes, teamwork makes the dream work."

Fascinated, Aja watched as Lavender expertly sorted through the resumes, her long fingers tapping against the pages in a rhythmic pattern.

Initially hired to work a six-month contract at Exposé, Lavender was now a full-time employee leading the development team.

After a few minutes, Lavender sat back in her chair and looked up at Aja and Zaria. "Well, these three are definitely promising," she said, pointing to three resumes that were now sitting at the top of one pile.

Aja leaned forward to glance at the names Lavender had singled out, her curiosity getting the better of her cautious approach. "Why those three?" she asked.

"There's a mix of experience here," Lavender explained, tapping the first resume. "Take this one. Jasper has worked with some start-ups, and he's got a real entrepreneurial spirit. Could be good for innovation."

She shifted to the next one. "Elise comes from a corporate background—strong in process and structure. Good counterbalance to Jasper."

Then she paused at the third resume, her eyes lighting up a bit more. "And this one—Kai—has some serious coding chops. Plus, they've been freelancing across multiple platforms and technologies. Agile, adaptive, I'm sure they could come in and hit the ground running."

Aja considered Lavender's assessment. She was good at this;

after all, Aja hadn't been wrong in hiring her. Maybe it was time to let go of the reins a little.

"Okay, I'll schedule interviews with them," Aja said decisively.

Lavender and Zaria exchanged a look that bordered on conspiratorial before Lavender spoke up again.

"How about this? Give me until tomorrow afternoon," Lavender said confidently. "I'll call them first and do a phone screening. By then, I'll know who we should bring in for an in-person meeting."

"Sounds perfect," Aja agreed, relieved and admittedly impressed by how swiftly Lavender had taken charge.

Lavender gathered the chosen resumes and stood up. "I'll get on it first thing tomorrow. And Aja," she paused, holding Aja's gaze, "trust isn't just about believing in your team's abilities. It's also about letting go so they can prove themselves."

Zaria clapped her hands together once Lavender had left the room. "See? Problem solved. Now, let's head out to Black Women LIT and network."

Aja dragged herself into her condo, closing the front door firmly behind her. She loved her home on the top floor of a small midtown Atlanta building but she couldn't enjoy it right now. Dropping her bags and stretching her arms above her head, she just wanted to make a beeline for her room. She and Zaria made some good connections at the event for Black women tech enthusiasts but now she just wanted a hot shower and her bed.

However, just as she was about to head to the bathroom, her phone rang, jolting her back to reality. She considered ignoring it but when she saw it was her grandmother Inez, or Nezzie, as all the grandkids called her, she couldn't just let it go to voicemail.

"Aja, how you holding up, baby girl?" Her grandmother asked, with her Texas twang.

"Nezzie, everything okay?" She asked. "You usually don't call me this late."

"I'm calling to check on you. Now why didn't you tell me your mama passed? London mentioned it and I said, let me call Aja, cause Lord knows, she won't ask for help when she needs it."

Aja sighed at the dig. Her grandmother was worried, she could tell. "I'm okay. They want me to go to Barbados and handle things, but I'm just going to get my lawyer to find someone to represent me there."

"You sure you're alright? She was still your mother, even if she wasn't around. Now, It's okay to not be okay, you don't have to prove you're strong to nobody."

What was she supposed to feel right now? "I'm fine, I guess."

Aja pushed herself up from the bed to grab her water bottle thinking about Diana Lewis. She had vague memories of a mother with long jet black hair. In one instance she was playing in her mother's hair, doing her version of a braid, then her mother shooed her away. She'd thought her mother was the prettiest mom ever.

"Okay, well, you know I'm here if you need me." Nezzie continued. "And, Aja, hear me out. I think you need to go take care of your mama. Just because she left and didn't look back, doesn't mean you shouldn't do the right thing. You're her only child. You should see to it that her body is laid to rest proper."

"How do you know I'm her only child?" Aja placed the bottle on the counter. She needed something stronger to have this conversation but the water would do. "It's not like she sent postcards or emails checking in. She could have a house full of kids."

"Well, your dad told me he wanted more kids, but she said one was enough. I think there's more to that story but you'll have to ask him. He wouldn't tell me much."

Aja's mouth dropped. She stared at the phone. "Why is this the first time I'm hearing all of this?"

Forget the damn water. Aja pulled a bottle of white wine

from a beverage fridge in the large island in her kitchen. The unit allowed her to set the wine at whatever temperature she desired. Best upgrade ever.

"You know how your daddy is. Easier to pry pearls from an oyster than to get him to share his feelings."

Unless those feelings were displeasure, Aja wanted to say but she worked on getting her wine bottle uncorked instead. Her relationship with her father was complicated. She and her half brother, Ash, were, no matter how much effort they exerted, not living up to his idea of their potential.

She knew her father loved her but he never told her he was proud of her. Not after the full academic scholarship to Clark Atlanta University (he was disappointed she hadn't chosen to attend Spelman), or the Young Entrepreneur grant she'd gotten (he thought she should have gone to business school instead) nor had he congratulated her when she was selected as one of Georgia's Forty Under Forty.

She pushed her daddy issues aside for the time being.

"Nezzie," she sighed, staring at the half glass of wine in front of her. "I don't know anything about my mother. I don't want whatever she left me. I don't know what her final wishes were, where she wanted to be buried or if she preferred cremation. I have no idea and Dad has never talked about her with me. She is-was, I mean-a stranger to me."

"She was still your mother," Nezzie said firmly. "Maybe she had her reasons for leaving. Maybe you'll find answers there, maybe not, but you one hundred percent won't find them by sticking your head in the sand and thinking it will all go away. You've always been an inquisitive child, too much for your own good most times, and I know you're going to want closure."

Aja's shoulders slumped. Her grandmother had a point. She had hoped that she could find a lawyer to handle the affairs on her behalf but she hadn't had any luck thus far.

"Baby girl, I know it's a lot, but think about it some tonight." She heard the squeal of her grandmother's favorite recliner and knew the older woman was rising, probably to make herself a cup of tea. "And call me if you need to talk. But call before Blue Bloods. You know I don't talk on the phone while Tom Selleck is on."

"Of course," Aja chuckled, taking a sip of her wine. "I'll think about it."

"Good, that's all I'm asking."

"Bye, Nezzie, I will talk to you tomorrow."

CHAPTER 4

Del strode into Exposé the following workday and noted there was still a stack of boxes in a corner. The outer office was quiet; there was no receptionist at the front desk ready to greet visitors. As he peered closer, the desk looked like it hadn't had an occupant in a while. There was no dust or clutter but it gave off an air of desertion, as if the previous occupant swept everything into a box and carted it away.

He waited, debated on taking a seat in one of two open chairs in the lobby. He chose the seat closest to the entrance. He should have called Aja, but what exactly would he have said? Sorry I blurted that assessment about your business to everyone at the party?

As he sat there, contemplating running out before anyone caught him, he couldn't help but feel guilty about his actions. He'd been in his feelings because Aja had been dismissive of his life's work and he'd needed to prove to her she was wrong.

Now here he was, foolishly sitting in the middle of a deserted space, wondering where everyone was when the smell of food hit him. He groaned. It was lunch time, which explained the absence of people in the office.

He stood and turned to leave, bundling his coat around him. The high temperature that day was only going to hit forty degrees.

Del was retrieving a leather glove he'd dropped when London strode into the lobby, pulling on a deep plum colored peacoat.

"Hey Del, you here to see Aja?" She grinned at him as she buttoned the coat.

Del stuffed the glove into his pocket and straightened up. "Yes, I am, but realized it's lunch time so..." He trailed off, not sure how to finish without sounding even more foolish than he felt.

"About Barbados, right? I think she should go, but that's just me."

London's casual confirmation caught Del by surprise and he nodded. "I was hoping to catch her, maybe give her some additional details on her mother's last wishes." He was trying to convince the wrong person, he realized. "Anyway, I'll save that for her. How are you today? Staying warm?"

"Trying to," London rubbed her hands together. "We're going to brave the cold and try the new Greek restaurant across the street." She motioned toward the window.

He glanced out in the same direction. "I haven't been to that one but I love Greek food. Hope it's good. Is Aja here?"

"She's here, she decided to get her scarf from her car before we head out." London leaned in like she had a secret. "I convinced her to take a lunch break for once." She tilted her head. "You love Greek food, you should join us...I'd love to hear more about Barbados."

He started to politely decline, he was busy, there were other things he could be doing, but before he could say another word, Aja bustled into the lobby, huffing like she'd taken the stairs at full speed.

Her eyes widened when she saw him. "Del?"

"Hey, I was just in the neighborhood," Del lied smoothly, his voice more confident than he felt. He shifted on his feet, then added, "Thought I'd stop by and see if you had made any decisions about your mother's estate."

Del noticed Aja was wearing the same bold lip color she'd worn the night of the party. Somehow, even buttoned up in her wool coat, she managed to give off a sexy vibe. He imagined her licking those full red lips in anticipation and had to stop the train of thought before it was obvious to the women that his mind was at the bottom of the gutter.

Her phone rang before she could respond. She pulled it out of her purse and sighed. "One second, I need to take this."

Aja stepped away, leaving him standing with London.

"You'll join us for lunch? Or you meeting a special someone?" London asked.

"No, but I'm pretty certain your cousin would object to my presence. I don't seem to be one of her favorite people."

London waved a dismissive hand. "Oh, don't mind her. Come with us so you can tell me about the beaches and warm weather. I hate winter."

In his mind, he declined but his stomach overrode the command. "Sure, I can grab something to go, I don't have another client until three."

"Good. This will be fun. Oh, maybe you can give me some suggestions. I usually order the same thing when I get Greek food." She rubbed her hands together.

Aja returned a few minutes later. "You ready, London? Del, I can check my schedule-"

London cut Aja off. "Del's coming too. He loves Greek food."

Del watched Aja. To her credit, the only indication that she was not thrilled to have him tag along was an almost imperceptible twitch of her eye.

"Right. The more, the merrier, I guess. Let's go."

Impressed, he hid a smirk.

Aja turned on her heel, heading toward the door leading to the elevator.

Del motioned for London to lead the way and opened the door for her. Aja was holding the elevator when they stepped into the hallway.

The restaurant was warm and inviting, the smell of garlic, oregano and sizzling meat heavy in the air. A few people stood in line waiting to place their orders while others sat at square tables for two or four. While the place wasn't packed, it seemed to be off to a good start. The servers, clad in khakis and tees with the restaurant logo on them, hustled colorful plates back and forth.

The line to order moved quickly and Aja placed her order, receiving a number card to place on the table they selected. She picked a table for four near the rear and took a seat.

She moved, he noted, like a woman who knew exactly what she wanted and how to get it, exuding confidence and self-assurance.

"Del, what are you getting?" London asked him, still holding a menu.

"I'm getting the lamb souvlaki. It's grilled lamb on a skewer with Greek salad and pita bread." He said, the mere thought of grilled meat making his mouth water.

"Ooo, I'll try that, oh, that's my phone," he heard the faint ringtone, which sounded suspiciously like the theme song from Jurassic Park, coming from the large purse slung over London's shoulder.

"Hey, Sweetiekins, what's up?" She glanced up at him, an embarrassed half grin on her face. "You did? Where are you?"

London motioned for Del to step ahead of her to the counter where a bored twenty-something stood waiting to take his order. Once his order was placed and paid for, he stepped back to where London stood.

After ending her call, she motioned him over to the table where Aja sat. "Umm, that was Donovan. He brought me lunch and he's standing in the office waiting for me. Sorry to desert you both," she said and hurried off.

Del sat. "I guess we got ghosted for Sweetiekins?"

Aja nodded, rolling her eyes in mock annoyance. "Yep, it's new love so they're pretty extra sometimes. I'm happy for her though."

As she shrugged out of her coat, Del reached over to help her, noting the snug cowl neck sweater that hugged her curves.

She scooted her chair up to the table and met his gaze. "I owe you an apology. I shouldn't have insulted your profession at Mia's party. That was rude of me."

He raised a brow, surprised at her admission. "I say we agree to forgive each other? I was way out of line."

Aja gave him a small nod. "Deal."

Del cleared his throat, feeling a weight lift off his chest now that they'd acknowledged their bad behavior. He had been carrying that conversation around with him for days, wondering why he'd taken such offense. "Thank you for understanding. I know I can be a bit intense about my work, but it's something I love and take seriously."

Aja fiddled with the silverware on the table. "I can tell. You have a passion for what you do." She looked up at him again, her brown eyes meeting his. "What do you know, we're alike in that regard."

"We've agreed on two things today...you think hell is freezing over?"

He was rewarded with a half-smile.

Del figured he was about to piss her off again but he couldn't help it. He wanted to know more about her.

"London told me you don't take lunch often," Del said, crossing his arms and leaning on the table.

She glanced up at Del in surprise. "No. I tend to work straight through lunch most days. But she wore me down today. Sounds like maybe she did the same to you?"

He tilted his head back and forth. "Yeah, I suppose she did. Didn't take much though, I'm starving."

Resting a hand under his chin, he said, "I get the impression you would have preferred a stick in the eye to eating with me."

"Hmm. That's overly dramatic," Aja said as a petite server with blue ombre hair set their food down and swiped the number card. Del thanked the woman, who nodded and hurried away.

"But I'm not wrong, am I?" He pressed, and wondered why he cared.

She regarded him. "Most people have an angle and because I haven't figured out yours yet, I don't know what to make of you." She took a bite of the pita. "I know you want me to go to Barbados. But there's something else going on."

Del watched Aja carefully, his curiosity piqued. He had never been one to hide his intentions or play games, so he was a little taken aback by her blunt assessment of him.

Aja was far more accurate than she knew. He sighed, sticking a wedge of bread in his mouth, buying time before he answered. He reached for another piece. "Tell you what, it's clear you're not ready to talk about it, so I won't mention Barbados for the rest of the meal. We'll find something else to talk about."

Her eyes narrowed, like she knew she was being set up, "Sure," she said slowly.

Del grabbed the lamb souvlaki, taking a big bite. The meat was tender and delicious. He was going to need a nap once he got back to his office.

He decided to steer the conversation toward neutral ground. "Tell me about your work," Del suggested. "What are you so focused on that's got you skipping meals?"

Aja frowned as she stabbed an olive. "Why are you so fascinated with my work habits?"

"I like studying human nature...especially the habits of entrepreneurs," he shrugged, wiping his mouth. "We're trailblazers and risk takers but we have our flaws. I like to help shed light on them and provide solutions to manage them. So... what are you working on?"

Aja toyed with her salad. "Everything and nothing. And for what it's worth, I work through lunch so I can leave by six most days."

"Hmm. Your husband doesn't want you working late?"

She was now attacking the salad with her fork, punching it like he was sure she wanted to punch him.

"My life is structured so that I don't have to answer to anyone about my time or my business."

He smirked, impressed that she'd managed to answer fully without telling him anything. "That was my idea of a bad joke. Don't tell me you're logging in once you get home. That time counts too."

A furtive, guilty look crossed her face then she sat up. "I have a lot to do and I can get more done at home where I'm not constantly being interrupted." She paused to glare at him. "Why all the questions? Are you trying to convince me I need your coaching services again?"

Why he wanted to know was a valid question. Del wasn't sure she was ready to hear the truth yet. "No, I honestly have more clients than I can manage at this point, but I'm asking because I see the burn out looming. I've been there and don't wish it upon anyone, especially this early in your entrepreneur journey." He dipped his souvlaki into the tzatziki sauce. Perfection. He'd have to remember this place next time he was in the area.

He tried another tack. "I saw you in the Atlanta Business Weekly. The Forty Women Under Forty article."

"Yeah, since you read that, you know I don't have a husband." She pursed her lips like she'd tasted a rotten tomato.

He knew the reason for the displeasure on her face. The article read more like a Top Forty Bachelorette spread than a piece on the accomplishments of the participants. He recalled the article stating that Aja was still single and searching for a special someone. He was sure the writer wouldn't have dared put anything like that in a piece featuring men.

"Assuming we both like to know who we're dealing with before we meet, I'm willing to bet good money that you've already run me through whatever systems you use."

"Actually, I didn't, just a basic Google search." she admitted. "You have some high-profile clients."

Del had to suppress the urge to grin. Aja sounded almost impressed.

She was referring to his handful of reality star clients. That was the thing with word of mouth, it tended to keep you in a particular industry. But he didn't want to bore her talking about himself. "I also read that you have three other full-time employees?"

She nodded. "I do. But I'm not burned out. I love what I do." The words came out like she was trying to convince herself.

"You can love what you do and still be on the brink of burnout. Here, try this lamb," He slid a hunk of the tender meat onto her salad plate then poured a bit of the creamy white sauce on the side.

Aja eyed the meat then him and after a moment of hesitation, used her fork to stab the lamb, sliding it through the sauce. "Not bad," she said after taking a bite. "Why are you asking about my staff?"

"You said you can't take time off to travel right now. I'm wondering if you've fully empowered your team to run the business while you're gone. Are you training someone to take your place?"

She dropped the fork. "Ours is a small operation. I'm not where I need a succession plan just yet."

"Succession plan?" he chuckled, paused to sip his water. "No. What I mean is, if you're unavailable for a couple of days, could your business function without you?"

Aja looked as if she was considering his words carefully. She picked up her fork and began twirling her salad around absent-mindedly. "I suppose my team could manage for a few days without me," she admitted with hesitation, "but I'm not sure what kind of chaos I'd come back to."

Del raised an eyebrow at this, curious about the dynamics of her business. "Chaos? That sounds like you don't completely trust them to handle things on their own."

She frowned. "It's not that I don't trust them, it's just that I know more about how to get things done. It's usually quicker for me to just take care of whatever it is."

Del shook his head in disbelief. "Aja, that's exactly the problem. You're working in your business, not on it. You have to let them learn, make mistakes, and grow. You can't build a scalable business if you have to put out every fire yourself."

She set her fork aside and folded her arms across her chest. "Why do I feel like I'm in the hot seat, defending my business and my decisions?"

He'd pushed the issue too far and now she was in defensive mode. He gave her a wry smile. "I slipped into coaching mode, didn't I?"

She smirked, her eyes narrowing slightly. "Just a bit. Should I expect a bill for this session?"

Del laughed, appreciating her dry sense of humor. "Nope. Just giving you something to think about." he leaned in, resting his elbows on the table. "Tell me one thing no one knows about you."

CHAPTER 5

Aja

Aja picked up her fork, took another bite of her salad as she tried to come up with a suitable answer. She wasn't going to reveal her deepest secret, but she was curious to see where Del was going with the conversation. "Wait...you've asked me a million questions. You go first."

He stroked his beard. "You can't laugh or make light; I'm baring my soul here."

Aja nodded, placing her fork on the side of her plate. She swallowed a bite of crisp lettuce and cherry tomatoes mingled with feta cheese. "I promise," she said, 'I won't laugh."

Del cleared his throat and leaned in closer. "If my clients ever found out...I don't know..."

"Del," Aja said, her voice low and firm. "What you say will never leave this table."

He picked at the corners of his napkin, his gaze darting around the restaurant before landing back on her. Finally, he drew in a deep breath, as if pulling from a well of courage deep inside him.

"You know Publix has those holiday commercials, right? Do you shop there?"

Aja raised her eyebrows. Why was he asking about the grocery store? "Yep, there's one on my way home."

"I've actually gotten prickly eyed watching them," he said, dropping his head. "Especially the one with the stepdad where she calls him 'Chris' until her wedding day when she calls him 'Dad'. Gets me every time."

Aja blinked, not sure what to say. Del, the confident celebrity coach, softened by a Publix commercial? She had to admit, she hadn't seen that coming at all.

"That's... " she began, pausing when she saw him raise an eyebrow at her, a defensive look in his eyes.

Adorable was the first word that popped into her mind but she doubted he'd take that well. Instead, she said, "That's human, Del. It means you're not a robot. We all have our soft spots."

He nodded, a flash of relief crossing his face as he placed more lamb on her plate. "Your turn."

Well," she said finally, "I've been thinking about a dating app."

Del stopped eating and studied her. "Really? I'd think in your line of business, a dating app would be the last place you'd look for a connection."

"Oh God no, not for me. I meant developing a dating app." She immediately took a forkful of the meat, running it through the sauce and popping it into her mouth.

Next time she came here, she was definitely getting the lamb.

"Ah...got it. But," he said. "Isn't that the exact opposite of what you do?"

"Well, we would just be using our tools in a different way. We could weed out the catfish before they're approved for a profile. And even though I advise them against jumping right back into the dating pool once they find out they've been catfished, most don't listen."

"I bet Andre would sign up to be matched." Del stroked his chin. "You could develop the underlying technology and sell it to the big players for a nine figure payout."

Aja frowned. "Wait, why would Andre sign up? Aren't you two...together?"

"Me and Andre?" he tilted his head like the concept had never occurred to him. "Nah, we've been friends since we got out of college. She's like a sister to me."

She tried to wrap her mind around this new information. "But at the party, the way you two moved..." She didn't want to say it out loud but she'd felt like a voyeur watching them move sensually to the music.

Del chuckled, shaking his head. 'Ah, that's just how we are. We've been each other's wingmen and dance partners for so long it comes naturally to us. Trust me, though, there's nothing romantic between us. She's looking for her next husband."

"I see," she said, taking a sip of her water. And she'd vowed that she would never let him see her dance. "Anyway, my dating app idea is a huge investment. Maybe in a few years."

"It's probably more doable than you think."

~

Aja paced her office, restless, replaying her conversation with Del the previous day.

Even though she'd initially been irritated with London for inviting him to join them then abandoning her, she'd enjoyed her lunch with Del.

Would they hang out the same way if she went to Barbados?

She sat down, intending to focus on work.

Rubbing her arms, she sighed as she watched her email notifications pop up. Everyone expected her to drop whatever she was doing to take care of their requests. Zaria wanted her to sign off on a larger than usual discount for a new client, one of the contractors was trying to outfit a new home office on her dime, Lavender needed approval to change the scope of her current project.

There was no way she could leave the country right now.

Aja grabbed her phone and pulled Del's business card from her desk drawer.

She added him to her contacts and started a new text.

> It's Aja. I can't-

The phone shook as an incoming call interrupted her typing.

Her father's name and face showed on the display. She frowned. Why was he calling her in the middle of the day?

"Hey, Dad, everything okay?"

"Aja, your grandmother told me that your mother passed away?"

Straight to the point, as always. "Hello to you too," she muttered. "Yes, it happened last week, I guess."

"You guess?" His voice was tinged with something that sounded like disappointment, or maybe it was concern–she couldn't tell. "Aja, this is important. You're the next of kin."

She pressed her fingers to her temples, a headache looming at the base of her skull. "I know, Dad, it's just—"

"Did you call Bernard yet? His firm can handle the estate stuff for you. Let them worry about all of that."

"No, I haven't called him. I was trying to find an estate lawyer in Barbados but haven't had much time." She felt like she was making excuses.

"That's why you need to call Bernard. He can sort out everything there on your behalf, including the sale of the properties or whatever she had."

"I was thinking of taking some time off to go there and handle things in person." Aja admitted.

Her father paused for a moment, the silence stretching between them like a taut wire. "In person?" he finally said, his voice laced with surprise.

She heard him sigh deeply. "That's not a good idea, Aja."

Aja leaned back in her chair, feeling the weight of his words.

Her father had always had the power to control her, to push her into succumbing to his will.

Normally she complied without resentment, but today she felt like rebelling. "Why not?"

"You're just going to waltz into another country and do what exactly? You don't know anything about her life."

When she didn't respond, he sighed again. "She betrayed us. She walked away from us and you don't owe her anything," he said sharply.

"What if this isn't for her but for me, Dad?" Aja asked softly.

She couldn't see it but knew there was a disapproving frown on her father's face. She took a deep breath, steeling herself for his judgment.

"Aja, you have a business to run and people depending on you for their livelihood. Your cousin needs that job and you're just going to run off for a woman that left her child behind? What sense does that make?"

"Dad, I have to go." She rubbed her forehead in frustration. "I've got work to do."

"Yes, you do. Now forget this foolishness. Call Bernard, let them handle everything. Okay?"

She closed her eyes. Maybe her father was right. "Right. Bye, Dad. I'll talk to you later."

Aja stared at her phone after her father ended the call.

Her father's words echoed in her mind and she realized with a start that he was still harboring a lot of bitterness and anger toward her mother. She was angry at her mother as well but she also wanted closure.

He was right; she had a business to run, responsibilities to uphold. But more than that, she had questions that needed answers. Who was Diana Lewis?

Maybe she could find something in Barbados that would answer this question and many others that had festered in her mind for years.

Aja stared at the keys on her laptop. She had emails to answer, issues to resolve, but suddenly, none of that seemed important.

She opened her text messaging app and saw the message she'd been composing to Del before her father called.

Aja erased the previous words and sent a new message.

Aja: Del, it's Aja. I'll go.

Decision made, she sent out an urgent meeting request and got to work making notes.

~

Taking deep breaths and trying not to freak out about what she was about to do. Aja reviewed her notes for the hundredth time. She could really use a shot of something, whether it was expresso or tequila was up for debate. Either one would work at this point.

Her team, as she liked to call her full time employees, was gathering in the tiny conference room of the office gearing up to hear what she had to say.

She adjusted her suit jacket after glancing at herself in the full length mirror on the back of her office door. Power suits were her thing, they made her feel like she was capable of keeping the ship that she called her company afloat every day. Today she had on her favorite: a pinstriped tailored jacket and matching tuxedo pants with patent leather stilettos.

Breathing out, she worked on projecting an air of authority like she knew exactly what she was doing. No matter how far from the truth that was. Fake it till you make it, right?

Scooping up her laptop, she headed for the conference room.

When she stepped into the small space, she closed the door behind her.

The casual conversation stopped. Three sets of eyes were on her, expectantly. They'd left the head of the table seat for her. Aja walked over and sat down. London was sitting to her left, her laptop open, ready to take notes. Zaria had taken the seat at the opposite end of the table and her newest full-time employee, Lavender, sat across from London on her right.

"Ladies, thank you for meeting with me on short notice. I know everyone is busy so we'll get down to business." She made eye contact with each woman. She was proud of her team.

Lavender spoke first. "You're not selling the business, are you?" she asked suddenly.

"What? No," Aja raised an eyebrow at her. "What makes you think that?"

"Usually what happens when you get called into an emergency meeting at the last minute. And it would be my luck just as I'm getting everything sorted," She grumbled.

Aja sighed. Sometimes being the boss sucked. "No. To be clear, I am not selling the business. As you all know, my mother recently passed. I've decided to take a couple weeks off to handle my mother's estate in Barbados."

The room was silent for a beat then Zaria spoke up. "I'm glad you're going. You could use the time off." She motioned to the rest of the women. "We'll handle everything here while you're gone."

Good. That was what Aja wanted to hear. She would also have to make sure she checked in regularly without seeming like she was micromanaging. She had to let go and trust her team to handle things, even if it was done in a way different from how she might handle them.

"Yes, that's what we need to talk about now. I'll need to offload a lot of my meetings and other duties to you." She turned to Lavender. "Zaria will be taking over for me while I'm out but Lavender, I'd like for you to run the initial interviews for the open positions. I'll still want to do the final round but send me your recommendations on who moves forward. "

Lavender nodded as she typed on her laptop. "Will do." She looked up at Aja. "And I'm sorry for your loss. Losing your Mum is never easy."

Aja nodded. She was trying to get to a better place in dealing with everyone's well-meaning comments about her mother. No one seemed to understand that she'd mourned the loss of her mother long ago. They took their relationships with their mothers, no matter how dysfunctional, for granted. "Thank you."

She referred to her notes on her laptop. The condolences had knocked her off track slightly. "We're supposed to do a demo of the new onboarding app a week from today. I don't want to reschedule that just yet but I don't know what I'm walking into once I get there. I'm not sure if I'll have good internet or what kinds of demands will be made on my time. Let's keep it on the calendar for now. I'll update you once I know more."

London looked up. "Where are you going to stay? And what city are you going to, anyway?"

Aja glanced at her cousin, her father's words playing on a loop. *Your cousin needs that job.* She pushed the words away and focused. "My mother lived on the west coast, Saint James parish." She hesitated before continuing. "Del referred me to a small boutique hotel near my mother's glass studio, an area called Holetown."

Zaria looked up from her laptop. "You didn't tell me that. Are you sure you trust staying someplace that's not an international chain? Did you look the place up? Is it in a good area?"

Aja smirked. "You doubt our resident expert? His family is from there. I would think he'd know better than the travel review sites."

"I mean, I guess, but seriously did you look it up?" Zaria's hands were poised over the keys. "What's the name of it?"

Aja sighed, knowing her best friend meant well. "Sapphire Cove Resort."

London tapped her keyboard, typing faster than Zaria. "It's well rated and in a good location." London said. "And it's adults only."

"That sounds perfect!" Lavender said, grinning at Aja.

"London, make sure you send us all the contact info in case

we need to reach Aja," Zaria turned back to her. "But I'm only going to contact you if something is horribly wrong." Zaria said quickly.

Aja ran a hand over her forehead. "If something happens, I want to know sooner rather than later. So don't hesitate to call me."

"I can handle things here. You just take care of business there. What are you going to do about your mother's remains and funeral services?"

Aja shrugged. As far as she knew, her mother didn't have any other close family. She knew her mother's parents had died long ago, before Aja was born. She had no siblings and she had no idea if her mother had grandparents. Which meant the arrangements would fall on her shoulders. "I hadn't really thought about it. I guess if she had any last wishes, she would have expressed them to Del." She sounded bitter, she knew, but it couldn't be helped.

"Del is who again?" Lavender asked. "Did we run any checks on him? What's his full name, I can run one now."

"He may have been Aja's mother's boyfriend." London said. "If it's true, I wouldn't blame her. He's very easy on the eyes. Right, Aja?"

Easy on the eyes wasn't the half of it. But she kept that to herself. "He's not bad looking," she said, then turned to Lavender. "I ran a preliminary check on him already. He's the executor of my mother's estate. But thank you, Lavender, I appreciate you looking out." She said and managed a smile.

London looked up from her laptop. "Holetown is a touristy area, there's plenty of restaurants and nightlife there, so you shouldn't stand out too much from the locals." She paused, "you're going to take casual clothes, right? Leave the suits at home?"

Aja frowned, looking down at her suit. She'd planned on taking a couple of suits just in case she needed to appear professional. "I'm not going there to sunbathe, I'm going to handle business. I need the right attire for that."

Crinkling her nose, London glanced at her laptop again. "The weather there today is," she tapped the screen. "Sunny, no rain with a high temp of...wait for it...eighty-five degrees. In February. While here, there's a chance of snow flurries and freezing rain later on. Take advantage and wear some shorts."

Zaria piped up. "It wouldn't hurt for you to explore the island a bit. When's the last time you took a vacation?"

Aja started to remind them that she didn't have time to vacation and make sure they got their paychecks on time and in full. But she stopped, considering the question. When was the last time she'd been somewhere for fun and not work?

"It's been a while. We'll leave it at that." she said finally, hoping that was the end of that line of questioning.

"Well, you and I haven't been anywhere together since, hell, when we took that trip to Mexico for our thirtieth birthdays. Ooo, I could go with you if you need company."

Aja shook her head. "No, you need to stay and hold things down here. We've got that big presentation."

Zaria nodded then crossed her arms on the desk, pushing her laptop away. "Have you been anywhere since Cabo five years ago?"

"I've been building this business for the last four years so no," she said, not wanting to dwell on how long she'd been grinding away at her business. "Let's get back on track."

Lavender interrupted. "Since you haven't gone on holiday in five years, you need to take some time for yourself. I'm with London, pack some shorts. And a bikini or two."

"Um, do we need to leave early today so we can go shopping?" Zaria sat up. "The resort wear is out so we can find you some cute beach outfits."

Aja blinked, realizing her team had gone silent, waiting for her to speak. "What?"

"Zaria asked if you wanted to go shopping, which you should," London said as Lavender's head bobbed in agreement.

"And," she paused, then rushed ahead. "you should consider taking Nezziw with you for moral support."

"Nezzie?" Aja frowned. She hadn't considered taking her grandmother along.

"Oh that's a good idea!" Lavender said. "She can keep you company."

"Yes, she's wanted to go since she found out Rihanna is from there. You know how much she loves Rihanna," London leaned in. "I think she'd enjoy it."

Aja rolled her eyes. Her grandmother had what Aja considered a borderline unhealthy obsession with the pop star.

Tenting her fingers, Zaria leaned back in her seat. "Maybe you should take her. Since you're making me stay here in the frigid cold."

"Way warmer here than New York," Lavender pointed out, "Or Manchester. I don't miss those winters."

"But it's eighty-five there. We could be on the beach right now surrounded by Bajan men offering us drinks and debauchery." Zaria said.

"And that's why I need you to stay here," Aja pointed out, as she tapped her fingernails on the wood conference table. Taking Nezzie meant they'd get a chance to bond a bit. Her grandmother loved to explore new places and didn't get around as much after her husband died. "I could drag Nezzie along," she said aloud.

Aja turned to London. "So, question for you. Did you and Donovan cook up that convenient lunch scheme yesterday?"

Zaria looked up from her phone. "What happened at lunch yesterday? I thought you all were going to try the new Greek place?"

Aja pursed her lips at her cousin, who had a suspiciously innocent look on her face and wouldn't meet her eyes. "London begged me to go with her to the Greek place since Lavender was unavailable," she told Zaria. "I'm sloppy seconds, but whatever."

"No, you're not," London cut in. "You never go to lunch so I thought I'd drag you out for once."

"Anyway, I went to the garage to get my scarf since it was so cold yesterday and the next thing I know, Del is standing in the lobby and London's invited him to lunch with us."

She crossed her arms. "You want to finish the story, cousin?"

London raised her hands in defense. "I swear I didn't plan any of that! The man said he loved Greek food...I took it as a hint and invited him along. Then Donovan calls me asking where I am because he brought us lunch." She lifted a shoulder. "You looked like you were in good hands."

Zaria put a hand under her chin and smirked at Aja. "Oh, so you had lunch with Mr. Parris. How did that go?"

Before Aja could answer, London jumped in. "I did ask if he was meeting a special someone for lunch and he alluded that there wasn't."

Zaria's eyes got wide. "He's going back for the service, right?" She put her elbows on the conference room table. "You should have a beach fling with him. I certainly would."

"We know you would," Aja said, "but I'm going to take care of her affairs and that's it."

Zaria eyed her and Aja dropped her gaze. She pulled up her schedule to distract herself from her best friend's scrutiny.

"Is our official meeting over?" Zaria glanced around the table.

"Pretty much." Aja closed her laptop. "I covered everything on my agenda."

"Okay, let's get into it," Zaria leaned back, crossing her arms. "What did you and Del talk about yesterday? And why didn't you tell me you had lunch with him?"

She weighed her words carefully. "He has very strong opinions about how I'm running my business which I didn't ask him for." She didn't want to let on that she'd spent the better part of the last twenty four hours thinking about him and his words.

"Is he trying to bring you on as a client?"

"No, I asked him that and he said he's got plenty of clients and didn't need the likes of me."

Zaria scowled. "Shut up. He didn't say that, did he?"

"Not quite, but that was the tone I got."

"You seemed to be offline for a while yesterday. You sure you two didn't hit it off?" Zaria asked.

"Okay, as far as I know I don't need to check in when I come back from lunch."

"Just making sure you didn't sneak off for a quickie like this one probably did." Zaria nodded, jerking a thumb toward London, who ducked her head, all but admitting her guilt.

"Really, London? We work in this space." Aja chided, eager to change the subject.

"No, we were in my office," she emphasized. "Eating lunch."

"Oh, I'm sure he was eating all right," Zaria said under her breath.

London threw a pen at her.

"Anyway, back to Del. You really think he was seeing Aunt Diana?" London asked, then turned to Lavender. "He has this accent...he's from Barbados, and, whew, it screams sex on somebody's beach."

Aja stopped herself from rolling her eyes. Del's accent wasn't that sexy.

"Ooo, and he was seeing your mum before she passed?" Lavender perked up.

Aja motioned for the women to calm down. The meeting had gone off the rails but supposed she had gone over what she needed to. She rubbed her forehead. "I don't know. But that's not any of our concern given they were both well over eighteen."

She said all of this without meeting Zaria's gaze, hoping that she was more convincing than she felt. Her curiosity around her mother's relationship with Del Parris bothered her on several levels which she didn't understand. She wasn't interested in the man, why should she care if he was dating her mother?

"That's all I had to cover. I'll let you all know my travel dates," she stood and gathered her laptop, ready to leave the room.

Lavender threw her hands up. "Okay, well, safe travels. On that note, I've got a call in a few with one of our applicants so I must run." She scooped up her laptop and wiggled her fingers at them as she strode out.

Aja watched the tall woman leave. Lavender had been a blessing to the company and Aja had recently brought the expert software engineer on as a permanent employee after her initial six month contract lapsed.

London gathered her things. "Okay, I'll go by after work and help Nezzie pack. Just let us know the itinerary."

Once London was gone, Aja stood and tucked her laptop under her arm in an attempt to ignore Zaria, who was still seated.

"Not so fast, Lewis, take a seat." Zaria pointed at the seat across from her.

Aja felt like she'd been caught by the principal smoking in the ladies room. "Last I checked, you report to me but whatever. I really don't have time. I need to make our travel arrangements and get my appointments rescheduled."

But she sat down.

"It's just you and me. Talk to me." Zaria tented her hands. "Are you sure you're going to be okay handling your mother's affairs? And is Del going to be there?"

"Yes, he said he's flying in to help with the process and that he wanted to attend the service."

Zaria nodded. "Please be careful while you're there. And don't hesitate to call us if you need to."

Aja waved her off. "I'll be fine. This will hopefully be a quick trip and I'll be back home before you know it."

CHAPTER 6

Del

el paced the passenger pickup area at Grantley Adams International Airport, his hands shoved deep into the pockets of his faded denim jeans.

He scanned the arrivals board for the hundredth time, waiting for the update that Aja and her grandmother's flight had arrived in Barbados.

As the minutes ticked by, Del's anxiety grew. What if Aja had changed her mind and decided not to come?

He knew she'd struggled with leaving her team in charge of her business for the next couple of weeks, maybe she'd had a change of heart and decided she was needed in Atlanta.

Del wanted this trip to go well. Aja mentioned that this was her first time on the island and he felt a sudden, unexpected urge to show her his birthplace, his beautiful country. He scowled at his own sentimentality. This wasn't about showing off or impressing anyone; they were here to sort Diana's affairs and move on.

He rubbed a handkerchief from his pocket across his forehead. The afternoon air was still and hot, prompting him to wish he'd worn a lighter shirt. His navy blue button down, which had seemed like a good idea earlier that morning when it was cool and rainy, felt like a wool blanket wrapped around his chest.

His eyes flicked to the arrivals board again, verifying the flight had landed.

Anticipation had Del's heart racing. He hadn't seen Aja since their impromptu lunch but they'd exchanged plenty of texts coordinating their trip. He was looking forward to seeing Aja outside of her office on his turf.

He smiled at the memory of Diana's pride whenever she talked about her daughter.

Although Aja hadn't known it, Diana kept tabs on her daughter's accomplishments and shared them with Del. "You know my daughter was featured in Georgia Trend magazine?" she'd pointed out one day, holding the magazine with Aja's picture up to her camera like a proud hen.

"Why don't you email her? That's an excellent reason to reach out," he'd suggested. "You can congratulate her on being featured."

Her smile dimmed. "She doesn't want to hear from me," Diana said, sighing and lowering the magazine. "I'll just be a distraction for her."

Del had pushed his point further but Diana ignored him, choosing to change the subject instead.

"When are you going to settle down?" She'd asked. "Your thirties are almost over, Del. It's time you thought about babies and a little Del running around while you teach him cricket."

His turn to change the subject. Marriage wasn't for him. He'd opened his heart before and that hadn't gone well. He'd had to pick up the broken parts and move on. Now he enjoyed his life. He had women friends and lovers, but no one was exclusive and most were okay with that.

Del sat in the baggage claim area, watching the weary passengers as they retrieved their bags and hugged loved ones or searched for signs denoting the various resorts on the island.

As he watched a family of three, two adults and a daughter

who looked to be about five or six, locate their luggage he thought again about Diana, revealing her truth about her own family to him.

"Don't do like I did and take a family for granted. I thought I was trapped and it was only going to get worse. My husband wanted more kids, kept throwing hints that he wanted a son. While he was out making moves, growing his company, I was supposed to take care of Aja and the house," she paused, running a hand over her throat. "But the thought of playing the stay-at-home mom role all day everyday was overwhelming," she said softly.

Sighing in defeat, Diana stared out the window. "I regret it wholeheartedly but it's done. I made my choice and I have to live with those consequences. I hope my daughter doesn't do the same thing."

Drumming his fingers against the armrest, Del watched as the family he'd been observing disappeared into the throng of arrivals. That little girl, happily tugging her princess themed suitcase, was about Aja's age when Diana left.

Could Aja ever perceive her mother's flight as anything other than abandonment? Would she want to hear her mother's reasoning from him, a practical stranger observing her family's dysfunction up close? Or would she consider him overstepping?

His phone buzzed and he pulled it from his pocket. There was a text message from Aja.

Aja: Finished with immigration.

Heading toward baggage claim.

He stroked his chin and banged out a reply.

Del: All good. I'm in the seating area by the carousels.

Del decided to stand, but found himself pacing back and forth through the carousel areas, waiting for a glimpse of Aja.

Then, as if he'd conjured her up, she appeared.

She was wearing a floppy beach hat and oversized shades that made Del think of her mother. The shades coupled with the sundress she wore gave her an air of celebrity mystery. Like she was on a secret getaway in between movie shoots. She lifted the shades off, scanning the area for him. He was directly in front of her and when their eyes met, something deep in Del had him stop and stare.

Out of nowhere, he had the urge to lift her off the strappy sandals she wore and kiss her in greeting. Like they hadn't seen each other in months, when In reality, he'd last seen her only a few days ago.

He couldn't put his finger on it, he thought but as he watched her walk toward him, he realized what it was. Aja was dressed more casually than he'd ever seen, and she looked like she was on vacation. Or at least the beginning of a vacation.

He strode forward. "Welcome to Barbados," he said warmly to them.

He turned to Aja's grandmother, bowing slightly to the petite woman and extending his hand. "Mrs. Lewis, I'm Del. It's nice to meet you."

"None of that formal stuff! Call me Inez or Nezzie," Nezzie grabbed him in a bear hug, nearly knocking him over. The petite woman was stronger than she looked.

She stood back, taking him in. "You know, you remind me of a young Sidney Poitier...you favor him and that accent sounds a bit like his," She waved a hand. "You probably don't even know who I'm talking about...before your time."

"Ah, *Guess Who's Coming to Dinner, The Defiant Ones*, and my favorite, *In the Heat of the Night* to name a few," Del smirked at the pleased surprise on Nezzie's face.

She clutched his arm. "You do know him. But he was from

the Bahamas, I believe. Oh, I had such a crush on him. I loved his movies."

Del nodded. "Me too. When we moved to Atlanta, we had a cable hookup but we only got Turner Classic Movies and TNT, so I watched a lot of classic films."

"I watch TCM too." Nezzie patted his arm like they were old friends. "We'll have to compare notes while we're here."

"Anytime, Ms. Nezzie. How was your flight?"

"A little bumpy leaving Atlanta but other than that, not too bad." She grinned, reminding him of a little girl eager to explore. "Where are we going first? Beach, rum shack?"

"Neither. We've got to get to the funeral home before they close," Aja said, looking at her smartwatch as she approached. She glanced up at Del and they awkwardly stared at each other. Del held out a hand for her bag. She motioned toward her grandmother's bags with a slight sigh.

Del raised an eyebrow. Nezzie had clearly packed everything she owned. There were two large suitcases and a duffle bag. Del motioned to an eager porter that hovered near them. The porter returned with a luggage cart and heaved the bags on the cart. Del grabbed Nezzie's tote as she gave him a grateful smile. "Thank you. I don't get around as well as I used to but I do okay." She turned to Aja, beaming and taking her arm. "We're here! I can't believe my grandbaby brought me to Barbados."

Aja patted Nezzie's arm. "Anything for you, Nezzie."

Del watched the exchange between Aja and her grandmother, an unfamiliar warmth spreading in his chest. He could tell they were close and he couldn't help but feel a twinge of jealousy. Growing up without his own grandparents had been tough for him, but seeing Aja's loving relationship with Nezzie made him realize how much he had missed out on.

He led the way to his rented SUV,. "This airport is considered the hub for the eastern Caribbean countries," he said, opening the back to put their bags inside. "And we're on the southeast side of the island, not far from Bridgetown."

With the bags and passengers settled, Del got on the road.

"I see they drive on the opposite side of the road here," Nezzie's phone rang loudly. "Oh, I didn't think I'd have service," she answered the call. "Hey, Dina! Yeah, we just landed...girl it's beautiful."

Del chuckled as the older woman chatted with her friend.

He glanced at Aja in the passenger seat. She was quiet, too quiet for his taste. Which meant she was probably overthinking something.

"You okay over there?" Del asked.

She turned to him, and he could tell she started to tell him she was fine, everything was okay but something in her let down her guard. "No," her voice low, "I don't know what this trip will bring but my gut is telling me to be wary, on guard."

That admission, he knew, was a big deal for her.

Before he could speak, she went on. "What if I find out something about my mother that I wish I hadn't? What if I can't handle seeing her body after all these years?"

Keeping his eyes on the road ahead, Del reassured her. "We can do whatever you're comfortable with. If you want to do a viewing, we can or you can choose not to."

Aja rubbed her arms as if to warm herself. "My dad told me not to do this, I think he might have been right," she said.

He glanced sideways at her. "How so?"

She sighed, a world of uncertainty weighing her voice down. "He thinks I should leave things as they are, let the lawyers sort it all out. I thought I was strong enough to face it, but now that I'm here, it's real and I feel like I'm in over my head."

Del navigated a slight curve in the road, the ocean's vast expanse visible on one side. "Those doubts are natural, Aja. But you're not alone. I'm here and I'll do what I can. I know how things work on this island."

"I appreciate that but I can figure things out on my own," Aja said. "I'm sure you have better things to do."

He wasn't surprised at her comment. He knew she wouldn't

relinquish control easily. "I'm here to help. Your mother was my client but she was also my friend. I want to make sure she's taken care of. She would want me to help you."

He left it at that. No need to tell her that he knew she was used to depending only on herself, thinking she was the only one who could fix things. He knew that pressure and wanted, for some reason he couldn't fully explain, show her that she didn't have to be a superhero all the time.

They arrived at the funeral home and Del stepped out of the car and went around to help Nezzie. Aja had already gotten out and was waiting for them on the sidewalk. The warm Caribbean sun glared down on them as they made their way to the front door.

Del reached for the handle but it wouldn't budge. He checked the time on his phone. The sign said the location would be open until five o'clock and according to his phone, they had about thirty minutes until closing.

Del peered in. The place was deserted and the lights were out. Taking his phone out, he dialed the number on the sign.

After three rings, a perky female voice responded.

Del explained that they were standing outside, hoping to talk to the funeral director.

"De office is closed until Monday. Plumbing issue," the woman told him.

Del thanked her and ended the call.

"They had to close early and won't reopen until Monday," He glanced at Aja then back at Nezzie, who stood with her hands on her hips.

Aja sighed heavily before she spoke, "Okay, not a great start to this trip. Let's go to the hotel and check in. Maybe I can respond to some emails before everyone leaves for the weekend."

Nezzie scowled at her. "Aja, you spent both flights working. You need to call it quits for the day. Now," she turned to Del, "once we put our stuff down, we're gonna find me something good to eat and drink, right, Del?"

"Yes, ma'am," he smirked, seeing exactly where Aja got her take charge attitude.

As they drove to the hotel, Del stole glances at Aja, noting the tension in her posture. She sat in the passenger seat with her laptop open on her lap, typing away furiously.

He glanced at Nezzie through the rearview mirror. She was looking out the window, taking in the sights. Her face was relaxed and there was a slight smile playing on her lips. Del could tell she was enjoying every minute of her trip.

At that moment, Del made a decision to ensure that both Aja and Nezzie had an experience on the island that would be a memorable one. He'd show them the Barbados he knew, the one that went beyond tourist attractions and beach views.

They pulled up to the resort, a small colonial-style beachfront nestled against a backdrop of palm trees and azure skies.

Del helped Nezzie out of the car before unloading the luggage.

A tall young man stood waiting on their approach.

"Welcome to Sapphire Cove," he bowed his head. "I'm Zade and I'll be taking care of you. Can I interest you lovely ladies in a rum punch while we get you situated?"

Nezzie fanned herself. "Oh yes. I'll take one."

Aja shook her head. "Not right now. I'd like to get the wi-fi password and get settled."

As Zade checked Aja and Nezzie in, Del narrowed his eyes. couldn't help but notice the way the younger man kept stealing glances at Aja. It made a small wave of jealousy wash over him. He didn't know why he felt that way, but he didn't like it. He had only just met Aja, and yet the idea of anyone else looking at her with interest made him feel irrationally possessive.

He shook his head, trying to shake off the feeling. It wasn't like him to be possessive over someone he barely knew. He watched as Zade handed them their room keys, his hands touching Aja's for a beat too long.

"Anything you need, you let me know," Zade said, his meaning crystal clear to Del.

Del wanted to walk over and tell the younger man to mind his damn manners.

"Thank you," Aja said, smiling back at the man.

Enough of this. Del strode to the counter, directly facing the younger man. "Zade, big man, could you make sure their bags get up to their room quickly?"

The grin slid off his face. "Of course."

He picked up the phone and spoke softly into the receiver.

A man in a tropical shirt with a name tag on it that said Theo appeared and loaded the bags onto a cart.

Aja was watching him, her eyebrow raised.

Unwilling to meet her questioning gaze, Del glanced at his phone. "I've got to run for a bit," he said. "My aunt's got me running errands for her today. I'll text you when I'm done."

"Okay, I'm sure she's glad to have you staying with her for a while."

He shook his head. "Long story but my cousin and his kids moved back in with my aunt so I'm staying here as well."

Aja seemed taken aback by this news but before she could comment, Theo spoke up. "Ladies, I'll show you to your room and give you a tour of the resort."

As they walked away, Del watched them go, feeling a sense of unease, like something wasn't quite right. He didn't quite understand why, but he felt protective of Aja and Nezzie. He knew the island like the back of his hand—the friendly faces, the hidden spots of paradise, but also the potential for small-time scams and tourist traps.

Before long, he found himself heading to the parking lot with a sense of urgency, his mind already planning the day ahead. He'd take care of his aunt's list as quickly as possible; then he'd turn his attention back to the women.

CHAPTER 7

Aja

Aja watched as Del hurried toward his SUV.

He had seemed aggravated by the exchange between her and Zade at the desk, which surprised her. She hadn't thought Del was interested in her like that and she assumed he wasn't paying attention. But clearly he had been, even if his expression didn't change and he didn't say anything.

Since the party, when their hands touched and they'd both ignored the spark, she'd been more aware of Del. Despite knowing he didn't mess with American women. And despite seeing he clearly had a deep affection for her mother. She wasn't sure he'd acknowledged those feelings himself but she'd made it her business to read people and they were there.

Zade's flirtation with her shouldn't have mattered to him.

His relationship with Andre shouldn't have mattered to her.

She pushed these thoughts away and focused on the path she and Nezzie were taking toward their room.

As they strode through the courtyard of the resort, Aja took in the Mediterranean style archways and large palm trees artfully placed throughout the property.

"What a beautiful place," Nezzie exclaimed, sipping her punch as they walked through the pool area. "I don't know whether I want to hit the beach first or the pool. Maybe I'll do both!"

The Sapphire Cove Resort's multi-level pool snaked across the rear of the resort and the sound of the waterfall that carried water from one pool to another was soothing. Despite her protestations to anyone that mentioned the trip that she was coming here just to bury her mother, Aja found herself wanting to spend time in one of the poolside loungers.

She let out a heavy sigh. Yeah, right. Her brain would never slow down long enough for her to relax. She was constantly thinking of the things she needed to do once she got back in front of her laptop.

Dragging her focus from the pool, Aja scanned the rest of the resort.

There were a total of five buildings, each with three floors. Theo led them to a unit right behind the pool bar on the first floor. Aja frowned. She should have specified a higher floor; those were generally thought to be safer as intruders had fewer access points. But the moment she stepped into the room and saw there was a patio that gave her direct access to the beach, she perked up.

Theo set their luggage against the wall, giving them tips about room service, the restaurants on property and invited them to a weekly welcome reception that evening before leaving them to get settled.

"Which bed do you want?" Aja asked as Nezzie marveled at the room.

"Doesn't matter to me," Nezzie said, slurping the last of her rum punch. "Aja, this place is too nice, how much is it? You need to let me give you something toward it."

Aja rolled her eyes at Nezzie's offer to pay for part of their room.

Her grandmother had been hounding her since Aja invited her, trying in vain to pry the cost of the trip out of Aja. She knew that if she revealed how much the trip cost, her grandmother would worry Aja couldn't afford it. "Nezzie! This is a gift. Don't worry about it. I'm happy that you came with me."

There were two queen beds and a sitting area with armchairs that faced the ocean.

She took the bed closest to the door as she pulled her suitcase open and started unpacking.

"I just don't want you spending all your money on me. You have enough to pay for and who knows what kind of money we'll need for the funeral." Nezzie wrung her hands, looking around the spacious suite.

She smiled at her petite grandmother and rushed over to hug her. "Nezzie, I promise I can handle it. I wanted to do this for us. It's been a while since we hung out together."

Nezzie nodded, took Aja's hand. "I know, baby girl. I just don't want you to think you have to do everything alone."

"You're here, that's all I need." Aja squeezed her hand and led her to the patio doors. "Come outside...we've got beach access."

Aja unlocked the patio doors and slid one open. She and Nezzie stepped onto the small deck facing the ocean. Closing her eyes, Aja breathed in the sea air.

Nezzie stood, hands on her hips, watching the waves crash against the rocky coastline. "I tell you what, I gotta give it to Diana, she came to a beautiful island to spend her last days. This is the Caribbean Sea side, right?"

Aja nodded. "Yes. We're on the west coast of the island."

"I've always loved the beach," Nezzie mused, taking a seat on the metal patio chair, "Tried to convince your grandfather we should move to California when we first got married but he couldn't imagine leaving Atlanta." Her voice was wistful. "I hope Diana found happiness here."

"We won't ever know," Aja said then turned to her grandmother. "What was my mother like, really? What kind of woman was she?"

Nezzie clasped her hands together in her lap.

"Honestly, Diana always seemed a little flighty to me. I think she thought we were beneath her since your grandfather and I didn't go to college, but she tolerated us. You know, she treated you more like an accessory than a child. You were always dressed to the nines in frilly dresses, the cutest little chocolate doll I'd ever seen," she chuckled. "But she should have let you play more, you know, get dirty. She was always worried about you messing up your hair or your clothes, but that's what kids are supposed to do."

Aja stared at her grandmother. Even now she didn't like to do things that would mess up her clothes. Was her mother's quest to keep her clean and neat why she sometimes felt like she couldn't fully unwind?

A gust of sea air blew Nezzie's hair into her face and she tucked it behind her ear. "Or maybe boys are just different. I swear I could only keep my twins clean and presentable for so long. They barely sat still in church and as soon as we got home, you know they couldn't wait to get out of their church clothes. Your dad especially," she sighed. "He hated getting dressed up when he was younger. Now, of course, I rarely see him in casual wear."

Aja couldn't picture her stern, no-nonsense father squirming in church.

"Did Diana ever try to contact us after she left?"

Her grandmother's face fell. "Not that I know of. Your father hired a private investigator to find her...she was somewhere in California at that point, and tried to reach out to her a few times, but she never responded," Nezzie rubbed her arm. "I'm sorry, baby girl."

Aja's shoulders slumped. Growing up, she'd always hoped that her mother would come back, that they could have a chance to reconcile. But now, she knew it would never happen.

"Did she tell you or Dad why she was leaving?" Aja asked, not sure if she really wanted to know the answer.

Nezzie shook her head. "No, she just said she needed to find herself. She didn't tell anyone where she was going. As far as we knew, she had no relatives, her parents died before she met your dad," she rubbed her arms. "You know, when Diana left, it changed your dad. He wasn't the same. I was so worried about both of you."

Aja sat in silence, digesting the new information about her mother. She couldn't believe that someone could just leave their family without a second thought.

"Did Dad ever talk about her to you?" she asked, breaking the silence.

"Not too much," Nezzie replied. "He was always very guarded when it came to her. I could tell he was hurt and angry after she left, but I also knew they were having problems before, but he wouldn't talk about it."

Aja's heart ached for both her grandmother and father.

The two of them sat in silence for a few more minutes, watching the waves crash against the rocks below. The sun began to set in the distance, casting a beautiful orange glow over everything.

Her father never wanted to talk about her mother and Aja had eventually stopped asking, pushing her mother's memory into the recesses of her mind. Now, with her mother's death, everything was resurfacing, demanding to be examined.

Would this trip provide closure, as she'd told her father, or was she setting herself up for further pain?

Needing to pull herself out of her melancholy, Aja stood up, brushing the sand off her legs. "Enough sadness for now. Let's go get something to eat."

Aja watched her grandmother order the drink special of the day, a soft orange colored frozen concoction served in a tall, curvy glass complete with a cherry and an orange slice.

"Make it two, please," she said as she reviewed the menu in front of her.

They ordered cutters, a popular local sandwich made with fried flying fish, and settled in at the bar.

As soon as the bartender set their drinks down, Nezzie took a sip, turning to Aja with a gleam in her soft brown eyes. Aja braced herself. She knew that look meant her grandmother was up to something. "Now, that Del seems nice and I didn't see a ring," she raised her eyebrows, grinning at her.

Aja immediately shook her head. "Nope. Don't get any ideas. I'm pretty sure he had a thing for my mother," she said, convincing herself as much as Nezzie, "and even if he did, it doesn't matter. I'm not interested in him like that."

"Why do you think that? He was her, what did you call it, a life coach, right?" Nezzie asked.

"Yep, life and spiritual coach," Aja nodded, stirring her drink. "But it's not just that. The way he talked about her, the intensity in his eyes. It was more than professional respect or friendship."

Nezzie pursed her lips thoughtfully, taking another sip of her drink. "Maybe," she conceded, "or maybe you're seeing things that aren't there because you're looking for a reason not to get close to anyone. Del might just be a good man who admired your mother."

"But what if he's interested in me because he can no longer have her?" Aja asked.

"Anything's possible," Nezzie finally said, her voice gentle. "People can find themselves attracted to what's familiar, what reminds them of something they can't have anymore. But, consider this, isn't it also possible that he sees something special in you, Aja? Something entirely separate from your mother? You've grown up to be an amazing woman, despite not having your birth mother around."

Aja considered Nezzie's words as she sipped her drink. "Thanks but I'm not interested in hooking up with someone, I need to focus on the task at hand so I can get back to Atlanta."

Nezzie raised her hands in surrender. "Okay, okay. How about we talk about what we want to do while we're here? I heard there's a great sunset cruise we could go on."

An older man with a full head of wavy salt and pepper hair and a matching Hawaiian shirt and shorts ambled by, nodding at them in greeting.

Aja watched her grandmother subtly bat her lashes at the man. Her mouth dropped. "Do you know that man?"

"Nope. Wasn't he nice looking?" Nezzie nudged Aja. "You know I think that's his real hair, too."

"London was right, I need to keep an eye on you," Aja said, only half-joking.

"Pffft," she waved a dismissive hand. "Your cousin needs to mind her business. He's probably here with his wife. Anyway, since the funeral home won't be open tomorrow, what are we doing?"

Aja could think of a million things she could work on while she wasn't in the office but maybe she would take a small break over the weekend. "I'm going to see what I can get done tomorrow morning then we can maybe do the cruise that evening."

Another server in a starched white shirt appeared with their food, cautioning them that the plates were hot.

Aja thanked the server. "There's a spa on the property, would you like to get a massage or facial tomorrow?"

Nezzie's eyes lit up. "Oh, a massage sounds lovely. I haven't had one in ages."

Aja smiled. "We'll do that. We can make appointments after we finish eating."

Despite her grandmother's lively company, Aja found her mind wandering. She wondered if Del was planning to return any time soon.

Why was she so concerned with his whereabouts? His family was here; surely he was spending time with them? She should take a walk, maybe that would distract her from wondering where he was.

Once they were done eating, Aja rose, stretching her legs. "I'm going to check with the front desk about the spa and take a walk around the resort, you want to come?"

Nezzie shook her head. "Nah, I'm enjoying the scenery, you go on ahead. I'll be here."

"Okay, I'll be back." She patted her grandmother's shoulder and made her way to the reception area.

As she passed the pool, she scanned the guests.

She was, on a subconscious level, also looking for Del, even though she had no idea what she'd say to him if she did run into him. "Hey, let's talk about your relationship with my mother." Or "Hey, apparently my mother and I have the same taste in men."

That thought made her shudder.

When she reached the front desk, Zade was gone, a young woman with honey colored locs standing in his place. "Good evening," she said warmly.

Aja made the spa reservations and then set out to walk along the beach.

The sun was beginning to set, casting a warm pink and orange glow across the sky.

Slipping her sandals off, she wriggled her toes in the sand. The sugary sand was cool under her feet, and the sound of the waves crashing against the shore was rhythmic and soothing.

For just a moment, Aja let her imagination run untended. In the image, Del took her hand as they strolled across the picturesque beach.

At some point, they stopped as he pointed at the sunset and the next thing she knew, his lips found hers and...

Aja froze, dropping her shoes.

Where the hell had that come from? Now she was fantasizing about kissing him?

She shook her head, trying to rid herself of the thought. He was probably back with his family, enjoying their company, not thinking about her at all. And besides, she had more important things to focus on.

She turned, shoving her feet back into her shoes and trudged back toward the bar.

The seats surrounding the bar were empty when she walked up and Aja frowned.

Where was Nezzie?

She glanced around the pool. The women were still there, drinking and laughing loudly but there was no sign of her grandmother.

Aja walked to the covered lounge area where a DJ was setting up.

She started to ask him if he'd seen a woman in her seventies with a purple caftan when she spotted her grandmother talking animatedly with another older woman.

Aja approached the pair.

"There you are," Nezzie exclaimed, like Aja was the one not where she was supposed to be. "This is Jewel Forrester, Aja."

Aja studied the woman, realizing she wasn't her grandmother's age at all. The woman, tall with a generous full figure, had deep bronze skin, and looked to be in her late forties. She had a few fine lines around the eyes and mouth but she seemed to be comfortable in her skin.

Nezzie continued. "Jewel, this is my granddaughter, Aja. She's got a tech company," Nezzie didn't wait for Aja's confirmation, "and they look into online dating schemes for people, like that show *Catfish*."

She nudged Aja. "See if you can help Jewel, my allergies are flaring up and I need to run back to the room."

Aja blinked at her grandmother for a full moment. She hadn't realized her grandmother knew so much about her company. Usually she told people Aja did "something on the internet" and left it at that.

Before she could process this new information, Jewel spoke up, taking her hand. "Nice to meet you, Aja. Your grandmother and I were just talking about life and all its twists and turns."

Aja nodded. "Nice meeting you too."

Nezzie sneezed and excused herself.

As Nezzie strode off, Jewel motioned to the chairs. "We should sit. I was telling Inez that I met this man online and he's been wonderful but I'm wondering if he's really who he says he is."

Aja felt a familiar tingle run through her as she listened to Jewel's story. This was her passion; helping people desperate to know the truth about who they were talking to online.

She took the seat offered to her, the entrepreneur in her instantly switching into professional mode, even as the staff buzzed around, getting the stage ready for that night's performer.

"Tell me more about this man," Aja prompted as they settled into the woven lounge chairs.

Jewel nodded. "His name is Malik, and he says he's from New York but he lives in Atlanta now. But I don't know if any of that is true."

Aja nodded, making a note on her phone. She'd do more digging once she was in front of her laptop.

"Where did you meet Malik and how long have you been talking to him?"

Jewel's eyes lit up. "He's an artist and we connected in an online group for art lovers. We've been talking for a few months now, but we haven't met up yet."

Aja listened intently, taking notes as Jewel spoke.

"I mentioned how much I love having fresh flowers in my house and he's surprised me a few times with a delivery from local florists."

She looked up from her phone. "Why do you think he's not who he says he is?"

Jewel hesitated, her brows furrowing. "It's maybe nothing but I never gave him my home address. I'd guess that info is fairly easy to find if you dig for it, but still…"

"Have you asked him about it?" Aja asked.

Jewel shook her head, not meeting Aja's eyes. "I didn't want to make a fuss. You know, keep the peace."

Aja leaned back in her chair, observing Jewel with a thoughtful gaze. She had seen this pattern all too often: people tricked by those who preyed on their vulnerability, their desire for companionship.

Jewel held up a finger. "Another thing, he's promised to come to the island to meet me in person but he's always canceled at the last minute, saying he's got to travel for work."

Nodding, Aja continued to make notes. She was familiar with these forms of evasive behavior. "We'll see what we can find out."

Jewel sighed as she ran her fingers up and down the stem of her wine glass. "Thank you. I just...I want to believe he is who he says he is. But there's this little voice inside me that keeps saying otherwise."

CHAPTER 3

Del

Del strode through the resort lobby toward his room. He'd spent the better part of the afternoon helping his aunt get the supplies she needed for a party she was catering. His Aunt Felicity was a feisty woman in her mid-fifties who embodied the term hustle. She was always on the go, doing something to bring money into the household. Now that her son, Rashad, was back in her house after his divorce, she'd welcomed Del and his rented SUV with open arms and immediately put him to work.

He'd driven around the area where he'd grown up and marveled at all the things that had changed. And all the things that remained the same. New luxury resorts on one end that appealed to the tourists but in the areas not so near the beach, the streets were quieter, the houses more run down, and the familiar neighbors seemed to have aged overnight.

The weight of the day pressed at his back and shoulders and he was tempted to head up to his room for a hot shower but he caught sight of Aja and her grandmother walking toward the restaurant and lounge area.

"Del," Aja said, a hint of panic in her voice. "Nezzie's allergies are bothering her, do you know where the nearest pharmacy is?"

"Of course," he replied, trying to hide the smile on his face. "There's a pharmacy just down the road, I can take you there."

Aja nodded, and Del turned to Nezzie. "Other than the allergies, are you enjoying the island so far?"

Nezzie, tissue in hand, rubbed at her nose. "Yeah, and once I take something, I'll be fine, it'll probably knock me out." She turned away from them, a loud sneeze shaking her small frame.

"I knew there was something I forgot. Should have packed my normal allergy meds," she sneezed again. "I'm going back to the room."

Del motioned for Aja to follow him. "Let's go so we can get back quickly."

Leading Aja down the street, Del pointed at a brightly lit restaurant across from them. "This place here has been open since I was a kid. But my aunt dated one of the owner's sons and when they broke up, she forbade any of us to eat there."

Aja laughed, a light sound that made Del smile. "That sounds exactly like something my best friend would do," she said. "Except we'd never be able to eat or drink anywhere in Atlanta because I swear she's dated every straight man in the greater metro area."

"Really? And what about you? You dating your way through the men in the Atlanta metro area too?"

Del balled a fist at his side. What made him throw that question at her? She was barely eating lunch most days; he was willing to bet his coaching income that she wasn't casually dating. Or was she?

But something deep within him wanted to know.

She stopped walking. "Are you?" she asked pointedly, turning toward him.

"Me?" Del stalled.

"Yes, you. Before you tell me that I should be dating to find balance in my life or some other woo-woo bullshit, are you dating?" She motioned like a magician, waving her hand. "Is your work-life balance in sync with your auras?"

He blinked at her then gave her a slow, easy grin, appreciating her feisty side. "Nope."

Aja let out a frustrated sigh. "Meaning what? Or is this more of your coaching technique designed to get into my head?" she huffed as they entered the pharmacy.

The blast of air conditioning hit him, cooling his skin and Del paused a moment, enjoying the reprieve from the heat. "No, honestly, my work-life balance is mostly work. There's zero life," Del said finally.

"Which means I don't have the time or patience for dating."

"Hmm," she said noncommittally.

They walked down tidy aisles lined with brightly colored packages until they found the allergy medication. She bent to select a box from the lower shelves.

Del stood behind her, allowing his gaze to slowly meander over her curves, the way her dress hugged her hips, and showed off her toned arms. He cleared his throat, feeling a heat that had nothing to do with the humid outdoor air.

Aja straightened up, clutching the box in her hand. "This one should work."

She headed toward the line for checkout and Del grabbed a few items he'd neglected to pack then stood behind her.

As they waited, Del smirked at her. "Woo-woo bullshit, huh?"

"Okay, maybe that wasn't called for, but I sensed a wellness lecture brewing." She turned to look up at him, her brown eyes flashing.

"I wasn't planning on lecturing, I was just curious," he said.

Aja's eyes held his for a moment longer than necessary, and it was clear there was an unspoken question there, something that he knew neither of them wanted to voice just yet. "You know what they say about curiosity and cats," she said wryly.

Del's smirk graduated to full-blown laughter. "Well, good thing I'm not a cat."

Aja shook her head in amusement. "You're a mess."

"So I've been told." he said, shrugging. "What are you doing for the rest of the evening?"

Aja shifted, lifting a shoulder, "I haven't really thought about it beyond making sure Nezzie's okay."

Del nodded, "Of course. But maybe after that, we could talk about Diana's service? And when you want to check out her house and the studio?"

Aja looked away. "Right. Umm, yeah, we can do that."

"Or not. I just figured you might want to get the planning done as soon as possible." Del watched her closely, trying to gauge her mood.

"I do, I just," she sighed, turning to face him fully. "It's been a long day and I know I have run it into the ground that I wanted to get everything done as soon as possible, but I think I need a break tonight."

They were next in line. A bored cashier reached for the box of pills, offered a half hearted greeting and gave Aja the total.

Aja swiped her card and took the pills, declining a shopping bag.

Del nodded, handing his toiletries to the cashier, "I get it. We can talk about it tomorrow."

Aja smiled, relieved. "Thank you."

As they made their way back to the resort, Aja turned to him. "Is there a place nearby where I can get a drink and dessert? I'd give my pinky toe for something sweet right now."

Del raised a brow at her. He could run with that but he'd be a gentleman. "You're in luck. There's a place down the road, it's got the best rum cake on the island and their drinks are potent."

Aja's face lit up at the prospect. "Rum cake sounds perfect," she said, holding up the pills. "Let me run these up to my grandmother. I'll be right back."

Del watched as Aja's figure disappeared around the corner, her steps quick with purpose.

Aja wasn't at all like he imagined. Diana had spoken proudly about Aja's accomplishments and he'd expected an aggressive, take-no-prisoners world-weary woman who'd fought to make her business successful. He'd expected her to wear a thick coat of armor and give off a "I don't need a man" vibe.

Instead, he found someone who was both strong and vulnerable, a combination that intrigued him more than he wanted to admit.

Aja returned, her steps quick like they were on a schedule and running late.

"How's Ms. Nezzie?"

Aja smiled. "Good. She's taken a couple of pills and she's watching Blue Bloods so she's happy. To the rum cake?"

"To the rum cake," Del confirmed, matching her light tone.

They walked side by side down the road, the sun now fully set, and the stars twinkling in the sky.

The street was quiet, safe for an occasional bus or private car zooming past, their headlights cutting swathes of light through the tropical night air.

The place he had in mind was nestled between a craft shop and a small guesthouse, its sign swinging gently in the breeze. The front was painted a vibrant turquoise and as they entered, soca music spilled from speakers tucked away in the rafters, blending seamlessly with the murmur of waves in the distance.

Inside, the ambiance was a cozy blend of Caribbean charm and understated elegance. Bamboo tables were scattered across the open-air patio, each one adorned with a flickering candle encased in glass, casting warm circles of light on the smooth mahogany tabletops.

Del and Aja took a seat at a table with an unobstructed view of the sea, the moonlight sketching silver pathways across the water's surface.

"Do you know what you want to drink or do you need a menu? We'll order at the bar." Del said, rising to his feet.

Aja peered at him and he could see her wheels turning. "The rum cake, of course. And a glass of water."

"Not living dangerously yet?" Del chided. "You sure you don't want a rum drink?"

"Let me try the cake first," she said with a grin.

Del returned to the table and set a tall glass of ice water in front of Aja then settled into his seat with his rum and Coke.

"I'm beginning to see why my mother moved here. It seems peaceful, very laid back." Aja said.

Del chuckled, taking a sip from his drink. "Yeah, it definitely has its charms."

She nodded. "You think you'll ever move back?"

He considered the question as he took another sip. "I doubt it. I'm used to the U.S. now. What about you? Ever want to move somewhere else?"

"I think about the Pacific Northwest a lot. It's exactly the opposite of Atlanta in terms of geography. I don't know if I'd want to move there permanently but maybe for a year. I could get a little cabin in the mountains and enjoy the fresh air."

"Really? You don't really strike me as the rustic type. I'm thinking your cabin would be some five thousand square foot log palace with heated floors and an indoor pool," Del smirked.

"That sounds kind of nice, actually," Aja said, as a server slid a hunk of dark rum cake and a scoop of ice cream toward her. "But, I'm serious, I could live in a small place. You make me sound like some bougie princess."

Del lifted a brow but didn't say anything.

She dropped her fork, putting her hands on her hips. "I'm not, you know."

Del held up his hands. "Hey, I didn't say anything."

Aja rolled her eyes, but there was a hint of amusement in her expression. "Anyway, you said earlier that you don't have time or patience for dating?" She took a forkful of cake. "Wow...that's strong. Plenty of rum."

Del tilted his head. "You like it?"

"It's rich, maybe too rich for me," she said, taking a gulp of water. "But I want to talk about the ideas you had around my dating app. Would you be willing to try it out once it's done?"

He winced. "Umm...I'd rather invest in it," he said with a snort. "I have zero desire to use an app to find love."

"Oh, you'd rather go old school and meet women in person?" Aja put her fork down and sat back in her seat. "And what about investing in things you believe in?"

"Don't get me wrong. I believe in the idea, people are always going to want to connect and a lot of people want an easy, proven way of doing that," Del said.

His eyes met hers. "But yes, I prefer the old school way... meeting by chance and getting to know each other face to face, the anticipation of seeing them making your day brighter, being near them and feeling that spark of awareness," Del swirled his drink, the ice clinking against the glass. "You can't replicate that with an algorithm."

Aja leaned forward, her elbows on the table, her eyes bright with enthusiasm. "To me, there's room for both. Chance encounters and technology-assisted connections. Really just different paths leading to potentially the same destination."

Del listened, admiring the conviction in her voice. "I'm frankly surprised you feel that way, seeing as how online dating scams keep you in business."

Aja gave a shrug. "True, but my company is not trying to stop people from using technology, we protect them from those who misuse it."

"You should include that in your intro video. I see you on a stage like Steve Jobs, unveiling your dating app to the world," Del said, thinking that he could spend the rest of his time on the island vibing with her, listening to her talk about her passions.

She picked up her fork, tapping the tines against the white dessert plate. "You're gassing me up. If I didn't know better, I'd think you were trying to entice me to..." Aja paused, exhaling. "hire you as my coach."

"No," Del said, and took another sip from his drink. "I'm not trying to do either one. I believe you're destined for greater things."

"How are you so sure about that? We barely know each other," Aja leaned toward him and he could see the skepticism in her face, but there was a shadow of vulnerability that flashed before she could squelch it.

He weighed the question, debating on how he wanted to answer. Thanks to Diana, he knew more about Aja than she would probably be comfortable with. Diana had confided that her ex-husband, Aja's father, was exacting and hard to please. She saw that in all of Aja's accolades, deep down, Aja just wanted her father's approval. "Sometimes you just know," he said, immediately regretting the inadequate words.

But he didn't retract them, and the silence that hung between them felt as heavy as the humid Caribbean air. They locked eyes and Del could see her assessing him in that way of hers, trying to discern the truth.

Aja crossed her arms, a soft smirk playing on her lips. "Is that your best pickup line?" she asked, her gaze steady.

He chuckled, running a hand over his beard. "Nah. I know better than to use a line on you."

His honesty seemed to surprise her.

"Good answer," she said, leaning back in her chair. She studied him for a moment before speaking again. "You're not trying to become my coach...are you looking to get something from my mother's estate?"

"No." Del paused, his glass midway to his lips. He set the drink down, wanted to make sure his message was loud and clear. His gaze met hers, an intensity simmering within them. "My interest in you is purely personal."

Again, the silence between them stretched, humming with an unspoken energy. Her eyes widened a fraction and then narrowed just as quickly, as if she were trying to read some hidden meaning in his statement.

"Personal," she repeated, and there was a throaty edge to her voice that sent a thrill down his spine. "As in?"

"In that I enjoy your company," he said simply, knowing that any additional explanation would only cloud the situation. "I find our conversations stimulating and your determination admirable."

Aja blinked, tilting her head as she processed his words. "That's...refreshing," she confessed, her tone wavering between incredulous and intrigued.

She reached for her drink, taking a sip as she watched him over the rim of her glass. Her fingers traced the round edge of her drink, thoughtful. "Did you and my mother have a thing for each other?" Aja asked, her eyes never leaving his.

Del stiffened slightly, taken aback by the sudden change in topic. The question was fair, given his close association with Diana. But the answer was complicated.

"No, we were friends. Nothing more." He tried to keep his tone casual, not wanting to give any indication that there had been something more between them.

"And you didn't meet up with her here on the island?" Aja persisted, her brown eyes bore into him and he struggled to maintain eye contact with her.

After a beat, he shook his head. "I haven't been back here in years."

Aja studied him for a moment longer. "Okay," she said, taking another sip of her drink. Del released a silent breath, hoping his answers were enough to satisfy her curiosity.

"Del," she asked softly. "Why exactly are you here helping me?"

Del took a long, sip from his glass, savoring the potent rum before placing it back onto the table. He leaned back, fingers steepling as he regarded her with his steady, unwavering gaze. "Why do you think I'm here?"

Her eyes met his, a spark of defiance igniting within their depths. "I don't know," she replied. "That's why I'm asking."

"I'm here because your mother needed me to be," Del said after a moment, letting the words hang in the air between them. "She would want me to help you."

CHAPTER 9
Aja

Aja rose to the rich, offkey voice of her grandmother singing in the shower. She sat up, blinking and taking in the brightness of the morning. The sun was just rising and there was a hazy quality to the morning.

For a brief moment, she struggled to remember where she was. She took in the room with its dark colonial style furniture. She was still in Barbados. And last night, in a fit of desperation, she'd all but accused Del of being in love with her mother.

Slinking back under the covers, Aja groaned in frustration. Del had expressed interest in her and in return, she'd grilled him like she'd caught him stealing from her.

What was wrong with her?

If she was being one hundred percent honest with herself, she didn't know what to make of Del. While she was sitting at the table with him the night before, Aja considered two things: he didn't date American women and he might have had a romantic relationship with her mother.

Which, if both were true, were contradictory. She'd checked and learned her mother Diana was still technically an American even though she was living in Barbados.

Things didn't add up for her.

That was the only reason. Not because she was curious about him. Not because she was toying with the idea of a vacation fling and he fit the bill perfectly.

Sitting up, Aja scanned the room, forcing thoughts of Del away. She wasn't any closer to figuring him out and should focus on something else. Her laptop bag sat perched against the small writing desk and Aja decided she'd log in and see if she could get some work done while her grandmother was in the shower.

Her grandmother, always an early riser, was now belting out a Rihanna song with all the enthusiasm of a hopeful reality show competitor.

Nezzie seemed to be having a good time, she'd at least concede that.

Initially, Aja had reservations about bringing her grandmother along on this trip; she tended to get more done when she was on her own and thought the older woman might slow her down but she was glad she'd brought her.

Nezzie padded out of the bathroom wrapped in a fluffy white bath sheet and Aja's shower cap.

She turned to Aja, seeming to notice her for the first time. "About time you got up," she said, a sly smile spreading across her face. "You and Del have a good time? Y'all were out pretty late."

"Not that late." Aja said, scanning her inbox for any urgent issues. Everything seemed to be under control. Lavender had sent her the two top candidates for the open developer job but she could review those on Monday. She logged off and closed the laptop. "I wanted to get dessert so we went to this little spot that had rum cake." Putting the laptop back in her bag, she regarded Nezzie. "How are your allergies this morning?"

"Much better. My nose and throat were desert dry when I woke up, but I'll be fine," she said.

Nezzie selected an orange and yellow sundress from the closet. "Jewel invited us over for lunch. She said she's within walking distance of our hotel."

"You two certainly hit it off," Aja grabbed her toiletries bag, intent on taking a quick shower.

"We both like to talk," Nezzie said with a grin, "but I think Jewel is lonely. She's made a few friends on the island but her kids are still in the U.S.. Made me realize I'm lucky that my kids and most of my grandkids live nearby."

Aja frowned. "It's just her here?"

Nezzie nodded, taking the shower cap off and pulling soft rollers out of her silver hair.

"Yep. But she said she'd always wanted to retire on a Caribbean island. She loves it here."

Nezzie ran her fingers through her hair, loosening the curls. "I'm going to get us some coffee and maybe some fruit, you want anything else?"

"No, that should hold me until lunch."

In the shower, Aja let the warm water run over her as she considered her grandmother's thoughts about Jewel. Unfortunately, Jewel seemed like a scammer's perfect prey: new to the area, no family nearby, lonely and wanting to fit in.

She turned the knob to make the water a little hotter and let her mind form the questions she'd ask Jewel when they met. Jewel said they met on social media and Aja wanted to know how the man might have found her and if there was anything publicly available about Jewel's situation.

After getting dressed in a pair of shorts and a colorful top Zaria insisted she buy, Aja joined Nezzie on the patio. Nezzie was sitting in one of the vinyl chairs, humming a tune and seeming lost in thought.

The patio had two vinyl chairs and a small round table where Nezzie had placed two cups of coffee along with a large plate of pineapple, strawberries, and papaya.

Nezzie turned to Aja. "One other thing...after lunch Jewel wants me to go on a rum tour with her."

Who was this person sitting next to her? "Really? I didn't think you liked rum."

Nezzie sighed wistfully. "I like rum, it just makes me do irresponsible things, you know, so I don't fool with it most days, but since this is Barbados and I'm on vacation, I'm doing what the locals do."

"Well, okay, as long as one of you is able to drive home," Aja said slyly.

"Yes, ma'am," Nezzie rolled her eyes. "Anyway, Del called me first thing this morning. He wanted to see how my allergies were and asked if I needed anything else from the pharmacy."

"Wait, what?" Aja's head shot up. "How does he have your number?"

Nezzie stirred her coffee. "I gave it to him when you were checking us in. Always good for everyone to be able to reach each other. If something happens to you, he can call me."

Aja narrowed her eyes. She had a feeling there was more to her grandmother's explanation.

Watching Nezzie, who seemed to be studying the fruit plate intensely, Aja waited.

"He also wanted to take us over to Diana's studio and house today," Nezzie glanced back toward the patio doors. "I told him I had plans and that you would go."

And there it was.

"He said he'll be in the lobby."

Aja's heart raced at the thought of spending more time alone with Del. She knew she wouldn't be able to avoid him for the rest of the trip but she'd hoped to put off their next meeting until Monday when they went back to the funeral home.

Aja watched a man and his dog as they played fetch on the shore. "Let me get this straight. You're basically abandoning your oldest grandchild to go drink rum and who knows what else with a woman you just met?"

"You've always been too melodramatic for your own good." Nezzie rolled her eyes and sipped her coffee. "I'm giving you space so you can go see what's up with that sexy young man," she reached over, snagging a piece of pineapple. "You can't tell me you don't think he's attractive."

Aja sighed. Things weren't that simple. "Doesn't matter what I think, Nezzie, he doesn't date American women."

Nezzie licked a finger. "Why not?"

"I didn't ask. Not my concern." Aja gulped her cooling coffee.

"Hmm. Well, he likes you, American or not. I can tell." She peered at Aja over her sunglasses, "Better question: is he worthy of your time?"

Aja bit into a plump strawberry and wanted to sigh. Even the fruit here tasted like paradise. She leaned back in her chair to stare at the clear blue sky above. She pondered on Nezzie's words, wondering when her grandmother had turned into a relationship sage. Or perhaps she'd always been one and Aja had just never paid attention.

Was Del Parris worthy of her time? Maybe.

"A little island fling would do you a world of good, I think. Just be prepared."

Aja blinked. What was Nezzie saying?

Nezzie leaned in. "We can stop and get you some condoms."

Aja's mouth dropped. Granted, Nezzie had always tried to impress upon Aja and London that they could come to her if they had questions about sex when they were teens, but this was too much. "No. Umm...what exactly did you two talk about earlier?"

"Nothing much. I like hearing him speak with that accent of his, don't you?" Nezzie winked at her.

Aja rolled her eyes, trying to hide the blush that crept up her cheeks. She was a grown woman, but still felt like a kid talking about her sex life with her grandmother. Time to change the subject. "Let's go get our massages."

Jewel's home was a small bungalow with white walls and a red roof. The front yard was filled with vibrant flowers of all colors, and a small porch overlooked a compact backyard. Inside, the home was cozy and decorated with local art. Jewel greeted them with open arms and led them into her colorful kitchen, telling them the food would be ready in a few minutes. The smell of grilled fish and spices filled the air, and Aja's stomach growled in anticipation.

They sat down at the dining table, and Jewel served them a feast of grilled marlin, macaroni pie, sweet plantains, and rice and peas. Jewel held up a pitcher containing a deep red beverage. "Have either of you had sorrel drink before?"

Aja and Nezzie both shook their heads.

"Sorrel is very popular in the Caribbean. It's made from red sorrel leaves, either dried or fresh then we add spices like ginger, cinnamon, clove, and orange peel, add some sugar then we boil it and let it sit overnight. You can add rum but I left that out this time."

"That sounds good, I want to try a bit," Nezzie said, holding up her glass.

Aja accepted a glass and took a small sip. The drink was a nice blend of sweet and spicy and she nodded in appreciation. "You're from the States, right? How did you learn to cook the local food?"

Jewel smiled. "Cooking classes and talking to local restaurant owners that would tolerate me. I've always loved to cook so I learned to cook Bajan food."

"Everything is delicious, Jewel," Nezzie said. "I don't know if I can go back to regular macaroni and cheese after tasting this macaroni pie."

Jewel laughed. "Thank you, Nezzie." She turned her gaze to the pie, and Aja was instantly intrigued. The dish was prepared with long tubular macaroni, mixed with a special blend of sharp cheddar and mild cheeses before being baked until the top had turned into a golden-brown crust. It was served in large squares, and it held its shape firmly.

After lunch, they took their glasses of sorrel out to Jewel's deck. Even though she wasn't directly on the beach, they could hear the waves crashing in and smell the sea air. Aja marveled at the bright blue sky and the warm sun on her skin. It was nice to be outside, enjoying eighty-degree weather, on a perfect day in Barbados. If she were back at home in Atlanta, she'd be bundled up in her drafty home office, trying to catch up on her work.

Jewel leaned back in her chair and took a deep breath. "So, Aja, I wanted to show you some of the emails I've gotten from Malik."

Aja set her glass down and gave Jewel her full attention. "Sure, I can take a look. Do you want to forward them to me?"

Jewel waved her off. "I printed them out. Let me get them."

She hurried back into the house.

Nezzie slurped her drink. "I really hope this man is okay. Jewel's a nice woman."

Jewel returned with several pages of printed emails and handed them to Aja. Aja skimmed through, looking for any obvious red flags. In one of the messages, Malik said that he wanted to come see her in Barbados, but he was waiting on some money owed to him by his clients. While he didn't outright ask for money, Aja was sure that if Jewel offered, he'd jump at the chance.

"Do you mainly communicate with him via email?" Aja asked, not looking up from the pages.

"Mostly texts. Though I'm not really a big texter," Jewel admitted.

Making a mental note, Aja asked, "How often do you call each other?"

"Maybe once a week. He works a lot and if he calls, it's usually when he's on the road."

Nezzie grunted. "He's probably married."

Aja raised an eyebrow at Nezzie's comment but continued to read through the emails. Malik seemed genuine in his interest in Jewel, but there was something that made Aja uneasy. She couldn't quite put her finger on it, but her instincts were telling her to investigate further.

She held the stack up. "Can I hold on to these for a day or so? I don't see anything particularly suspicious, but I'll do some digging and see if I can find anything else."

"Thank you, I really appreciate it." She glanced at her watch. "Well, Ms. Inez, our tour starts in about thirty minutes, you ready to head out?"

"Oh yes. I can't wait. Do you mind dropping Aja off at our hotel? She's meeting someone there." Nezzie asked sweetly, glancing at Aja.

Aja stood, stretching. "Actually, I think I'll walk back. It's a nice day and it'll give me some time to clear my head."

Nezzie patted her arm. "Have fun and don't worry about rushing back. Tell Del I said hi."

Aja placed Jewel's emails in her tote. As she made her way back to the hotel, her thoughts strayed to Del. She was anxious about seeing him again. Would they be awkward, each treading carefully over last night's conversation?

When she approached the reception area, she saw Del was already there, chatting with the clerk.

He was wearing a lilac linen shirt and a pair of white walking shorts. Aja couldn't help but notice how well the clothes fit him. The color brought out the deep brown of his eyes and the fabric seemed to hug his toned muscles in all the right places.

She approached him slowly, taking in the sight of him. Her heart skipped a beat when he turned to look at her, his gaze intense.

"Hey," she said, a little breathless. Del gave her a slow smile that stirred something warm and fluttery deep in her stomach.

"Aja," he said, not taking his eyes off her face. "how was lunch?"

"It was good," she said, her voice a bit husky. She tried to sound casual, almost uninterested, but the warmth of his gaze was making it hard for her to focus on anything else. "I think I like Bajan food, at least what Jewel made, especially the macaroni pie... have you had that before? Wait, of course you have," she huffed, trying to stop the onslaught of words spilling from her mouth. "Should we go?" she gestured toward the street.

He cocked an eyebrow at her. "You okay?"

"I'm fine," Aja said, flashing what she hoped was a convincing smile. "Sorry, I'm still adjusting to the heat."

Del chuckled, the rich sound making Aja's heart thump wildly in her chest. "Yeah, I got some bottled water in the car if you need it." He motioned for her to precede him. As she walked past him, she caught a whiff of him and nearly swooned. He smelled good, she realized. More than good. He smelled amazing. Normally, Del smelled faintly of leather and a spicy aftershave but today she couldn't put her finger on the scent. She stopped, studying him. "What are you wearing?"

He froze like she'd told him to stand still.

"Fragrance wise, I mean. Is it cologne or..." she let her words trail off. Maybe she was getting too personal.

Del looked slightly uncomfortable. "Does it smell too strong? Apparently, my mother's new thing is making shea butter and she shoved some samples of it in my bag before I left. She's been hounding me to try it and let her know what I think."

Aja pursed her lips. The woman should call it *Sex in a Jar*. "It's very nice," she said finally.

"Does that mean you like it?" Del narrowed his eyes.

She nodded slowly. She wanted to bury her face in his neck but she figured there was no way to phrase that without sounding creepy.

A sly grin spread across his face. "I'll tell her you found me irresistible after I put it on."

Her eyes widened. "I didn't say all that...it's, you smell good, is all I'm saying."

She could just shut up now.

"Ah...you think I smell good. Even better."

She rolled her eyes. He might as well start strutting like a peacock. "Let's go."

CHAPTER 10

Aja

After they were buckled into his rental car, Del turned to Aja. "We should go by Diana's studio, if you're up for it. Make sure everything is okay."

She wasn't up for it, she wanted to scream. But throwing a tantrum wasn't going to make the task go away.

The weight of responsibility draped over Aja's shoulders like a heavy, scratchy wool cloak, but she knew she had to be the one to handle this situation.

Part of her wanted to rebel, to throw her hands up and retreat to the beach for the day. But she wouldn't. She would put her big girl panties on and take charge, as she always did.

Aja took a deep breath and nodded. "Sure, let's go check on it," she said, trying to sound confident. But inside, she was tense with anxiety. She had no idea what she was getting into or what she would find once she was surrounded by her mother's things.

Del started the car and added the address to his GPS then they drove toward Diana's studio. Aja tried to push her worries about her mother's things out of her mind and focus on the present.

As she watched the colorful houses dotted along the street, she wondered if she should have asked her grandmother to come with her. Nezzie had a way of rolling up her sleeves and getting things done, a trait Aja was proud to inherit. She knew her grandmother would have come if Aja had asked her to, but no, Nezzie deserved to enjoy her trip with her new friend.

She turned to Del. "How far are we from the studio?"

He checked his phone. "About ten minutes. I promise we'll be in and out."

She nodded, crossing her arms.

As Del drove, Aja stared at the passing landscape of Holetown, the quaint beachside charm a stark contrast to the anxiety building inside her. She tried to relax, taking deep breaths but her body remained on high alert.

When they arrived at the studio, Aja hesitated before getting out. Del looked at her with concern. "Do you want to stay in the car?"

Aja shook her head. "No, I need to do this." She undid her seatbelt and pulled the door handle.

Del reached over, stopping her, and took her hand. "I'm here, Aja. We'll do what you can and if not, just say the word and we'll go, okay? I got you."

Some of the pressure in her chest eased at his words.

Aja stepped out of the car, squinting at the bright sunlight. The studio was a quaint stone building nestled between a fabric store and a bakery.

As they walked toward the studio, Aja replayed Del's words on a loop.

Just say the word and we'll go. I got you.

She struggled with admitting she needed help, with admitting that she wasn't as strong as everyone assumed she was.

Del used a key from his pocket to unlock the door and it creaked as Del held it open for her. He handed her the key.

As Aja entered, a familiar scent she hadn't smelled in years hit her. Chanel perfume.

Aja closed her eyes, seeing her mother in her pink robe, spritzing the scent on her neck and wrists. Aja would watch in wonder as her mother then applied her makeup and dressed for the day. She'd thought her mother was the most beautiful woman in the world and she'd just wanted to spray on a little bit of her mother's favorite scent. Aja, barely tall enough to reach the bottle on top of her mother's dresser, managed to slide the perfume closer to the edge. But the bottle slipped from her hands and shattered once it hit the floor.

Her mother had scolded her when she reached the room. "Aja! I told you not to get into my things! Of all the bottles, you had to waste my good Chanel! Go to your room," she'd hissed. Aja had run from the room, crying, and flung herself onto her bed.

Her mother had left them shortly after that incident and for years after, Aja was convinced she was the reason her mother left. If she hadn't been playing with her mother's things, she might have stayed.

Later, when Aja was old enough to go to the mall by herself, she had her father drop her off at Macy's one Saturday. She made a beeline for the perfume section and found the Chanel collection. Aja tried each scent until she recognized her mother's favorite. Chanel No. 5.

She purchased her first bottle of perfume using the allowance she earned for helping her dad with his business.

When Aja got home, she took the fancy box and stared at it then placed it in her dresser drawer. If her mother ever came back, she'd give her that bottle and everything would be as it was before.

Now, however, she knew that wasn't true. A few years ago, she'd run across that bottle while packing to move into her condo and donated it to a local women's shelter.

Aja opened her eyes and looked around the studio, taking a deep breath. The scent of Chanel No. 5 was still in the air, but it didn't have the same power over her as it used to.

"It's a little stuffy in here," Del said as he opened one of the windows.

The scent of the ocean breeze pulled Aja from her musing and she turned her attention to the room.

"So," Del approached her, "does creativity run in your family? Are you an artist by night?"

Aja gave a quick snort. "Not at all. I took a sketching class when I was in middle school but I wasn't good at it immediately so I abandoned it for coding camp."

"Ah, you can write software, I'm assuming?"

"I can do the basics, but I leave that to the professionals these days," she said, perusing a display case full of small glass seashells. "What about you? I have a feeling you have a creative side?"

He made a face. "Nope. I can't draw to save my life."

He paused, picking up one of the seashells. "But I will tell you a secret, if you promise not to laugh."

"Oh, I'll keep your secret but I don't know about the no laughter part," she said, biting her lip in anticipation. "Are you about to tell me you love Hallmark movies along with the Publix commercials?"

If his intention was to distract her, it was working.

"There's nothing wrong with Hallmark. But you have to promise," Del put the seashell back in its place on the display shelf. "This is serious business."

"Now I'm intrigued. What is this big secret? You took ballet and played the lead in Swan Lake?"

He rolled his eyes. "No."

She snapped her fingers. "I know...you went to clown college and do kid's parties on the weekends?"

Del let out a long, deep sigh. "Your imagination is something else. Nope."

"Okay, I give up," Aja tried to keep from grinning. "What is it? I won't laugh, I promise."

"I will probably live to regret this..." Del muttered.

"Spill it, Delford!"

He sighed. "I watched *Ghost* with my mom when I was about fourteen and I decided I wanted to create pottery because I thought it would get me girls."

"Wait, the movie with Whoopi Goldberg?" Aja had never

seen the whole movie, but she knew what he was talking about. The infamous pottery wheel scene.

"Yep."

Aja pursed her lips, trying desperately to hold back a giggle.

He continued, "I was going to be the instructor, leaning over, guiding the girl...our hands intertwined in the clay..."

Aja tried to hold it together. "Let me get this straight...you were going to be the Patrick Swayze of pottery?"

"Yeah, something like that."

Aja couldn't contain her laughter any longer. She covered her mouth. "Okay, don't leave me hanging, how did it go?"

"Are you laughing at my heartache?" Del said in mock horror.

Tears formed in her eyes. "No, of course not."

"My mom bought me some modeling clay and I made her a lumpy ashtray," he winced. "She doesn't even smoke."

Still chuckling, Aja shook her head. "I can't believe that didn't work."

"Hey, in my defense, I was a chubby teen with a thick accent and no athletic ability...I was desperate enough to try anything."

Surprised, Aja turned to study Del. His description of his younger self didn't align with the man she saw before her. Now, he was tall and muscular with an unmistakable Caribbean charm. Aja found it hard to imagine him as anything other than confident.

"You? Desperate?" she teased, nudging his arm with her elbow. "I would think the girls would love your accent," she said, knowing she could listen to him read a dictionary and find it fascinating.

"Nope. Kids being kids, I was told to go back to Jamaica, which I have never been to, and the school suggested speech therapy." He picked up a clear glass piece shaped like a seashell and handed it to Aja. "Look at the detail on this thing."

Aja took the piece in both hands. She marveled at how real it looked. "Speech therapy?" Aja was shocked, "Why?"

"For my accent," he shrugged. "They thought it would help me fit in."

Aja struggled to make sense of what he was saying. "I'm so confused. Go back to Jamaica?"

"A lot of Americans hear a Caribbean accent and assume the person is from Jamaica," he explained.

"I had a coworker from Kingston and you sound nothing alike...it's totally different," she said, annoyed by the ignorance she knew he faced. His voice was lyrical and held a sing-song rhythm that was uniquely Del's. She placed the seashell back on the shelf.

"Yeah. But that didn't matter much to them. And truth be told, it didn't matter much to me either. I just wanted to fit in," he confessed. "I went to speech therapy for a while and all it did was make me more conscious of my accent."

For a moment, Aja just stood there, silently taking in his words. Something about his story touched her, the vulnerability in his voice hitting her harder than she had expected.

"I think that's what drew me to Sidney Poitier. He grew up on Cat Island in the Bahamas and I figured if he could make a living as an actor, maybe I could too. I watched his movies over and and over, listening to his voice and emulating it."

Aja stared at Del, her analytical mind processing his truth. With his good looks and easy confidence, she'd assumed he'd been popular in school. Here was a man who had been subjected to prejudice and mockery in his youth, yet, instead of allowing that to define him, he'd used it as a stepping stone.

Del continued, "My interests shifted after that. I got more into drama and arts. I learned that people are more accepting when you're playing a character or telling a story than when you're just another dude with an accent."

"Okay, so you were acting. How did you get into coaching?"

"Well," Del began, rubbing his hands together. "Acting took me to university. I got a scholarship, you know. Drama and all that. But by the time I was in my final year, I was kind of over it all." He glanced at Aja, and she felt that familiar quiver in her gut.

"Really?" Aja asked, leaning in. Her curiosity was piqued, eager to understand this man who had captured her attention so unexpectedly.

"I guess...I realized that I wasn't acting because it was my passion. When it started, it was just a way for me to fit in," he explained. "It was a role I played. A major one, sure, but a role and I wasn't connected to it anymore."

"I started coaching purely by accident," he finally said, walking around the studio. "I was working as a recruiter and I would help applicants with their resumes. We got this tip that a big auto manufacturer on the south side of Atlanta near the airport was moving their plant out of the country and the layoffs would be huge. I was essentially helping people who had been at these jobs for years and years create resumes and apply for jobs online. A lot of them had no idea what they were going to do next."

Aja nodded. She remembered that plant closing was a huge loss for the state.

Aja walked around the space, taking in the glass sculptures that her mother had created. They were beautiful, intricate works. Aja ran her fingers over one of the larger pieces, feeling the smooth glass. The orb had ribbons of blue and purple running through it. She picked it up gingerly, using both hands, and stared at it. The sphere was heavy, like a miniature bowling ball. The vibrant cerulean blue and deep purple reminded her of a winding river. She held it as she listened to Del.

"I helped a lot of them get into training programs to upskill and I helped a few pivot into new careers. I realized I could make a business out of helping people realize their dreams. I love what I do."

His words echoed through the small studio, causing Aja's heart to swell with admiration for this man who had unexpectedly fallen into her life. The depth of his character astounded her.

"I wish I'd known you back in the pottery days," she said softly, "I would have told you I loved your accent just as it was."

Del turned his thoughtful gaze on her, an affectionate smile curving his lips. "Thank you, Aja. But back then, I was too caught up in my own insecurities to see that."

He turned away abruptly, like he'd revealed too much too soon. A sudden awkward silence filled the studio.

Sensing that Del might need a minute, Aja focused on the orb she held. She could stare at the piece for the rest of the day, following the path of each ribbon of color. Is that what her mother intended when she'd created the piece?

Carefully placing the sphere back on its stand, she made her way to the back of the studio. There were two doors on either side of her. One was marked "restroom" and the other "private". Aja tried the knob on the private room and pushed it open.

The room contained a small office with a single filing cabinet, an antique white desk and a rolling chair.

Artwork adorned each wall, colorful abstract paintings that Aja suspected were her mother's work as well.

She sat at the desk, feeling that she was somehow intruding on her mother's space.

Aja opened the top drawer of the desk, half-expecting to find it locked but it slid open easily. There was a manila folder inside it and Aja pulled it out.

She flipped through the papers inside, recognizing her mother's handwriting on some of the pages. It seemed to be a collection of notes and ideas for future glass sculptures.

Her curiosity piqued, Aja continued to rummage through the folder.

Two pictures slid out, landing on the floor by her feet. Aja bent to retrieve them as Del strode in.

"You're awfully quiet in here, thought I'd check on you," he said, walking over to her.

Aja held up one of the pictures. "Care to explain this?"

CHAPTER 11

Del

Del's pulse pounded in his head as he stared at the picture Aja had in her hand. His first impulse was to stall while he tried to come up with a plausible explanation. "Where was that?"

"In this folder," Aja said, enunciating each word. "You said you'd never met my mother in person. Yet here the two of you are, taking selfies."

Aja's voice was controlled but he could tell by her clenched jaw and narrowed eyes she was pissed. He knew he had messed up by lying to Aja and now he had to face the consequences. "Technically, you asked if I'd come here to meet her and that was true."

The look she gave him was pure ice. "You could have clarified."

He sighed heavily and decided to come clean. "I'm sorry, Aja, I lied to you. Your mother came to Atlanta but she swore me to secrecy."

Aja stared at him, her eyes filled with hurt and anger. "Why would she do that? And why would you lie to me?"

Del took a step closer to her, closing the distance between them. "Last year, when you did that panel discussion at Women In Technology, Diana had mentioned it to me and I suggested she attend. I thought it would be a good way to start mending her relationship with you but she didn't want to be disruptive." He took a seat opposite Aja. "She didn't know if you'd be happy to see her. She came to town then ultimately decided not to go to the event. We met up for dinner, that's when we took that picture. She told me never to say anything."

Aja crossed her arms. "Why did she leave me in the first place? Did she ever talk to you about that since you two seemed to be sharing so many damn secrets?"

Del heard the bitterness and the underlying pain. He rushed over to her and placed a hand on her shoulder, attempting to offer her some comfort. "Aja, honestly, from the bits and pieces that she told me about that time, I think she was suffering from depression," Del said with a sigh. "But she deeply regretted every day she wasn't with you. I do know that."

He squeezed her shoulder. "She loved you. She talked about how proud she was of you."

Aja pulled away. "I don't want to hear it, Del. I don't want to hear about how much my mother loved me. She left me and never looked back. She didn't even try to reach out to me. How could she possibly love me?"

Del could see the tears forming in Aja's eyes, and his heart ached for her. He knew that no matter what he said, it wouldn't take away the hurt and anger that Aja was feeling. But he had to try.

"Aja, I know it's hard to understand. But sometimes, people make mistakes. They do things that they regret later on. Your mother was one of those people. She never stopped loving you, and she would have done anything to make it up to you if she had the chance."

Aja turned her back on him, walking over to the window. She stared out at the peaceful Barbadian landscape, the water shimmering under the late afternoon sun. "You should have told me," she said, her voice barely above a whisper.

"I know." Del agreed quietly. He wished he could have done things differently, wished that he hadn't lied to Aja.

She scoffed. "And are you sure you were just friends? What were you to my mother? Surely not just her coach?"

"No, I swear, nothing like that. She was like a bonus mother to me."

Aja's face darkened as soon as he uttered the words. Del winced, wishing he could call them back.

Her fists clenched at her sides. "She abandons the daughter she gave birth to for the son she always wanted, is that right?" Her voice was controlled, but Del could see the anger simmering below the surface.

Abruptly, she stood up. "I need to get out of here."

He held up the car keys. "We can go-"

"No," she cut him off. "I need to be alone. I need some air."

Del watched as Aja strode out of the office, slamming the door behind her.

He heard the door to the shop close. He sighed, debating on whether he should go after her or give her some time to cool down. She was hurting, he knew.

He'd seen that same pain in Diana's eyes when she talked about her daughter.

He couldn't imagine what it must have been like for Diana to leave Aja.

Del ran a hand over his chin. He was on dangerous ground, caring more than he should about Aja. He should just leave it-and her-alone.

But he couldn't. The thought of Aja, alone and hurting, was unbearable. He stood up and headed out of the office, hoping to find Aja before she walked too far away.

As he walked down the street, wondering which way she would go, he instinctively turned toward the pathway leading to the beach.

Glancing around, out of the corner of his eye, he caught sight of a deep brown skinned man leaning against the corner of the shopping center, smoking a cigarette. The man was of average height, shorter than Del but bulkier. Del got the sense that he was trying to be more casual than he was. He could tell the man wasn't a local by his vacation dress but the man's clothes and demeanor didn't scream *tourist*.

As Del watched, the man took another deep drag then tossed the cigarette to the ground, stepping on it. Then he turned and entered the bakery.

Del turned his attention back to finding Aja.

The sun cast long shadows as he approached the beach. He squinted against the glare off the water, scanning the shoreline for Aja's silhouette. To his relief, he spotted her in the distance; a lone figure standing by the water's edge. The breeze tousled her hair as she stood with her body facing out toward the vast expanse of the ocean. Del slowed his pace as he approached, carefully observing her from behind. Her body was tense, her arms folded across her body shielding her from the world.

He approached her cautiously, unsure of how she would react.

"I'm sorry," he said after a moment of silence.

Aja didn't move, didn't acknowledge him. He watched as she slowly uncrossed her arms, her hands falling limp by her sides.

A lump developed in his throat and the urge to comfort her grew within him, but he held back, giving her space.

Del noticed her sandals behind her and picked them up, brushing the sand off. The silence stretched between them but he didn't rush to fill it. Instead, he held her shoes, hoping his presence would be enough for the moment.

Aja finally turned to him, eyes red from crying. "I just feel so lost, Del. I don't know what to do. I don't know how to forgive her for leaving me. Now she's gone, and I'll never have the chance to get closure."

Del's heart ached for her as he listened to her words. He knew the pain of not having closure all too well - his own father had left when he was young, never giving him an explanation or a chance to say goodbye.

But in that moment, all he could think about was Aja and how much she needed someone to be there for her.

He stepped closer, placing a hand on her back and pulling her into a hug. She stiffened at first, but then relaxed into his embrace and let out a sob.

"I know it's hard, Aja. But you don't have to forgive her right away. It's a process, and it will take time. Don't feel like you have to be strong and resilient all the time. It's perfectly okay to not be okay."

Aja chuckled into his chest. "That's the coach coming out again, isn't it?"

"No," he started to protest. "Well, maybe a little."

She pulled away, her gaze meeting his. "I find myself appreciating the coach more than I probably should. Thank you."

"You're welcome," he said, unable and unwilling to break the spell between them. Electricity coursed through him as she leaned in.

"Just know, this is not me being vulnerable," she said. And before he could ask what she meant, Aja's lips met his.

Del was momentarily stunned, unsure of how he should react. He hesitated for a beat but his body moved of its own accord, taking the lead. He dropped her sandals and wrapped his arms around her waist.

Her kiss was full of raw emotion, desperation, and longing. He could feel her pain, but also her desire.

As they embraced, Del could feel the tension and hesitation in Aja's body slowly dissipate as he ran reassuring hands over her back, conveying that she was not alone in her struggles.

Too soon for his liking, Aja pulled back, breaking the kiss she'd initiated. "I forgot where I was for a minute," she glanced around. "I don't normally do the PDA thing."

"You could have fooled me," Del smirked. "And what's wrong with a little public affection? You're in a whole different country."

"True, but still...I don't know why I just did that."

"And you're feeling what, now? Regret?" He told himself he didn't care about her answer. It was just a kiss, after all.

Aja shook her head. "No, I probably shouldn't tell you this, cause it's going straight to your head, but I was curious."

"Ah, so that was a curiosity kiss?"

"Yep, let's call it that." Aja slipped her sandals back on.

"Anything else you're curious about?" Del asked, a mischievous glint in his eye.

Aja turned to him, giving him a saucy smile. "Maybe."

Del cocked an eyebrow. "My curiosity is different from yours how? Remember you warned me about cats and curiosity?"

"Glad you were paying attention. We can go back to the store. I think I'm ready to work now." She was back in business mode, the vulnerability she'd revealed earlier gone.

Del followed Aja as they took the path back to the store, his mind racing with thoughts of the kiss.

They'd just complicated an already complex situation. Del knew Aja didn't believe he and her mother had just been good friends.

He knew he shouldn't have crossed that line but he couldn't resist her. She was the type of woman he'd sworn he'd never get involved with again: too driven, fiercely independent. At some point, she'd wonder why she kept him around and she'd be gone, taking his shredded heart with her.

Not gonna happen.

Once was enough.

He scowled and slowed, increasing the distance between them.

They reached the store and went inside, the cool air conditioning hitting his face. Aja must have turned the air on before she stormed out.

Aja looked around the space. "I guess I'll need to find

someone to help me sell everything. I don't know if she was renting or if she owned this place."

"She owned this studio."

Aja's eyebrows shot up. "She must have been making a good living with her work."

He nodded. "Diana got a lot of tourist business. She told me she loved to see the cruise ships dock because she would make a killing in one day. And she did glass making workshops."

"I can see why. Her work is exquisite."

Del leaned against the counter, his arms folded. "Yeah, it really is. I saw you eyeing one of the blue pieces. You should keep any pieces you like."

Aja looked at him, surprised.

"Why not? Technically they're yours now." Del felt his heart skip a beat as he watched the emotions play across Aja's face. She favored her mother so much.

"I never thought, well, that didn't occur to me. I guess they are," she said softly.

She made her way back to the blue and purple piece, almost as if she needed to convince herself that she owned it.

Del watched her curiously, wondering what was going through her mind. He knew she was still sorting through her emotions about her mother's passing, the sudden inheritance, and him.

He cleared his throat. "This is a lot to process in one day. Why don't we go for my second to do item today?"

He wiggled his eyebrows at her.

Aja's head tilted. "I'm also afraid to ask since you talked to my grandmother earlier, but what do you have planned?"

"Have you heard of Harrison's Cave?" When she shook her head, he continued. "It's a cave system full of underground rivers, waterfalls, stalactite and stalagmite formations. You take a tram down into the cave. I haven't been since I was a teenager," he stopped. Aja had a strange look on her face. "What? Not interested?"

Aja shook her head vigorously. "Actually, that sounds amazing. It's just that you said caves and all that came to mind was that movie, The Descent. You know, the horror flick where a group of girlfriends go on a caving expedition and things go very badly very quickly?"

Del rolled his eyes. "I saw that movie in the theater. Not my idea. Anyway, there are no creatures in the caves. They're huge and you'll be fine."

Aja motioned to her clothes. "Are we dressed for caving? Should I go back to the resort and change?"

"It's a tourist attraction. As long as you can walk in those," he pointed at her sandals, "you're good."

She gave him one of her radiant smiles. "Okay. I guess we'll see if there are creatures, I'd hate to say I told you so."

Del grinned at her, happy to see her playful side return. "I'll take my chances." He motioned at the orb, "you bringing that with you? There should be supplies to wrap it up so it doesn't get damaged."

They found a cache of packing and shipping supplies near the checkout counter. Aja carefully wrapped up the orb then they locked up the store.

Once they arrived at the cave system, they boarded the tram and descended into the cave. The air grew colder, and the sound of rushing water echoed around them. As they explored the cave, Del was in awe of the natural beauty of his country. But he was also acutely aware of Aja's presence next to him, seated so close, their thighs brushing, sending shivers through him.

The tram ride down into the cave was an adventure in itself, and as they stepped off the tram, Aja gasped softly. The cave was a natural wonder, with underground rivers and waterfalls cascading down the walls. The air was filled with the sound of dripping water and the rush of the underground streams.

Aja was mesmerized, and Del found himself watching her more than the caves. He also kept replaying that kiss. She said she was merely curious but he had a sinking feeling she had done it to hide her vulnerability. He scowled, not wanting to dwell on those thoughts.

As they rounded a corner and came upon a massive underground waterfall, Aja grabbed him. "Wow, this is a whole waterfall," she murmured. The water cascaded down into a crystal-clear pool that sparkled in the cave's low light.

"This is incredible," Aja breathed out, snapping pictures with her phone.

Del chuckled. "Told you it would be worth it."

The rest of the tour group milled around, taking pictures as the tour guide described the cave system. A young couple taking selfies in front of the waterfall approached Aja. "Would you mind taking a picture of us? We can do the same for you."

"Sure," Aja said, holding her hand out for their phone. "I love your dress," she told the woman, as she adjusted the phone and took a series of pictures.

The woman smoothed the teal and navy dress. "Thank you! I bought this in one of the boutiques in Bridgetown."

Del watched as Aja chatted with the couple, a small smile on his lips. He had to admit, he enjoyed seeing her interact with others. She had a way of making people feel at ease, even complete strangers.

"Why don't you two stand here," the woman motioned to a spot to the side of the waterfall, "this will make a perfect picture."

Del hesitated for a moment. He wasn't one for taking pictures, but he found himself nodding.

Aja handed the woman her phone and stood close to Del. At the last second, he snaked an arm around her waist.

"Oh, that's a nice one." The woman took a few more pictures then handed the phone back to Aja, who studied the pictures, nodded and passed her phone to him. "Did you want me to send these to you?"

He scrolled through the images.

"Yeah," he finally replied. "Send them to me."

Once he received the photos, Del reviewed them again closely.

In every picture, they were smiling, their bodies unconsciously leaning toward each other in a comfortable familiarity. It wasn't just the beautiful waterfall backdrop that made the images so striking; it was them together.

In the first photo, he noticed how Aja's eyes were wide with surprise; she hadn't expected him to slide his arm around her waist, he knew. But in the subsequent pictures, she'd relaxed and leaned into him. If he was honest with himself, a part of him wanted more of these moments - moments where they looked like a couple.

He took a deep breath as he tucked the phone back into his pocket. He felt a knot tightening in his stomach, fear and anticipation each warring for dominance. He realized then, in the belly of a massive cave system under his homeland, that he was beginning to fall for Aja.

The tour went on, with the guide pointing out different features of the cave - the odd-shaped formations of stalagmites, ceilings studded with stalactites, and the fossilized remnants of long-extinct creatures embedded in the rocky walls. Del found himself increasingly distracted. His gaze kept returning to Aja, who was wholly lost in the wonder of the caves, her face lit up with awe and excitement.

Gone was the prim entrepreneur in the business suits and heels who felt she had to be in control every second. This Aja next to him was casual, in shorts and flat sandals, her hair pulled back in a ponytail, laughing and pointing in wonder at the cave's formations. She exuded pure joy and he wondered about the last time she'd let herself enjoy the moment.

When they boarded the tram, Del found himself sitting closer to Aja than before. He was drawn to her, wanted to show her the world. He realized he didn't want the day to end.

"I loved the caves! I'm glad we did this," Aja said, breaking the silence between them.

"I'm glad you enjoyed it," Del replied, his voice steady despite the undercurrent of affection that surged through him.

As the tram rattled on, leaving behind the ethereal beauty of the caves, they sat shoulder to shoulder. Del felt a satisfying sense of connectedness.

The tram ride back to the surface felt far too short. As they emerged blinking into the sunlight, Del studied Aja's face. Her eyes were bright with excitement. He decided as much as he liked her in-charge boss mode, he liked this look on her. And he wouldn't mind being the cause of it more often.

He realized she'd said something and was waiting for his answer. "What did you say?"

"I asked if there's anywhere else you'd like to show me today," she replied, a hopeful spark in her eyes.

Del couldn't resist. "You sure you don't want to go back to the resort and create some spreadsheets?"

Aja punched him playfully on the arm, shaking her head as she laughed. "Oh, the life coach is auditioning for Amateur Night at the comedy club now?"

"I'm just checking. It's been what, a few hours since you left that laptop?" He grabbed her wrist like he was checking her pulse. "You sure you're not going through withdrawal?"

Aja swatted his hand away and stuck her tongue out at him, a playful glint in her eyes. "Very funny, Parris. Where to next?"

Del's hand brushed against Aja's cheek, tucking away a loose strand of hair. "I've been thinking about something. Remember that moment on the beach when you kissed me? What was that all about?"

CHAPTER 12

Aja

Aja ended the call and found Jewel's number. She looked over at Del, who seemed to be on alert. She hadn't paid attention to where they parked, she'd been so wrapped up in seizing the day and breaking her own rules.

Del pointed toward the left side of the lot. She followed him as she waited for Jewel to pick up.

No answer.

She left a quick, urgent message asking Jewel to call back as soon as possible, then slid the phone back into her pocket. Her thoughts raced, trying to piece together the fragments of information she had just received.

Del glanced at her, his brow furrowed with concern. "Everything alright?"

Aja tapped the phone against her thigh. "I don't know," she said slowly. "That was my grandmother. She said the man Jewel met online, Malik, is in town and Jewel is going to meet him."

"She's never met him before, I'm assuming?" Del asked, stroking his beard.

"No. I don't know what it is, but something in my gut says this is wrong and she shouldn't meet him," Aja finally said. "But she also told us that he's claimed he's coming then cancels at the last minute. Somehow this feels different from that."

Del nodded, his expression serious. "Trust your instincts. They're usually right. What do you want to do?"

Aja stopped walking and looked up at the tall palm trees that lined the edge of the parking lot, their fronds swaying slightly in the warm breeze. The island was breathtaking everywhere she looked but she couldn't enjoy the moment just yet. "Nezzie said Jewel mentioned a sunset cruise and Bridgetown? Does that help? We flew into Bridgetown, right?"

Aja waited for him to confirm then she continued. "Part of me wants to see if I can find her, just to make sure everything is okay, but is that overstepping?" she wondered aloud. "She asked me to look into him, not be her mother."

Del put his hand on her shoulder, a gesture she found comforting. "You're not overstepping. You're looking out for someone who may be in danger. She hired you to look into him for a reason, right?"

"She did. Worst case: I'm worrying for nothing and she fires me for getting in her business. I can live with that." Decision made, she wanted to get going to Bridgetown.

Del nodded. "Yep, a lot of the tour boats leave from Carlisle Bay. We can head there now. If it's a sunset cruise, it should be gearing up to leave in a little while."

Once they were on the road, Del glanced at her. "We can say we wanted to do the sunset cruise too and act like it's a coincidence."

"Not a bad idea." Aja agreed.

The drive to Bridgetown seemed to take forever. Aja tried to relax and take in the scenery but her thoughts kept straying back to Jewel. Why had Malik decided to pop up in Barbados? Aja tried again to reach Jewel, but the call went straight to voicemail. Aja's fingers drummed against the door handle. Del glanced at her but didn't comment.

They arrived at Carlisle Bay just as boats were beginning to fill with eager tourists. Del was right; a sunset cruise would be leaving soon, and they needed to find Jewel before it set sail.

Aja scanned the crowd, her eyes darting between the faces, looking for the bright colors Jewel favored.

Del parked the car, and they both got out quickly, heading toward the bustling area where tourists were gathered to enjoy the beach and cruises.

This was one of those moments when Aja wished she were taller. Her view was obstructed by clusters of tourists with sunhats and shoulder bags. The air was thick with the scent of sunscreen and saltwater, laughter and chatter filling the space between soca beats floating from a nearby beach bar. Aja blocked it all out as she focused on finding Jewel.

She reached for Del, tapping his arm and appreciating the solid muscle of his bicep. No time for that right now.

"Do you remember what she looks like?" Aja asked. "I know you only saw her briefly last night."

"Yeah, I think I'll know her when I see her. She's kind of tall, right?"

"I guess. She's taller than me and Nezzie."

He smirked. "That's not saying much," he chided.

Aja side-eyed him. "Since you're tall, help me look," Aja motioned toward the crowds.

"I got a better idea. Come here," he pointed at his back then crouched down.

Aja stared at Del's broad back. She could list at least ten reasons why she should stay on the ground and not get so close to him but she convinced herself this would help them find Jewel quicker.

She climbed onto his back, her arms finding their way around his neck. His hands gripped her thighs securely as he stood, lifting her above the crowd like a child at a parade.

Sweet Baby Jesus. She could feel his back muscles beneath his shirt and resisted the urge to run a hand slowly over his chest. He felt like heaven, his body warm and hard next to hers.

The thought made her nipples tighten and Aja forced herself to focus on the mission at hand.

From her higher vantage point, Aja scanned the crowds, her eyes searching intently for any sign of Jewel. The salty ocean breeze ruffled her hair as she surveyed the milling tourists. Her heart was racing, either from Del's closeness or the urgency of finding Jewel before it was too late, she wasn't sure which.

Aja's eyes narrowed as she caught a glimpse of vibrant colors in the distance. She tightened her grip on Del's shoulders. "I'm pretty sure that's her, over by the tour boats." She pointed toward the dock.

Del nodded and started weaving through the throngs of people, Aja clinging to his back as he moved with purpose. At one point, he slowed, tapping her bare thigh with his large hand. The touch jolted her, as if he'd zapped her with a taser.

"You okay back there?"

She let out a sharp breath and tried to focus. "Fine," she lied.

Del's grip on Aja's thighs tightened as he maneuvered through the crowd, drawing her closer. The warmth of his body and the firm press of his hands sent a shiver down her spine.

"You sure?" He stopped and turned to look at her.

His brown eyes met hers and the concern in them drew her in. She wanted to forget about Jewel and slide around him so they were chest to chest, face to face.

"Yes," she said breathlessly.

She blinked, coming to her senses.

He had asked if she was okay. She mentally shook herself out of her haze. "Yes, I'm fine. Let's get going."

He cocked a questioning eyebrow at her but resumed his brisk pace.

As they drew closer, Aja could make out Jewel's form in a flowing tropical print halter dress in shades of red and orange.

"Okay, maybe I should approach her alone," she said. "I don't want to scare her."

As they reached the dock, Aja slipped from Del's grip and

landed on her feet, adjusting her blouse which had ridden up during the piggyback ride. The immediate loss of warmth made her shiver despite the tropical heat.

She walked over to where Jewel was standing. The woman was alone and seemed deep in thought. "Jewel?"

Jewel jumped slightly and spun around toward Aja. "Oh, Aja!"

"Hey, I didn't mean to startle you. We were thinking about doing one of the sunset cruises," she said. "Have you done one before?"

Jewel glanced at her watch. "No, actually I haven't, but I have tickets for one leaving in a few," she gestured toward a queue of people waiting to board one of the catamarans. "My friend... canceled. Do you want the tickets? I don't want them to go to waste."

Aja waited for more detail, but Jewel remained silent. "Are you sure? Maybe you can reschedule?"

Jewel shook her head quickly. "No, I'm not going." She pulled the tickets from her bag. "Take them. Enjoy it, I insist." She handed Aja the tickets.

"Let me pay you for them. How much?"

Jewel waved her off. "No, this is on me as a thank you for checking into that thing I asked you about," Jewel lowered her voice. "I don't think I need your help anymore. I think that's over with."

Taken aback, Aja frowned. "Did something happen?"

Jewel's gaze dropped and she shoved her hands into the pockets on her dress. "I don't want to get into it right now," she replied in a hushed voice. "You should go get in line, looks like they've almost finished boarding."

Aja looked over her shoulder at the dwindling line, then back at Jewel. "Alright, if you're sure. And if you change your mind or need anything, let me know. I'll be here for the next two weeks."

Jewel returned the smile, though hers was tinged with sadness. "Thank you, Aja. Enjoy the cruise."

With that, Jewel turned and raised a hand in greeting to Del then set off in the opposite direction.

Aja watched her go, a sense of dread seeping through her. Aja was willing to bet money Jewel was meeting Malik for the cruise but Jewel hadn't mentioned him. Maybe she was embarrassed to tell Aja she'd made plans with the very man she'd asked Aja to investigate.

She sighed. Jewel might confide in Nezzie about the botched plans; she'd have to wait and see.

Turning back, she handed the tickets to Del, who had been waiting for her silently. "She said her friend canceled and she insisted I take the tickets." She gestured toward the boat. "You want to go?"

She waited for his answer, feeling like a teenager asking the cute boy to the prom.

Del looked at the tickets in his hand, then back at Aja, seeming to consider her offer. "A sunset cruise with a beautiful woman? I guess I can make time," he teased.

"Well, thank you for your sacrifice." She put her hands together as if in prayer.

They slipped into the queue just as the last few passengers were getting checked in.

As she waited for the passengers ahead of them to get settled, Aja turned back to Del and found him studying her. "What?" She asked.

"Nothing," he said with an easy grin. "You never fail to amaze me."

"It's my sarcastic wit, isn't it?"

"Nope. I've learned that it takes a while to peel back the business-owner-boss layer but when you do, it's like you're a kid again, excited and eager to experience life. I like it."

Aja felt her cheeks flush at his words. She tried to play it off with a shrug. "Life's too short to not be excited about the little things, right?"

"Exactly! I think I'm rubbing off on you." He gave her a smirk, clearly proud of himself.

Aja rolled her eyes.

A crew member checked their tickets and advised them to leave their shoes in a plastic container on the dock before they boarded. Aja slipped out of her sandals and waited for Del to remove his sneakers and socks. Another crew member helped her step onto the boat. Aja took in her surroundings as they settled into the last available bench near the stern. There was a bar and two buffet tables near their seats.

Del rose. "Can't do a proper sunset cruise without a drink. Rum punch?"

She might as well try the rum punch. "Sure, but I'd also like some water." Del bowed and headed toward the bar.

When he returned with two bottles, she quickly opened hers and took a long drink. The ice cold water felt good going down. She hadn't realized how thirsty she was.

A crew member called for their attention, introduced the staff then started the safety presentation. Aja noted the location of the life jackets and watched closely as the speaker demonstrated putting one on and securing it. While she knew odds were slim they'd need life jackets on this excursion, she'd rather be prepared.

After the safety presentation concluded, the crew prepared to set sail and cranked up a soca song with a slower tempo that Aja found herself thinking was the perfect song for a cruise at sunset. She swayed to the beat slightly, lost in her own world as the catamaran set sail. The sun was just beginning its descent and the sea breeze felt good against her skin. She closed her eyes, determined to let go of all her worries about Jewel, her business and her mother.

Aja felt Del's presence behind her seconds before he slid his hands up her arms. Immediately his touch caused a chain reaction, from the goosebumps on her arms to the electric current that raced through her blood.

"You cold?" Del's voice, his accent even more pronounced, was a low murmur in her ear.

Aja opened her eyes. She shook her head, looking up into Del's warm brown eyes. "I'm fine."

"That you are," he agreed, pulling her closer to his chest. "But are you cold?"

His scent and nearness were more intoxicating than any cocktail from the bar.

"Not at all. And if I didn't know better, I'd think you were trying to shoot your shot." Aja murmured, turning back to take in the waves.

"Oh, should I?" Del asked, nuzzling her neck. His tone was light but there was an undercurrent of something more that made her heart beat faster.

"Maybe you should." The words slipped out before she could run them through her internal filters. But she meant every word, she realized.

She barely knew him, yet here she was, leaning into his touch and encouraging him to make a move. She couldn't deny there was something about Del that drew her in, something magnetic and irresistible.

"If I didn't know better, I'd think you were issuing me an invitation," he said into her ear.

Aja swore her toes were close to curling.

She turned back to face him. "You gonna RSVP, Parris?"

He tilted her chin up so that she was looking directly into his eyes. They were a warm brown, resembling the Barbadian soil underneath the gleaming sun. "Consider this my RSVP," he murmured, leaning down to capture her lips in a slow, lingering kiss. His hand cupped the back of her neck. Unlike their earlier kiss where she'd caught him by surprise, Del was the driver this time, taking what she offered and demanding more. He drew her closer, his tongue exploring the contours of her mouth. Aja had always rolled her eyes when women gushed about kisses that made their knees weak but she was a believer now. She was certain her knees would give out at any moment.

Thankfully, Del's arms were around her, holding her steady while his mouth continued its intoxicating assault. The taste of him, a heady mix of rum punch and something distinctly Del, had her pressing closer still. He withdrew slightly, allowing her to catch her breath before he recaptured her lips for another lingering kiss. His hand, which had been steady on the small of her back, now roamed up and down her spine, sending tingles of anticipation throughout her body.

A cheer from their fellow passengers broke them apart. Aja turned back to the sea to see the sun dipping below the horizon in a blaze of pink and orange. The catamaran had stopped and everyone was watching the sunset, glasses raised in a toast to the end of another beautiful day. The world around them seemed to be on pause as they took in the beauty of nature's free show.

Del's hand still rested on her lower back, his thumb absentmindedly drawing circles against the fabric of her shirt. She felt him press a soft kiss on her temple. "Beautiful, isn't it?"

"Beyond beautiful," Aja answered, not certain if she were talking about the sunset or the man whose arms were wrapped around her. She worried about Jewel but there wasn't much she could do if Jewel didn't want her help.

Del pulled her closer, as if sensing her thoughts. "You've done everything you could. Sometimes, you need to let people walk their own path. You can't protect them from everything."

"I know," Aja murmured, leaning further into him. "But I have a feeling the Jewel drama is far from over."

CHAPTER 13

Del

Night had fallen by the time they got back to the resort. As they strolled slowly through the courtyard, their bodies close but not touching, Del wanted to prolong the evening. He was enjoying Aja's company and wasn't ready to let her go. But as he glanced at her, he could tell she was deep in thought. Probably overanalyzing their attraction and figuring out how to let him know this wasn't going to happen.

He let out a soft sigh. "What's on your mind, Aja?"

"I had a good time tonight, outside of the Jewel incident. I wish Jewel had trusted me enough to tell me the truth, but I get it, I guess," Aja stopped walking, looked up at him. "She just met me, she doesn't know anything about me."

"She may come around," he said.

Aja nodded, but her expression remained troubled. They resumed walking and stopped in front of Aja's door.

There was a silky pink scarf tied around the handle.

Aja frowned. "Does this mean what I think it means?"

Del shrugged. "What does it mean?"

She let out an exasperated sigh and hissed, "It means my seventy-year-old grandmother is getting more action than I am and has sexiled me from the room for who knows how long."

"For real, Ms. Nezzie's got company?" He couldn't say he was surprised. Ms. Nezzie was a big flirt.

Aja put her ear to the door then jumped back like the door was too hot to touch. "Oh, jeez...they're still...you know what, let's go," Aja said, pulling him toward the stairs.

"I can't believe Nezzie is hooking up with someone on this trip," Aja muttered, shaking her head in disbelief. "I mean, I love that for her, but damn... I was not prepared for that."

Del chuckled, finding Aja's reaction quite endearing. "Well, it seems like Ms. Nezzie is living her best life. But now that you need a place to hang out, why don't we see what games they have in the game room? I think there's a bar up there as well if we want drinks."

Secretly, he was glad Aja wasn't going back to her room for the moment.

"Sure, why not? It's not like I have anywhere else to go right now." Aja glanced one last time toward her room. "And I could definitely use a drink after that little surprise."

The game room was attached to a rooftop bar above the main buffet restaurant. As they climbed the stairs, loud eighties music thumped from the area. The rooftop bar was packed and Del could see that there were several couples dancing and enjoying the music. Inside the game room, a raucous foursome was playing pool and there were a couple tables dedicated to card games and dominoes. Everyone looked like they were having a good time but the vibe was wrong. He wanted a spot where they could be somewhat alone.

He turned to address Aja. "They must be doing one of their themed dance parties tonight. Feel like dancing?"

Aja leaned in. "Not at all," she said loudly. "I can't hear myself think."

Del nodded in understanding. The music was definitely too loud for any meaningful conversation. Del led the way back down the stairs to the courtyard. "Well, we can order room service from my room," he said, studying her face. "Up to you."

Aja hesitated then seemed to make up her mind. "Let's do room service."

"You're safe, I'm not going to try anything, if that's your hesitation," he told her.

"What if part of me wants you to," she said softly. "And I'm trying to talk myself out of doing something rash that we both might regret?"

Del's heart skipped a beat at Aja's words. He could see the conflict in her eyes, and he knew she was struggling with her feelings toward him. He wanted to take her in his arms and tell her that she didn't have to hold back anymore, that they could explore this attraction between them together.

"We're going to order room service and sit on the balcony watching the waves roll in. That's it," he said, trying to convince himself as well. He could refrain from touching her, as long as she didn't do anything he found sexy. He groaned inwardly. It was going to be a long night.

He led the way to his room on the top level of the resort as anticipation and tension rose within him in equal measure. He didn't want Aja to feel anything other than comfortable in his space and he could feel the hesitation from her almost like a weight pulling them beneath the ocean.

Stopping in front of his door, Del turned to Aja. "Hey."

She was right behind him when he'd stopped. She backed up a half step, peering up at him with a slight smirk. "Yes?"

"Before we go in, I'm establishing that I'm going to be real with you while you're here. No BS. If you want to know something, just ask," he said, wondering if his words would circle back to bite him.

Aja nodded, her gaze steady on his face. "I appreciate that," she said, "And I promise to do the same."

Aja held up a finger. "I do have a question." She covered her mouth with her hand like she was trying to come up with the best way to say what she needed to say.

Del stood there outside his hotel room waiting, scanning his brain for any possible thing she might ask about him. What could she ask? About his past relationships?

"Shoot," Del said, bracing himself, his heart pounding in his chest.

Finally she spoke. "Why are we standing here when all I want right now is for you to open this door and toss me on your bed?"

Del blinked, taken aback by her frankness.

The look in her eyes said she meant every word and Del's blood rushed straight to his groin. Since their first kiss, he'd been trying to keep a respectful distance despite the powerful attraction between them. But Aja's bold declaration shattered the last of his restraint.

He fumbled with the key card, almost dropping it before he could hold it up to the sensor.

The little green light flashed, and the lock clicked open. Without a word, Del pulled Aja inside. His room was dominated by a king-sized bed in the center and a spacious balcony that offered an unparalleled view of the ocean.

Closing the door behind them, he started to ask if she was sure she wanted to do this, but Aja was already sliding the door open and stepping out on his balcony. "Wow," she held out her arms. "This view is even better than my room."

Del followed her out, mesmerized by the sight of her leaned against the metal railing, her hair blowing in the breeze. He felt that familiar tug whenever she was near, pulling him into her energy.

The moonlight illuminated her features and Del marveled at how stunning Aja was. He invaded her space, pressing his body to hers, pinning her against the railing.

"You still want room service?" He scanned her face, wanting to know if she had doubts.

"Not unless that's your coy way of asking if I want you to service me...otherwise, not right now," she sighed into his chest.

She pulled away. "Which I hope I've made clear that I do."

He closed his eyes, tried to hide his elation. "Yeah, I got the not-so-subtle hints."

Del gently cupped her cheek, his thumb tracing her jawline. Her eyes fluttered closed at his touch, sending a thrill through his veins. He leaned down and pressed his lips to hers, feeling like he was finally where he was meant to be.

He kissed her, meaning to take it slow but the kiss evolved, intensified, threatening to drown him. He pulled back, let his lips trace a path down her neck, his hands roaming over her body, memorizing every curve and dip. Aja let out a small moan as his mouth found its way to her collarbone, nibbling at the soft scented skin there.

Her hands roamed over his head as he lifted her up, sitting her on the metal railing of the balcony. Del stood between her legs, pressing against her as he continued to kiss and nuzzle at her neck.

She let out a soft sigh.

"My grandmother asked me this morning if I needed to go get condoms and I told her I didn't. Who knew she'd be right?"

He chuckled. "I love that woman. And I took care of that."

"Did you know something I didn't? You assumed I'd fall into your arms eventually?"

Del paused his kisses at the curve of her neck. "I tell my clients all the time...If you stay ready, you don't have to get ready. But seriously, I don't assume anything with you, Aja. I was just happy you agreed to come out with me today."

"You and that accent of yours are very persuasive. If I let you, you're going to charm me out of my clothes," she bit her lip, teasing him.

"Hey, I was willing to come in here, order food and watch tv," he leaned his forehead against hers. "You're the freaky one wanting to be tossed on the bed."

"Which I'm still waiting on," she said, stroking the back of his neck with feather light touches that had him ready to explode with anticipation.

"So impatient," he murmured against her ear, letting his

breath fan over the sensitive spot behind it. "Slow down. We've got all night and I intend to take my time with you."

He peeled his shirt off and chucked it aside, revealing his well-muscled torso. Aja's eyes were riveted on him, her lips parting slightly as she drank in the sight of him. She reached out a hand and traced a finger along his chest, across the ridges of his abs. Del shivered under her touch, feeling his control slipping.

"Let's go inside," she whispered.

Del scooped her up into his arms, carrying her through the patio doors into the cool interior of the room. He held her above the bed like he meant to drop her and Aja squealed. "Okay, maybe I don't actually-"

With a wicked grin, Del dumped her onto the bed.

Aja bounced slightly as she landed, letting out a surprised "Oh" that faded into a deep sigh as Del grabbed her ankle, his intent clear in his eyes.

Removing her sandals, Del proceeded to explore every inch of her, his fingers just grazing the surface of her skin. His mouth followed suit, leaving a trail of featherlight kisses along her brown shapely legs. He heard her catch her breath and he couldn't help but smirk, feeling a thrill at having her at his mercy.

"Del..." she muttered beneath her breath, her words swallowed by the tension in the air.

Hovering above her, he paused to trace the curve of her hips, his fingers dipping beneath the band of her shorts. He leaned down to kiss her navel, hearing her sharp intake of breath as his lips met her skin. Slowly, torturously, he unbuttoned her shorts and eased them off, revealing a pair of tiny black panties.

His gaze fixed on the revealed skin, his heartbeat quickened as he took in every inch of her. Del felt a swell of desire stronger than any he'd ever experienced before. Del brushed a thumb across the satin edge of her underwear, his touch eliciting a shuttered sigh from her.

He moved closer, nestling between her legs. Aja closed her

eyes, arching her back slightly as Del's hands traced paths up and down her thighs.

"Del...you're literally killing me," she began, her voice a husky whisper that nearly undid him. But he had promised to take things slow, and he was nothing if not a man of his word.

"Mmm...patience, love," he murmured in response, his voice thick with need.

He unbuttoned the frilly blouse she wore.

Slowly, he slid it off her shoulders and down her arms, leaving her in her bra. His mouth nearly watered at the sight of her dark skin against the black lace, the curve of her full breasts. He let his fingers trace the soft swell above the lace, watching as her eyes fluttered closed and she bit down on her lower lip.

Tugging at her bra cups, he freed each breast and drew one into his mouth. Aja's head rolled back as he tongued the now rock hard nipple.

She gasped, her hand gripping his shoulder. "Del," Aja breathed, her chest arching toward him. He switched to the other breast, giving it the same attention until she was squirming beneath him.

"Relax," he murmured against her skin, his hands palming her breasts. "I've got you."

Aja's breath came in shallow gasps, her chest rising and falling with each one. Del took his time, kissing and tasting, his tongue dancing in a rhythm that was as old as time itself. By the time he reached the hem of her panties, Aja was trembling beneath him.

"Del," she whimpered his name again, "Please."

He glanced up at her, surprised by the urgency in her voice. Her gaze was heavy with desire and anticipation. She was beautiful like this - flushed and breathless and aching for him. The sight of her filled Del with a fierce need to claim her, to make her his in every way possible.

With a swift tug, he removed the final barrier between them, revealing Aja in all her glory.

He kissed a path from her navel downwards, each kiss leaving

Aja quivering with need. She writhed beneath him as his lips found the most sensitive part of her, her hands grabbing fistfuls of the sheets.

"Don't stop...please," she moaned, her voice a broken whisper.

Del smiled against her, savoring the taste of her on his tongue. He was only too happy to oblige her. His smile was hungry, predatory even, as he lowered his mouth to her again. His movements were slow and thorough, their intent to send ripples of pleasure through Aja's body. Soon she was crying out in ecstasy, her body arching off the bed.

"Oh God..." Her exclamation was almost a plea, her eyes meeting his as she convulsed.

He shifted his body up, climbing next to her on the bed. His hands continued their dance over the planes of her body, soft touches that left a trail of goosebumps in their wake. Her eyes slid closed, her chest rising and falling slowly. The glow of satisfaction painted an ethereal sheen on her skin.

"Del," she murmured, reaching out to pull him closer. Her hand found the waistband of his shorts, fingers playing with the button. He could feel her trembling, the heat of her body against him.

Gently, Aja worked on his button and zipper while she watched him through half-lidded eyes, a devilish grin tugging at the corners of her mouth.

"Your turn," she said, her voice thick with seduction as she finally managed to undo his shorts. Her hand slipped beneath the waistband of his boxers, her fingertips brushing against him. The contact sent a thrill up his spine.

Aja's hand snaked its way back to him. Her touch was electric and sent shivers of anticipation down his spine. He watched as she explored him, the curiosity in her eyes mirroring his own when he had explored her. It was a sight that enthralled him to no end - Aja, naked and flushed, with this look of pure lust in her eyes.

A slow stroking rhythm began, her warm hands beginning to know him as thoroughly as he had explored her. The sensation was exquisite, a heady mix of pleasure and torture that left him gasping. He threaded his fingers through her hair, guiding her downward until she was eye level with his arousal.

Aja licked her lips then wrapped them around him. Del's eyes crossed, rolled back in his head as euphoria flooded through him. His fingers tightened in her hair, his other hand gripping the sheets tightly. Aja's mouth worked expertly, her eyes never leaving his. The sight of her, the feel of her was enough to drive him wild.

"Shit, Aja," Del groaned, his voice husky. He was trembling, every nerve ending screaming for release. His breaths came in ragged gasps as he lost himself in in the warm wetness of her mouth. The rhythm built, a crescendo sweeping over him like a hurricane. His body was on fire, the desire for her consuming him.

Slowly, Del reached down, pulling her up to him. His voice was ragged as he spoke. "Aja," he said, his voice thick with need. "Baby, stop...come here," he gasped suddenly, pulling away from her with a groan. He wanted this to last, he didn't want it to end this quickly. He wanted to savor the moment, to embed it in his memory forever.

With a gentle tug, he pulled Aja back up to him and kissed her deeply.

He could taste himself on her tongue, the flavor mingling with her natural sweetness. He moaned into her mouth, his hands roaming over her back, pulling her flush against him. His arousal throbbed between them, begging for attention.

"Hold on," he gasped, reaching behind him for the nightstand.

His hand closed around a small, foil packet. He tore it open with practiced ease, rolling the condom onto himself. His fingers trembled with anticipation, his heart pounding in his chest.

He flipped their positions, settling Aja beneath him. His hand coasted up her thigh, the sensation making her gasp. Her legs wrapped around him, pulling him closer. Their bodies fit together perfectly—like two pieces of a puzzle clicking into place—and he reveled in the feeling.

With one smooth thrust, he was inside her.

Aja let out a soft gasp, her fingers digging into his shoulders. Her body welcomed him, warm and wet, guiding him to her depths. He paused for a moment, letting both of them adjust then he began with slow, deliberate movements, each thrust intended to draw out as much pleasure as possible. Aja met him stroke for stroke, their bodies moving in sync.

His hand found hers and he laced their fingers together, pressing it into the mattress next to her head.

"Aja," he breathed out in a half-whisper, half-groan. He looked down at her beneath him, her eyes were closed and her lips slightly parted. The glow on her face was more than just sweat—it was pure ecstasy. He quickened his pace, leaning down to capture her lips once again, swallowing her gasps and moans. He loved the way she responded, the way her body arched up into his with every thrust, the soft noises that escaped her lips when he hit just the right spot.

He moved one hand down to where their bodies joined, his fingers finding that sensitive spot that made her gasp and writhe beneath him. The other hand remained intertwined with hers.

As his thrusts became more urgent, she clenched around him, a sure sign of her impending climax. The sensation almost undid him, but he held on, wanting them to reach the peak together. He buried his face in her neck, nibbling and sucking on the sensitive skin there.

He could feel her release as she moaned his name. Another thrust and he was there, his body shaking with his own release. "Aja..." he said into her neck with a shutter.

Afterward, as they lay there panting, Aja sat up on her elbows, grinning at him. "Now we can order room service."

CHAPTER 14

Aja

Aja woke with a start. The sun was just starting to rise and it took her a moment to realize she wasn't in her own room. She tried to sit up but she was pinned under a large arm.

Right. She was in Del's bed after an epic night of the kind of sex she only heard about from Zaria.

Her attempt to wiggle out failed as the arm around her waist pulled her closer, and Del grunted something in his sleep, oblivious to the dawn breaking.

His breath was warm on the back of her neck, his body heat seeping through the thin sheet that covered them. She could feel the steady rhythm of his heart against her back, and for a moment, Aja considered staying.

She had to go. Extricating herself gingerly, Aja tried not to wake him. She stood up and tiptoed around the room, gathering her clothes scattered on the floor, intent on slinking back to her room before anyone caught her walk of shame.

"You sneaking out after taking advantage of me all night, Aja?" Del's voice, husky with sleep, startled Aja and she dropped her bra.

Busted, she turned to see Del propped on an elbow.

She wished he would cover up. She didn't need to be distracted by his bare chest right now.

"I took advantage of you, huh? That's the story you're going with?" She scooped her bra up, intending to slip it on.

"You did. I was trying to be a gentleman, but you insisted I throw you onto the bed," he shrugged, a sly grin on his face. "Who am I to refuse a beautiful woman?"

Aja rolled her eyes. She was not going to fall for his charm this morning. She wasn't going to get sucked into that melodic accent and that broad chest and the memory of those hands on her, stroking her. Not today.

She turned her back to him, struggling to put her bra on. Aja could feel his eyes on her. "I'm flattered, but I have things to do today and-"

"Let me help you with that," he said. Before she could refuse, he was behind her, his large hands covering hers.

Attempting to ignore the shiver that ran down her spine, she dropped her hands. He slid the straps down her arms and kneaded her breasts.

"What were you saying?" He asked, all innocence.

Aja lost her train of thought. For a moment, she was silent, as his hands roamed her skin making it impossible to think straight.

"This isn't really helping me get dressed," she said. leaning against him.

"No, I'm helping you relax," he murmured against her ear.

She watched as the bra slid to the floor.

"Del," she sighed but didn't resist as his hands began running over her shoulders and down her back, causing goosebumps to break out on her skin. She closed her eyes, swaying slightly against him.

"Mm-hmm," he said, his hands moving lower until they rested on her hips. Aja felt the heat of his body against her back, consuming every drop of her resolve.

She turned around slowly, finding herself trapped in the intensity of his gaze. "Del, I need to go," she managed to whisper.

She should push his hands away, find the rest of her clothes and make her way downstairs to her room.

His hands slid over her hips and thighs, tracing lazy circles as her resolve melted.

Aja couldn't believe she was considering staying in bed with Del instead of facing her responsibilities. His magical hands were making it hard to think about anything but how good his touch felt.

"What do we need to do today?"

His choice of pronouns had her heart skipping.

She closed her eyes and took a deep breath. He was distracting her on purpose and it was working. How would she let him go once they left the island?

"I need to see if my grandmother is okay," she hesitated, "and I should go to my mother's home and check it out."

As if on cue, Aja's phone rang. Reluctantly, she stepped out of Del's reach and picked the device up from the nightstand. "Well, good morning, Sunshine. Did you sleep well?"

"I did, not that we got much sleep," Nezzie answered, cheerful as ever. "Are you with Del?"

Aja sat on the bed, pulling the sheet up to her neck as if her grandmother were watching. "Yes, I had to go somewhere after I saw you had company."

She turned away from Del's smug smirk.

"Good. Why don't you both meet us for breakfast? I want to introduce you to someone," Nezzie said.

Aja groaned. While she was happy her grandmother was having a good time, she wasn't ready to meet Nezzie's new beau in person.

"Nezzie, I was planning to go take care of my mother's house first thing today," Aja looked over her shoulder at Del who was now stretched out across the bed, the sheet barely covering his essentials.

"Are you sure you're ready to do that?" Nezzie asked, concern in her voice. "I'll come with you."

"Oh no, you should enjoy your...friend, Del said he'd help," she glanced at him, hoping he was on board with her plans.

Del nodded and Aja's shoulders sank in relief. "Why don't we all meet for dinner tonight instead?"

"Okay, but are you sure you don't need me?" Nezzie sounded worried.

"I'm sure, Nezzie. Del will be there," Aja reassured her, feeling a strange warmth at the idea of having Del by her side. She hadn't known him long but she knew he would support her.

On the other side of the line, Nezzie sighed in resignation. "Alright, baby girl. I'll be here at the resort. They're doing bingo and aquacise for seniors later. You call me if you need me, you hear?"

"Yes, ma'am. Have fun." Aja ended the call.

"Looks like we have dinner plans, unless you've got something else to do?" Aja said, trying to be casual.

Chuckling, Del shook his head. "I wouldn't miss this dinner for the world. I can't wait to meet Ms. Nezzie's new friend."

"And you're okay with taking me to her house?" She asked again.

"Of course. But first," Del tugged her back into bed. "Let me wish you a good morning..."

Later that day, Del turned into a narrow driveway that led to a small pastel blue bungalow surrounded by wild and tall palm trees. Tucked away from Highway One, off a side street, Diana's house was nothing like Aja had imagined. She'd pictured a luxury condo. This place was more of a cozy artist's haven.

Del parked in front of the house and looked at her, worry etching lines into his forehead. "Are you sure you're up for this?" he asked, placing a hand over hers. She nodded, swallowing the lump that had formed in her throat. What would she find once she entered her mother's house?

Aja squared her shoulders as she and Del got out of the SUV. There was a covered patio with wild bougainvillea cascading over the front porch, and a bistro table with two chairs in the center.

"I gave you the keys, didn't I?" Del said, approaching the front door. "Open it, but let me check it out first."

Aja pulled the key ring from her tote and unlocked the door, pushing it open. The house was stuffy; the scent of Chanel heavy in the air.

Del stepped around her and Aja hung back, rethinking her decision to tackle the house today. The perfume smell was more potent now, trapped within the walls of the bungalow. Aja found she was having a hard time breathing. She hurried over to the patio and unlocked the door, but it wouldn't budge. She gave it another shove and it finally slid open. Fresh air flowed through the room and Aja breathed in deeply.

Del moved methodically through the rooms, checking each one as he passed. She watched him move with a confidence she found comforting. "All clear?" she called out.

"Clear as vodka on ice," he called out from what she presumed was her mother's bedroom, his voice echoing in the still quiet house.

"Somebody's ready for happy hour," she smirked, following the sound of his voice.

She found Del in a room bright with natural light. The walls were painted a soft lavender and adorned with paintings of seashells. A king-sized bed, neatly made with white linen sheets and heaps of fluffy pillows, sat prominently in the middle of the room.

Aja gasped softly.

The center of the dresser held a small photograph of a much younger Aja.

Emotions she couldn't name rushed over her. She picked up the frame, tracing the edges of her baby picture with trembling fingers. Her mother might have never been physically present in her life, but there was some solace in knowing a part of her had always been there.

Tears welled in her eyes, blurring and distorting the image of her younger self. Aja blinked them away, setting the picture frame carefully back on its place.

Del touched her arm. "You good, Aja?"

She shook her head, reaching for him.

He stepped closer, pulling her into his arms. "We can take this slow, okay?"

Aja steeled herself, refusing to give into the sadness that threatened to overwhelm her. She'd gone from longing for her mother when she was a child to being angry with her for leaving once she'd hit her teen years. That anger, Aja realized, hadn't gone away. She'd managed to tuck it away but now she had to deal with it.

"I'm okay," she lied, trying to convince herself more than Del. "Let's keep going."

Pulling away from Del, Aja stepped over to her mother's closet. There were lots of colorful pieces. Aja pulled out two dresses, one a rose colored chiffon and the other, a cream silk maxi. She held them both up. "Since you knew my mother better, which one do you think she liked best?"

Del stroked his chin. "The white one."

Aja held up the cream silk dress, her eyes studying it. It was classically beautiful and understated, much like Aja's style. She returned the pink chiffon dress back to its place in the closet before running her hand down the soft fabric of the cream dress.

"We'll take this to the funeral home for her to wear."

Del nodded, accepting her decision. "Good choice, the silk suits her," Del said, his voice thick. "Your mom had great taste and she loved dressing up. I think she'd approve."

Aja looked down at the dress for a moment longer before carefully folding it and placing it on the bed.

She turned to him. "Do you think she was happy here?"

Del stroked his beard and Aja saw him consider the question.

"I think she was trying to find happiness. She loved working in her studio, creating beautiful art and she loved this house," he gestured, "but she carried a lot of guilt and regret and it weighed her down some days."

He studied his hands. "When I first heard she was gone, I wondered if she...maybe wanted to escape her guilt," he said finally.

Aja's head snapped up at this. "You think she may have taken her own life?"

Del shook his head slowly. "I can't say. Now, don't get me wrong, she never indicated to me that she was in that state of mind, but her bad days could be really bad and I just wonder. The official word is that her boat capsized and she drowned but Diana was a strong swimmer. She boasted to me about that a couple of times," Del let out a deep breath. "The ocean can take out even the strongest swimmers...I just don't know."

Aja nodded silently as she absorbed Del's words. She thought of her mother, the artist, living alone in this house by the sea, painting seashells and creating beautiful works in glass while the guilt ate away at her.

That was odd. If her mother was indeed a strong swimmer, what happened to her boat that day? Aja made a mental note to take a closer look into her mother's cause of death.

Pulling open a dresser drawer, Aja busied herself with selecting undergarments and shoes for her mother's final rest. She picked up a pair of strappy gold heeled sandals, admiring them. Her mother's style was similar to Aja's and the sandals would go nicely with the dress.

"By any chance, did she tell you what her final wishes were? Is there a place she wanted to be buried?" Aja asked, placing the shoes in a small suitcase she found in the closet.

"She mentioned she wanted to be cremated," Del scratched at his chin, lost in thought. "The thought of being buried made her skin crawl, she told me once."

Aja nodded. "Was there a place here that she loved? Somewhere I can spread her ashes?"

Del paused, his brow furrowing. "She liked to drive over to Bathsheba and watch the surfers. That's on the eastern side of the island."

"Okay, I'd like to check it out." Aja said.

"We can do that. I'm going to take a look in her other room, see if I can find her important documents." Del gave her a comforting rub on the shoulder before he left the room.

Aja stood alone in the room, listening to Del's footsteps recede down the hallway. He'd been a rock through this process and Aja was grateful for his presence.

As she resumed packing, her eyes fell on a small jewelry box on the dresser. The box itself was an ornate piece of art, a mosaic of brilliant sea glass and tiny shells. Her mother's handiwork, no doubt. Aja opened it, revealing a few pieces of delicate gold and silver jewelry. There was a small folded note under the pieces and Aja picked it up, hesitant to delve into her mother's privacy. Clearly the note meant a lot to her if she'd stored it with her other valuables. She glanced up at the door, hoping Del wouldn't return and catch her then opened the note.

Here's a little something to mark the time until we meet again. XO

There was a florist's name and logo in the lower left-hand corner.

Aja sank onto the bed. Someone had sent her mother flowers and included a note that wasn't signed.

Were the flowers a regular thing, thus no name needed? Or was the sender attempting to remain confidential?

Del walked in at that point, holding a folder full of paperwork and an electronic device. "I think this is all of her current bills and this tablet but it's dead and I didn't see a charger," he frowned. "What's wrong?"

Aja glanced up at him. "I found this note in my mother's jewelry box."

Handing Del the note, she asked, "Did she mention she was seeing anyone?"

His brows furrowed, Del read the note. His face revealed nothing of the thoughts playing in his mind. "No, Aja," he said after a moment, handing it back to her. "She never hinted at seeing anyone new. This..." he motioned to the note, "this is news to me."

He ran a hand over his head. "It says 'until we meet again' which sounds to me like they weren't seeing each other regularly," he said.

"Be right back." With that, he dashed out of the room.

Aja continued to stare at the note. She wondered if this mystery suitor had anything to do with her mother's sudden death. Was it a serious relationship? And, if so, why was it so secretive?

Del returned holding a clear gourd shaped vase. "Diana liked elaborate design, so this stood out to me. Thinking that card came with flowers in this vase," he held it out.

"That makes sense. But she didn't mention him to you," Aja said, thinking aloud. "Any ideas on why she didn't?"

Del took a seat on the foot of the bed. "Hard to say. Diana always wanted to pry into my love life...telling me I needed to find someone and settle down and all, but she didn't talk about her own situation much." He stroked his beard. "I always got the sense it was an off limits topic for her and I didn't pry."

Aja's ears perked up. He talked to her mother about his love life. Interesting. "I'm curious...what advice did my mother give you about settling down?"

Del let out a slow breath. "Oh, Diana had a lot to say about love. She told me not to rush things, ever. That love should find me naturally and when it does, I shouldn't be afraid to embrace it."

He met Aja's gaze. "She also said that love wasn't about finding the perfect person, but learning to see an imperfect person perfectly. Then she told me she had a daughter about my age."

CHAPTER 15

Del

Del watched as the realization that her mother thought she and Del would be perfect together hit her.

The silence in the room grew as Del quietly observed Aja. Her mind was reeling; he could practically see her working through what she'd just learned.

He recalled all the times Diana had hinted about him needing company, someone special in his life. He never imagined she had her own daughter in mind for him.

Aja's voice interrupted his musings. "I was thinking I'd get answers when I came here, but it's been the exact opposite. I have a ton of questions and no answers."

Del took a seat on the bed beside her. "Would talking it out help?"

Aja turned toward him, but Del could tell she wasn't focused on him. "On one hand, she carried a lot of guilt, which may have led to her deciding not to fight for her life while she was in the water." Aja held up a finger. "But she had someone sending flowers and promising they'd meet."

Del agreed. "To me, it feels like a new relationship and maybe too new to share. Or maybe she just didn't want to tell me about it."

The thought didn't sit well with him. During their coaching sessions, when they were done with whatever they needed to talk about, Diana would veer into subjects close to her heart. She'd talk about her art, about Aja and her regret that she wasn't a part of her daughter's life.

She didn't tell him why she'd left her family in Atlanta all those years ago.

Now, he wished he'd probed more. But he'd respected her privacy, not wanting to overstep the boundaries of their professional relationship. After all, Diana had been his client, not his confidant.

"He might have been married," Aja said. "She probably wouldn't share if that was the case."

"Maybe," Del said. "Have you found anything else that might shed light on her relationship? Any men's clothes in the closet?"

Shaking her head, Aja stood up. "No, just her stuff. I want to take the dress to the cleaners, is there one nearby?"

"Should be. We'll find one," he hesitated, unsure of how she would react to his next question. "Do you want to start going through the house and deciding what you might want to keep?"

Aja put the dress and the other clothing items in her bag and turned to him. "I don't want much," she said quietly. "We're going to need several boxes to pack all of this stuff up, but I don't think I'm ready to tackle that today."

A pang of sympathy stirred in Del's chest as he observed Aja. This was a battle she had to fight alone, but he wished he could do more, offer more comfort. He gave her a small nod, attempting to mask the concern etched on his face.

"Take your time," Del murmured. "There's no rush."

Aja sighed deeply, looking around the room one last time before heading for the door.

As they left Diana's house, Del couldn't shake the feelings of sadness and emptiness that lingered in the air. He could only imagine the turmoil Aja must be feeling as she searched for answers about her mother's life.

~

Later that evening, Del and Aja were the first to arrive at the restaurant, an upscale seafood eatery directly on the beach.

The aroma of the sea mingled with the pungent scent of grilled seafood and garlic, the rustic decor and soft lights creating a warm, inviting atmosphere. They were led to a table by the window, giving them an uninterrupted view of the crashing waves under the setting sun.

As they waited for Nezzie and her date, Aja seemed lost in thought, her gaze focused on the expanse of the ocean beyond them. Del took a moment to truly appreciate her, studying her profile. She was beautiful, there was no denying that. But what drew him in more than her physical attractiveness was her resilience. Aja was used to doing everything herself, he could tell and he wondered if she'd ever really had anyone take care of her.

"This is a first. I've never been on a double date with my grandmother," she said, sitting up and placing her elbows on the table. "I don't know what to expect, so I'll apologize up front for whatever inappropriate things she says tonight."

Del chuckled, his eyes crinkling at the corners. "She's been okay the few times I've been around her. Or was she on her best behavior then?"

Aja rolled her eyes but smiled nonetheless. "Best behavior definitely. And once she gets a couple of drinks in her, she really loses her filter."

Just as she finished the sentence, the door swung open revealing Nezzie looking radiant in a floral print sundress, her silver hair pinned up in an elegant high bun. A tall, light brown skinned man that looked to be in his early seventies stood behind her, dressed in a crisp white linen shirt and chinos.

Del stood to greet them as they reached the table. "Nezzie, you look beautiful tonight," he complimented, earning a dazzling smile from Aja's grandmother.

"You are a charmer, Del Parris." She turned to the man, lacing her arm through his. "Aja, Del, this is Clayton Rummel, he's on vacation from Miami."

Aja's head snapped up and she stared at the man like she'd seen a ghost.

Del stuck his hand out. "Nice to meet you, man. Welcome to Barbados," Del said, eyeing Aja.

Clayton returned the handshake with a firm grip and a friendly smile. "Thanks, Del. It's a pleasure to meet both of you."

Aja seemed to snap out of her daze and stood from her seat to greet the man. "Nice to meet you, Clayton," she said in a polite but distant tone before taking her seat again.

As Nezzie and Clayton settled into their seats, laughter and light conversation flowed around the table. The server took their drink orders as they began talking about Clayton's vacation and his impressions of Barbados.

Aja watched her grandmother and Clayton with a slight smirk on her face, like she knew a secret. "Clayton, is this your first time in Barbados?"

The older man nodded with enthusiasm. "Yes, I joined a travel group for retirees...it's been fun. Usually we're doing stuff closer to home, like Key West and Tampa but this is their first international trip and my first trip to the Caribbean. I never got to travel much when I was working...I always thought my wife and I would do that when we retired," he said wistfully. "But she passed before we could take any trips together."

They all expressed condolences then an awkward silence descended over the table.

Del saw Nezzie give Clayton's hand a squeeze.

Nezzie's eyes softened, the twinkle that was usually there replaced by a flicker of understanding. "Life has a way of taking unexpected turns, doesn't it?" Nezzie said, offering him a comforting smile.

Clayton nodded, clearly appreciative of the gesture. "Yes, it does."

Del sipped his water as he watched Aja. She was subtle about it but he could tell she was observing Clayton. He knew that Aja was fiercely loyal to her family and would protect her grandmother at all costs but her focus on Clayton seemed extreme.

Del reached for Aja's hand under the table and Aja gave him a surprised glance before relaxing under his touch. "You good?"

She gave him a slight nod and some of the tension he felt eased.

"Did you do any sightseeing today?" Aja directed her question at her grandmother.

Nezzie perked up. "I have always loved architecture and I read that there are some plantation houses here that date back to the 1600s so we toured Sunbury Plantation, which is supposed to be one of the oldest on the island," Nezzie said, taking a pull from her glass of wine. "There are some beautiful antiques in the house, lots of original pieces from the colonial era."

"Sounds interesting," Aja responded, her eyes flicking to Clayton. "Did you enjoy it?"

Clayton gave a hearty laugh. "It was amazing. I had planned to take the walking tour of Bridgetown with our group but I ran into Inez by the pool and she talked me into going with her. Your grandmother is an excellent tour guide."

Del stifled a smile as the couple beamed at each other. Their attraction was obvious and he could tell they were enjoying their time together.

Clayton turned his attention to Aja and Del. "What is it you call Inez? Is it Nettie?"

Shaking her head, Nezzie placed her wine glass on the table. "It's Nezzie. When Aja was first learning to talk, I decided I didn't want to be called "Grandma" just yet...it made me feel older than my years."

She turned to Clayton. "What do your grandkids call you?"

The older man shrugged. "The oldest calls me Clay these days...I don't know about today's kids. No respect for their elders."

Nezzie picked up her glass again. "You know? Anyway, so I point to myself and say to her, 'I'm Nana,' This one," she pointed at Aja, "tilts her head at me like she's trying to figure out how to tell me I'm an idiot," Nezzie chuckled. "Then she points at me and says 'No, you're Nez' which stuck. And somehow it evolved to all my grandkids calling me Nezzie." She gave a what are you gonna do shrug and sipped her wine.

Clayton chuckled at the story, his eyes gleaming with amusement. "It's a unique name," he praised, sending Nezzie a fond look. "Has a ring of character to it."

"It does, doesn't it?" She grabbed Aja's hand. "This is my oldest grandbaby and she's been pretty much calling the shots since then."

Nezzie turned to Del. "When she told me she was taking me to Barbados, I hollered like I'd just won the lottery!" She let out a belly laugh.

Del found himself laughing along and he witnessed Aja's lips curve up into a genuine smile.

Aja wrapped her arm around Nezzie's shoulders, pulling her in for a hug, "I just wanted to give you something you'd enjoy," she confessed. "You deserve it."

The warmth in Aja's eyes as she looked at her grandmother was infectious. Del found himself fondly watching them as he admired their strong, deep, and unyielding bond.

Their food arrived then, effectively ending the reflective moment. The chatter resumed, flowing effortlessly around the table.

At one point, when Clayton excused himself in search of the men's room, Del leaned closer to Aja, inhaling her scent and anticipating when they'd be alone again. "Why were you eyeing him like he stole something? He strikes me as a good man."

"Long story. I'll tell you later," Aja muttered.

Del raised an eyebrow but let the subject rest for the moment. "Alright," he said and gave her hand a reassuring squeeze.

A slow melody began to play, enticing couples to abandon

their tables and sway gently to the rhythm on an impromptu dance floor by the bar.

Clayton strode back to their table and extended his hand to Nezzie. "Care to dance with me, pretty lady?"

Nezzie giggled like a schoolgirl. "Why, I thought you'd never ask, kind sir," she retorted playfully. They moved to the dance floor, their bodies slipping into a comfortable rhythm with the music.

Del watched as Clayton led Nezzie in the dance, his hand respectfully positioned on her waist. For an older guy, he seemed to move with grace and gentility.

"Ms. Nezzie seems like she's having a great time," Del said it softly, more like a wish rather than an observation.

"Yeah, but what happens after the vacation is over and they part ways? He lives in Miami. I can't see my grandmother moving to be with a man."

Del shrugged, "Well, maybe they don't have to decide anything right now. They're just enjoying each other's company."

Aja seemed to consider this before finally answering, "I guess. But I don't want her to get hurt."

Del followed her gaze back to the dance floor just in time to see Clayton dipping Nezzie, much to the delight of the surrounding guests who erupted in applause.

"Hmm...your grandmother got up to dance with no hesitation," he said pointedly, "But do I risk getting shot down for the third time? I don't know."

Del wanted to hold Aja in his arms again and the dance floor seemed as good an excuse as any, but she was staring at the couples moving around the floor, her spine straight.

Aja crossed her arms. "What do you mean, third time?"

"I first asked you at Mia's birthday party, where you didn't hesitate to shut me down," Del reminded her.

"Del, I-"

Aja's clutch, nestled in the space between their seats, vibrated.

"Let it go," Del said, turning to face her. He was filled with a sudden longing to hold her and for just a moment, forget about everything else.

Aja shook her head slowly. "It could be urgent," she said pulling the device from her bag.

She looked up from the screen. "It's Jewel," she said, easing out of her chair. "I'll just be a minute."

He sighed inwardly as Aja retreated to a quieter corner of the restaurant, her phone pressed tightly against her ear. With her gone, he found himself observing Clayton and Nezzie again.

They were in their own world, dancing and laughing together like teenagers. He envied their ease with each other.

Turning his gaze away, he picked up his glass of wine and took a hefty swig. The thought hit him like a fist to the jaw: Aja might as well have been talking about them when she considered what would happen when they left the island. And he had his suspicions that she might consider him an island fling and be done with him once they were back home. She wouldn't need him anymore.

He frowned, swirling the red liquid in his glass, lost in thought. He told himself that was fine with him; the last thing he wanted was a relationship. Casual suited him, so maybe the island fling was best.

She returned moments later, sliding into the chair beside him with an apologetic smile. "Sorry about that," she said softly, her gaze flitting briefly toward the dance floor where her grandmother was still twirling around like Cinderella at the ball. "Jewel wants me to continue investigating Malik."

Del stroked his beard. "I'm not surprised. Something's up with that one."

"Definitely. But I told her I'd talk to her more tomorrow," Aja said.

She fell silent then and Del could tell she wasn't thinking about Malik.

"I can't dance," she said suddenly. "I have zero rhythm."

She motioned at her grandmother and Clayton, who were

moving in sync like they'd been partners for years. "I don't know why that gene skipped me but it did."

Del started to tease her about being the only Black woman he knew that couldn't dance but as he took in her stiff posture and the pained look on her face, he could tell she was sincere. He watched her swallow, her eyes glossing over with disappointment.

A new song started, a slow, sultry ballad, and Del stood, holding his hand out. "Come on, we'll go slow," he leaned in close to her ear. "This is my excuse to hold you close."

Her lips pressed together, Aja studied him for a moment, obviously weighing her options. He held his breath, waiting, hoping she'd trust him.

"Alright...but don't say I didn't warn you," Aja said, rising and taking his hand.

He led her onto the dance floor, the gentle sway of the music pulling them into its rhythm. But as they reached an open spot on the dance floor, Aja hesitated, her shoulders raised. "Relax, I got you," he said, pivoting so that he was facing her. Del held her hand in his and with his other hand, guided her free hand on the small of his back.

"Just move with me," he murmured, inhaling the coconut scent of her hair.

She relaxed against him and he forced his body not to react to her nearness.

"I watched you dancing with Andre at Mia's party and I swore I'd never dance with you," Her confession was soft against his chest, sending shivers down his spine.

"Really? Why?" he asked.

"Because you made it look natural and effortless and you looked like you were having fun. I don't think I've ever danced and had fun doing it," she said.

He tightened his grip around her as they swayed with the rhythm.

"Fun fact," Aja said into his chest. "I tried out for this special summer dance camp and the captain of the team, this mean girl named Genevieve, pointed out that I was a rhythmless disaster and wondered why I was bothering to try out at all."

He rubbed her back, feeling the pain of her memory and wanting to soothe it away.

"That's harsh," he said, a frown furrowing his brow.

"Yeah, it was. I never set foot in a dance class or on a dance floor after that." She gave a slight laugh that sounded more like a sigh.

"This is the first time you've danced since you were a kid?" He couldn't help asking.

Aja nodded and nestled her head against the crook of his neck. "That happened when I was twelve, so yeah. This is almost a historical moment."

Del couldn't believe it. Aja hadn't danced in over twenty years? It seemed almost impossible to him, especially since she was such a natural at everything else she did. The coach in him wanted to probe deeper and ask more questions, but this wasn't the time for that. Instead, he simply held her tighter and focused on the music.

They danced slowly, their bodies swaying in time with the beat. Del could feel Aja relaxing more and more with each passing moment. "So, why are you giving my man Clayton the evil eye?"

Aja raised her head slightly. "Another small world story...I'm pretty sure he's the guy who got catfished in my cousin London's first investigation last year."

Del turned to peer at Clayton. "For real?"

He glanced at Aja, her eyebrows arching in amusement.

She shrugged nonchalantly, "Seems he has a thing for online dating. London figured out the whole scheme."

As the song ended, Del kept his hands on Aja's waist, not wanting to completely let go just yet. She looked up at him with a soft smile on her face.

"Thank you," she said quietly.

"For what?" Del asked, genuinely confused.

"For making me feel comfortable," she said. Her gaze was soft, yet intense. "You helped me face a fear I've been carrying for years."

Del felt a sudden warmth spread through his chest.

Lightly tracing circles on her waist, he replied, his voice equally soft, "Anytime, Aja."

An upbeat soca song started, breaking the trance between them. He tipped his head toward the rest of the couples now moving energetically to the faster tempo. "You want to learn how to dance to soca?"

Aja shook her head. "Baby steps. I'll let the pros–," she tilted her head toward her grandmother, who was winding her hips to the beat with Clayton, "--do their thing."

CHAPTER 16

Aja

"Do you want a viewing of the body before the cremation? Or would you rather have an urn on display? Meaning we cremate beforehand?" Aja and Nezzie were seated in a conference room in the funeral home they'd contacted the prior week.

Del had dropped them off, promising he'd return as soon as he could. Aja hadn't asked where he was off to so urgently and he hadn't given any details. Now her mind wandered, wondering what he was doing. A throat cleared and Aja looked up, realizing they were waiting on a response from her.

The funeral director, a stout man with slicked curly hair peered pointedly at her over round reading glasses. He spoke softly as if they were in the middle of a service. She had no idea there were so many options to choose from and the thought of choosing one made her head hurt. She glanced at Nezzie, who sat mesmerized by the local news station on a tv monitor above Aja's head.

"Nezzie, what do you think?"

Nezzie met her gaze. "Aja, honey, this is your choice. Do you think you need to see your mother for the last time?"

She started to say she didn't but maybe she should. "We'll do the viewing."

The director gave a nod of approval, typing with one finger on the laptop in front of him. "Very well, Miss Lewis, we'll prepare for a viewing before the cremation."

He pulled a brochure from a stack next to him. "We also offer urns for the cremains," he opened it and slid it over to her. "Take a look at these and let me know what you think."

Aja flipped through the pages. Each page featured several urns on it and the book was as thick as a fashion magazine. Too many choices. She nudged her grandmother. "See any that you like?"

"I'm not sure, baby girl..." Nezzie's voice trailed off. She bit her lower lip, her gaze shifting back to the screen above them.

"You're not even looking at them," Aja protested.

Nezzie shrugged. "Bigger things to worry about, Aja," she said, pointing at the television just as the weatherwoman began her tropical storm advisory.

Aja glanced up briefly. "It's not hurricane season, is it?"

"No, but that doesn't mean we can't get one. Mother Nature works on her own timeline." Nezzie pointed toward the screen. "That storm looks dangerous."

The funeral director studied the screen. "It's rare to get a hurricane this time of year."

"I'm trying to tell y'all that global warming is a thing, you know?" Nezzie folded her arms.

Aja sighed. She needed to get this meeting back on track. "Once I decide on these options, we need to choose a date for the service, right?"

"Yes, ma'am. Saturdays are most popular days but you can decide. Let me pull up the calendar."

The funeral director busied himself with his laptop, leaving Aja to stew over the brochures once again. Nezzie had gone quiet, her gaze fixed back onto the TV screen where the weatherwoman gestured animatedly toward a satellite map of the Caribbean Sea. A swirling mass of deep blues and purples hovered ominously over Barbados.

Trying to dismiss the foreboding image, Aja forced her

attention back onto the brochures. She absently picked one up and trailed her fingers over the glossy paper. What would her mother want? She bit her lip in frustration. She had no clue. She didn't know much of anything about her mother. Glancing up at the silk dress she'd placed on the coat rack when they'd entered the conference room, she knew her mother had good taste in clothing. She also knew, based on the decorating choices her mother made in her home and her glass studio that she loved color and fine art. She studied the brochures again. Pointing at a white marble urn with pewter trim, she said, "I'd like this one."

Nezzie turned to look. "Oh, that one is nice. Get me one like that too when I go."

Aja eyed her grandmother. "Still haven't looked at the other options..."

Nezzie pointed at the picture. "Not that it will matter to me, but it will go with your decor better. That way you can stick it on the mantle of that fancy fireplace of yours."

Aja couldn't help but laugh at Nezzie's casual approach to the prospect of her own death. "Don't talk like that, Nezzie," she scolded lightly.

"Like what?" Nezzie shrugged. "I'm not gonna live forever."

The funeral director cleared his throat, obviously trying to wrap up their appointment. "Ladies, if I might suggest you decide on a date before anything else? Whether or not the storm comes, we should have a plan."

"Alright," Aja nodded, turning back to the calendar on the laptop screen. "Let's check next Saturday."

The funeral director clicked through his booking schedule, pausing when he arrived at the following Saturday. "That's available," he said, pushing his reading glasses closer to his face. "Would you like me to book it?"

"Yes, please."

He nodded and began tapping at the keyboard again. As he worked, Aja glanced over at Nezzie. The elderly woman had turned back to the television, her lips pursed as she watched the weather forecaster tracking the storm.

She should make sure the date worked for Del as well. After firing off a quick text, Aja turned her attention back to the funeral director.

"Just getting confirmation that the date is good," she told him.

"Yes, of course," the funeral director confirmed, his fingers pausing over the keys.

"Thank you," Aja said, her mind racing with a dozen different tasks she needed to accomplish before the service. She was about to speak again when her phone buzzed against the table. Glancing down, she saw Del's confirmation. Next Saturday worked for him too. "We're good."

"Excellent," the funeral director tapped a few keys. "Now, about the arrangements. Considering the potential hurricane, there is a possibility we may need to adjust plans if the storm does intensify."

Aja nodded, her brows furrowing. "Yes, of course, we'll have to keep that in mind."

Nezzie finally tore her gaze away from the screen. "What does that mean, 'adjust plans'? You're not saying we should postpone it?"

"No, not necessarily," the funeral director leaned back in his chair, interlacing his fingers over his belly. "We have a few contingency plans in place, just in case. For instance, we could potentially bring the service forward or delay it a few days if the storm were to hit on that exact Saturday."

Aja glanced out the lone window in the room. The sky was calm and bright blue, the clouds fluffy and sparse. The serene scene was in stark contrast to the foreboding storm on the television screen earlier. "Well," she sighed, returning her gaze to the funeral director, "we'll have to hope for the best, won't we?"

"Of course," the man nodded, turning back to his screen.

"Let's talk about the program and the type of service you want to have..."

As he spoke, Aja's mind began to wander, his voice fading into the background. There were too many choices, too many decisions to be made. As an entrepreneur, Aja was used to making decisions quickly but she was out of her depth here.

Feeling a hand touch her arm, Aja looked down to see Nezzie offering a supportive squeeze. She fixed her granddaughter with a steady gaze. "Aja, it's going to be alright. We'll get through this," Nezzie turned to the funeral director. "Let's do a traditional service, nothing too showy."

Aja took her grandmother's hand and squeezed it, finding comfort in Nezzie's presence. She'd always been the force that held their family together. "With flowers," Aja added. "Lots of colorful flowers."

The funeral director gave her a warm smile. "Of course."

Aja's pulse raced. "One more thing, do you have any more details on how my mother died? I understand her boat capsized?"

The man hesitated. "Let me see what the coroner put in his report," he pecked at a few keys then ran a finger down the screen slowly. "Looks like cardiomegaly, or an enlarged heart, led to heart failure. She may have gotten dizzy and lost control of her boat."

Aja and Nezzie settled into their lounge chairs near the shallow end of the pool that wound through the boutique resort. Del had dropped them off and hurried away again. Again Aja pushed her growing irritation and anxiety about his absence to the back of her mind. He had family here; naturally he wanted to spend time with them. And it was way too early in their relationship for her to meet family, wasn't it? They hadn't even decided they were in a relationship.

She inhaled and let the air out slowly. She needed to calm down.

Aja shifted in her lounger. The sun above them was intense, and Aja was grateful for the large umbrella providing shade.

Nezzie placed her sun hat on her lap, squinting at her granddaughter. "Aja, you are a million miles away," she noted. "Is it all this business with the funeral or is something else going on?"

Aja hesitated, her gaze stuck on the cerulean water of the pool. She didn't know where to begin. While Nezzie knew her better than anyone else, Aja wasn't sure she wanted to unload all of her issues while they were supposed to be relaxing.

"I'm just... overwhelmed," Aja admitted finally. "Even with the funeral home handling most of the details, I feel like I should be doing something."

She picked at the edge of her beach towel. "I should be relaxing but I don't know if I remember how."

Nezzie sighed, pulling her sunglasses off. "Aja, you've always been a doer," she said matter-of-factly. "Even as a kid, you were the one trying to organize everything and take charge. But sometimes, you need to step back and let others help."

She motioned toward the pool. "If you really want to be busy, do a couple of laps in the water. It'll do you some good," she glanced around. "Or get Del to entertain you. Where did he say he was going, anyway?"

"He didn't," she said, trying to keep the testiness out of her voice. Nezzie raised an eyebrow at her.

"Ah, that's the issue." she said, chuckling. "You're wondering what Del's up to, aren't you?"

Aja scowled under Nezzie's knowing gaze. "I just find it odd that he drops us off and then disappears without a word," she said. "But that's his business, not mine."

"Sure, let you tell it," Nezzie put her shades back on and settled into her lounger.

Before Aja could respond, a voice called out from behind them, "Guess who?" They turned around to see London striding toward them with a grin on her face. Del trailed behind her and Aja's heart thudded with relief.

"London!" Aja sprang up from her chair, rushing to meet her cousin with a surprised laugh. She threw her arms around London, squeezing tight. "What are you doing here?"

"I figured you might need some help and if I asked, you'd just say you got it, so here I am." London said, rubbing Aja's back.

Aja turned to her grandmother, who didn't seem at all surprised to see London. "Did you know about this?"

Nezzie glanced up, peering over her shades. "Who do you think got Del to pick her up?"

Del flashed her a lopsided grin that gave her butterflies. "Ms. Nezzie twisted my arm and swore me to secrecy," he said, lifting a shoulder. "I had no choice."

Aja turned to London, a genuine smile on her face. "Well, I'm glad you're here," she admitted, hugging London once more.

Nezzie patted the empty lounger on the other side of her. "Come have a seat, Lulu, we'll get you a drink."

London accepted the invitation with a nod of thanks and collapsed onto the lounge chair, kicking off her sandals.

Aja glanced around then up at Del. "London, Where's your stuff? I can give you my room key,"

"Already taken care of," Del said. "Nezzie gave us her key and I put London's stuff in your room."

"Okay, good. We're kind of spread out but we'll make it work," Aja said.

Aja swung her feet to the ground, making room for Del to sit. Del took a seat on Aja's lounger then his gaze met hers. "You are always welcome to hang out in my room if you need more space."

Aja's heart fluttered at his offer, her cheeks tinting a rosy shade of pink. "Thank you Del, I might just take you up on that," she said, surprised at her own response.

London fanned herself beside Nezzie, a teasing tone in her voice, "Nezzie, you've been holding out on me."

"Oh, you don't know the half of it," Aja snorted then turned to her grandmother "You tell her about Clayton yet?"

London's head snapped up. "Clayton?"

Aja nodded. "Remember Clayton Rummel? He's vacationing here as well. Guess who's caught his eye?" She tilted her head toward Nezzie.

London's mouth dropped. "Shut the front door! For real?"

Nezzie looked like the cat that swallowed the canary. "We're both single and trying to mingle."

London rested her chin on her palm. "What are the odds?" She placed a hand on Nezzie's arm. "Did he tell you anything about his last online dating experience?"

"He told me a little about it...but he said he's done with dating sites," she glanced at her phone. "Tonight we're going to do that sunset cruise that Aja and Del went on," she told London. "You want to go with us?"

London shook her head. "Nah, I'm going to call Donovan in a bit and hang out here at the resort," she turned to Aja. "Unless there's something you need help with?"

"No, we got all of the funeral planning stuff done today, so nothing more needs to be done for now," Aja replied. "You just relax and enjoy your evening."

"Will do," London said. She laid back against the lounger, her eyes closing.

A server in a tropical shirt stopped by to take drink orders and Nezzie ordered a round of frozen margaritas for the group.

Aja settled into her lounger, watching Del. He had a slight frown on his face and she could tell he was miles away. She shifted her legs away from him, giving him more room to get comfortable. "Do you want to stretch out?"

Del shook his head, giving her a half smile that didn't reach his eyes. "I'm fine."

"What's wrong?" she asked softly. "I can tell something is on your mind."

He sighed, ran a hand over his beard. "Sounds like you made all the decisions about Diana's service already?"

Aja nodded slowly. "We did...what's the problem?"

Del shifted uncomfortably, his gaze straying to the beach. "No problem," he replied, though there was an edge to his voice that suggested otherwise. "I assumed you'd wait for me before you decided."

She stilled. "What are you talking about? You dropped us off and sped away like you had urgent business elsewhere," she said, her voice rising.

The server returned, placing their drinks on a small side table between Aja and Nezzie.

"Thank you," Nezzie said to the server. She turned back to face Aja. "Do you two need a moment?"

Aja looked back at Del, her eyes probing his face. His mouth was set in a firm line. Before she could answer, he stood up. "Yeah, we do. Excuse us."

Del reached out a hand, helping Aja up from her lounger, and led her away from the group. As they walked in silence toward the beach, Aja felt a knot twist in her stomach. "I don't understand this. You never said anything about wanting to have a say in my mother's service."

He stopped walking, turned on her. "Why would I be here otherwise, Aja?"

CHAPTER 17

Del

Del didn't wait for an answer. "Diana entrusted me with her estate and I understand now that she wanted us to work together to make sure she was taken care of."

Del resumed his pace, heading toward the path that led to the beach.

"Will you stop or at least slow down?" Aja called out behind him. He turned to find her jogging toward him.

"My crystal ball is out for repairs, so my mind reading skills are gone, Del. Why didn't you say you wanted me to wait for you?"

"I didn't realize I had to," he said tersely, halting as he waited for Aja to catch up with him. He saw the hurt in her eyes and knew he was being unfair but Diana's sudden passing had hit him harder than he had expected. She was not just a client but a friend; one who'd shared her dreams, fears, and hopes with him. Her absence felt like a gaping hole in his life and he wasn't sure how he'd move on.

"You just took off without a word, what was I supposed to do?" Aja asked again.

"I wanted to have a say in the service. Diana deserves a

goodbye that's true to who she was," Del said, keeping his voice hard.

"Nezzie and I did the best we could considering we don't know who the hell she was," Aja was defensive now. "I don't even know why I'm here. I should have listened to my dad and let the lawyers deal with all of this," she waved her arm in defeat. "She should have left everything to you since you were so fucking close."

Del turned to Aja, his grief-fueled rage simmering just beneath the surface. "You're right, maybe you should have let the lawyers deal with it," he said, turning again to walk away.

But Aja wasn't finished. She grabbed Del's wrist, bringing his retreat to a halt. "And maybe you should remember that I've lost my mother twice now," her voice trembled with raw emotion. "Instead you're rubbing it in my face that she didn't care about her only child enough to stick around."

Her words sliced through him, cutting through his own grief. He turned to look at her, breathing heavily. She was blinking rapidly, on the brink of tears and he saw the moment when she broke. She released his wrist and buried her face in her hands. Her shoulders shook and Del stood there, his guilt rendering him immobile.

"Aja," he said, finally making an attempt to reach out to her. But she was already walking away from him, her posture defeated. Del watched her, every instinct urging him to follow, but instead he remained rooted in place, his own fears keeping him from moving. He stared at the path she'd taken, probably back to her family. He tried to convince himself this was for the best. They both would leave the island and go back to their normal lives in Atlanta.

Slowly, he turned away from where she'd disappeared and headed in the opposite direction.

The colors of the sunset were streaking the sky in vibrant hues of orange and pink as Del made his way to the resort bar, thinking he and Aja should be enjoying this sunset together.

Instead he was alone, consumed by the argument, replaying it over and over in his mind. He slid onto a stool at the bar and signaled for a drink, intending to drown his sorrows in Bajan rum.

The bartender brought him a glass, filled to the brim with the amber liquid. Del raised it to his lips and took a gulp, letting the fiery liquid slide down his throat. He stopped himself from taking another large swallow. He didn't want numbness just yet; he wanted to feel every bit of his sorrow.

By the time he'd made his way through half the glass, the sun had fully set, leaving behind a clear star-filled sky. Del allowed himself a moment to appreciate the beauty of his country, then went back to his drink. He was determined to drag out every agonizing minute of his self-imposed punishment.

His fingers tightened around the glass as he thought about his words and Aja's pain. He had handled everything wrong. He realized he had been thoughtless, even cruel. All because he'd been in his feelings, thinking Aja didn't need his help.

Del took a shuddering breath, his eyes fixed on the twinkling lights reflecting off the sea. His hand reached up to rub his aching temples. The rum hadn't dulled the sharp edges of regret that were gnawing at him.

Del tipped his mostly empty glass toward him, watching a small piece of ice evaporate. He should quit while he was ahead and go up to his room. But why bother? Aja wouldn't be there.

"Is this seat taken?" a feminine voice beside him asked. Del looked up from his glass to the source of the voice-a striking woman with honey tipped locs and skin the color of cinnamon. She was in a flowing white sundress that accentuated her skin and her dark eyes held a faint hint of amusement as she regarded him.

"No, it's all yours," Del replied.

The woman gathered her dress and eased herself down on the stool next to him. "You look like you could use a friendly ear," she said, her voice tinged with a slight Southern accent he tried to place. Maybe one of the Carolinas, he guessed.

"Is it that obvious?" he asked, a hint of bitterness creeping into his voice.

The woman chuckled softly. "Only to someone who's spent their fair share of time on that side of a bar," she said, her eyes conveying her empathy. The bartender came over and she ordered a dirty martini.

"Lydia," she introduced herself, nodding at Del as the martini was placed before her. She smoothed her dress and turned toward the bartender. "Another drink for my friend here."

"No," Del said, holding up his hand. "One's enough for tonight."

Lydia turned to him, an eyebrow raised in surprise. "That's refreshing, a man who knows his limits." She took a slow sip of her drink, her eyes never leaving his. "So, what's got you staring into an empty glass alone on a beautiful night in paradise?"

He considered deflecting or giving her a vague, non-committal answer, but something in Lydia's eyes told him she wouldn't let it pass. "Stupid, heat of the moment thing. I said a lot I didn't mean," Del confessed, his voice low. "To someone I care about."

Lydia took another sip of her drink before responding. "Maybe that person needs space to cool down," she mused, her gaze on him. "If they care about you too, they'll be willing to talk and work things out when they're ready."

"Even if I was wrong?" he asked.

"Especially if you were wrong," Lydia replied, her voice firm. "Acknowledge it, apologize, do better. That's all we can do."

The sincerity in her words reached Del and he found himself opening up more than he'd expected. He told her about his argument with Aja, how hurt he'd been that she hadn't included him in planning Diana's service. With every word he spoke, the weight of his guilt seemed to lessen.

Lydia listened, a thoughtful expression on her face. When he was finished, she took another sip from her glass. "Sounds like you've both been hurt," she said, her voice soft but clear. "Everyone grieves differently."

"Do you think she'll forgive me?" he asked. When she didn't respond immediately, he sat back. "Would you forgive me if you were in this situation?"

"I'm not her," Lydia said, giving him a steady look. "And without knowing the full extent of your relationship, it's not really my place to say."

Del nodded, glancing down at his empty glass. "I get that," he admitted.

"However," Lydia continued, her voice softer now, "from what you've told me, it sounds like she means a lot to you. And if that's the case, then she's probably worth fighting for."

Del looked at Lydia, her words resonating within him. Yes, Aja was worth fighting for. He would do whatever it took to make things right between them again.

Del glanced at his phone, checking the time. He hesitated. It was nearly midnight. Was Aja still up, waiting for him to reach out and apologize or did she need more time? He felt torn, caught between the fear of making things worse or letting the silence between them grow.

Just as he was about to put his phone away, the room came alive with the sound of music. A local band had started their set, the slow, sensual rhythm of reggae filling every corner of the bar. Lydia perked up at this and turned to him with a half-smile.

"This is my favorite song. Dance with me?" she asked, extending her hand toward him. The unexpected offer threw him off balance and Del sat there, frozen in place.

She bit her lip. "Please?"

Del blinked at her, his mind racing. One dance wouldn't hurt, he reasoned and offered Lydia a small smile of his own. "If you insist."

Lydia winked. "I do. But I feel like I should know your name first?"

"Del," he said, taking her hand and leading her to the center of the floor in front of the band.

As they moved to the rhythm of the reggae band, Del found himself captivated by Lydia's grace. Her movements were fluid, her hips swaying to the beat of the music with a sensuality he couldn't ignore. They moved together like they'd been dance partners for years; she reminded him of Andre in that regard.

"Del, I hope she appreciates your skills," Lydia leaned in, speaking close to his ear. "If not, I could dance with you all night."

His eyes met hers and he saw something in her gaze; a playful challenge, a spark of interest.

But he could no longer deny it; his heart was elsewhere. "I appreciate it," Del said with a hint of regret in his voice, "but I can't take you up on that offer."

Lydia pulled back slightly, her eyes searching his. There was no judgment in her gaze, only understanding. She gave him a wistful smile. "Well, she's a lucky woman," she said softly. Her hands slipped from his, but not before giving them a gentle squeeze.

"Thank you, Lydia," he responded genuinely, feeling a deep appreciation for this stranger who had unknowingly helped him realize what he needed to do.

Just as they were about to step off the dance floor, Del happened to glance across the lounge area where a dessert and coffee bar were stationed. Aja stood there, holding a tray of paper coffee cups, staring at him.

A sudden jolt of panic surged within Del, his heart pounding against his chest. She had seen him dance with Lydia.

Shit. Hurriedly excusing himself from Lydia, Del crossed the room to Aja. He felt a strange mix of apprehension and relief; at least now he wouldn't have to wait any longer to have this conversation.

"Aja," he said, stopping a respectful distance from her. She turned fully toward him, setting the tray of coffee cups down on the bar.

"I need to explain..." he started, his voice hoarse with emotion. Aja said nothing, merely inclined her head slightly in acknowledgment of his words.

"Actually, Del, save it," she said, picking her tray back up. "Here I was thinking I'd hurt you and I was trying to give you space to grieve thinking you were alone but I guess you're good now, right?"

Del felt like he'd been punched in the gut. He opened his mouth to explain, to tell her that it wasn't what it looked like, but Aja held up a hand, silencing him.

"Let's not do this. Not here." she said tersely, tilting her head toward the people around them that were watching them with keen interest.

She moved to walk away, but Del reached out and gently took hold of her arm. Aja looked down at his hand then back up at him, her expression unreadable. "Aja, please..." Del pleaded, his voice barely a whisper. "Talk to me."

She shook her head. "There's nothing more to say."

Aja slipped her arm free from his grip, avoiding his gaze.

It was the finality in her voice that cut him the deepest; it left no room for negotiation or pleading. He watched as she turned on her heel and walked away from him for the second time that day, leaving him standing there alone with his heart pounding in his chest.

CHAPTER 18

Aja

Aja sat cross-legged, her eyes closed, trying to focus on her breathing as the meditation coach instructed.

Aja and London, along with a handful of other bleary-eyed vacationers, were sitting on the beach, doing sunrise meditation, a session offered by the resort. London was on her right, humming softly. Aja opened one eye. "You can't possibly be in a meditative state while you hum," she hissed.

The instructor gave them a warning glance.

"Yeah I can. And you can't be in one if you're worrying about me." London replied, keeping her eyes closed.

Aja scowled. This was a bad idea. She'd thought that trying a few minutes of meditation would allow her to clear her mind and allow her heart to start healing but it wasn't working. Thoughts of Del plagued her constantly, making her irritable and snippy.

London stopped humming. "How long do you think you can avoid him?"

She let out a long sigh. Why had she asked happy-go-lucky London to come along when all she wanted was quiet so she could wallow in self-pity? Nezzie would have been her first choice but she came in late after her date with Clayton and was still

181

sleeping. Then again, Nezzie wouldn't allow her to take her bad mood out on everyone else.

"I'm not avoiding anyone," she lied. Two days had passed since she'd caught Del dancing with that woman. Her heart dropped every time that image of them together flashed through her mind. The woman had that look on her face, the kind that Aja recognized instantly—one of attraction and admiration. She imagined she had that same look when Del was nearby.

She had been avoiding him, not that he had made any real efforts to approach her either. There had been texts from him the day after—asking her if they could talk—but she'd ignored them. She pushed the thought aside, trying to regain focus on her breathing again.

"Hmm. At my job, our fearless leader is always telling us to overcommunicate with our team and our clients, I would say that applies to personal relationships as well. Would you agree?"

She lifted an eyebrow. "Really? You're choosing this exact moment to toss my words back in my face?"

"I'm just saying...you should talk to him," London said. "He looked miserable when he came by last night."

Aja opened her eyes, dropping the pretense of meditation altogether. She stared hard at London.

"Wait. He came to our room? Why didn't you say anything earlier?" she asked, her tone sharper than intended.

The instructor shushed them and Aja rolled her eyes.

London stifled a yawn, "I tried to wait up for you but I finally gave up and went to bed. I thought you were with him...where did you go last night, anyway?"

The meditation session ended with a soft bell ringing and the instructor announcing in a calm voice, "Take a moment to bring yourself back from your inner journey."

Aja took that as her cue to get up. Sand stuck to her legs and she busied herself brushing it off. "I walked the beach for a long while."

London swiped at the sand on her legs. "Any epiphanies? Aha moments?"

Aja shook her head, her eyes still locked on the horizon where the sun had fully risen, casting a golden hue over the sea. "No, not really. Just more confusion," she admitted.

"Maybe you're looking for answers that are right in front of you," London said as they trudged back to the resort.

"Maybe." Aja wasn't ready to have this conversation. "Let's go grab Nezzie and have breakfast on the patio."

"Sounds good," London said.

When they reached the room, Nezzie was already dressed and putting the finishing touches on her make-up. "Good morning! Aja, someone just slid that letter under our door." She pointed at a sheet of paper on the nightstand.

"What does it say?" Aja asked, putting her flip-flops in the closet.

"I don't know, I was getting in the shower so I didn't have my reading glasses handy." Nezzie said.

London picked up the letter and read it aloud.

"Dear Guests, this is a follow-up warning regarding Hurricane Juno. The tropical storm has been upgraded to a Category 4 and is expected to make landfall in forty-eight hours. We advise all guests to prepare for potential evacuations and stay informed through our provided communication channels. Please attend the mandatory safety briefing at noon today in the main hall."

Aja crossed her arms, her mind running worst case scenarios. Hurricane Juno could be catastrophic. Her thoughts turned to Del once more. Was he preparing too?

She glanced at Nezzie, who met her eyes with a worried look of her own. "After breakfast, we should start packing just in case," Aja suggested, trying to keep her voice steady.

London folded the letter and placed it back on the nightstand. "Yep, good call. We'll get everything ready before the safety briefing."

Nodding, Aja took a critical look at herself in the full length mirror. She smoothed her hair and grabbed her floppy beach hat and her crossbody bag. She wondered if Del would attend the safety talk.

They made their way to the restaurant then settled into a table under a large umbrella with a view of the ocean. Nezzie immediately started building a colorful plate from the buffet, while London ordered a chai latte. Aja nibbled absentmindedly on a piece of pineapple, her thoughts drifting back to Del. She knew she owed him an apology for not giving him a say in her mother's arrangements and for assuming the worst when she saw him with that woman.

Aja's gaze drifted out to the horizon again. The day was bright and sunny. Only the violent waves crashing against the rocky coast hinted at the approaching storm.

London and Nezzie kept up a steady stream of chatter as they ate and Aja found herself nodding along, but her heart wasn't in it.

London turned to her. "You should just go up to his room, talk to him before the safety briefing."

Aja sighed, the weight of the impending conversation settling on her shoulders. "You're right," she said, pushing her plate away. "I shouldn't put this off any longer."

London gave her an encouraging smile. "You've got this. We'll meet you back in the room after breakfast."

Nezzie nodded in agreement, giving Aja's arm a reassuring squeeze.

The corridors of the resort were bustling with anxious guests and staff members preparing for the impending storm.

Aja's feet seemed to move of their own accord as she made her way through the resort, her pulse quickening with each step. She was halfway up the stairs to Del's floor when she heard her name.

"Excuse me, Ms. Lewis?"

Aja stopped and turned toward the voice.

Zade, the front desk clerk that had checked them in, stood a few feet from her.

His expression was a blend of concern and urgency. "I'm sorry to bother you, but we need all guests to verify their personal information at the front desk as part of our emergency protocol."

Aja nodded, though her mind was elsewhere. "Of course, I'll be there in a moment."

The young man smiled then glanced around him. "Ms. Lewis, a word please?"

Aja hesitated, her thoughts still lingering on her mission to find Del. She glanced back up the stairs, then nodded and stepped toward Zade.

"Is something wrong?" she asked, trying to mask her impatience.

Zade's deep brown eyes shifted nervously. "I thought you should know...the situation with Hurricane Juno is progressing faster than expected," his voice went lower. "We've received an update—it might make landfall sooner. If you are trying to go back home before it comes, you need to do so now."

Aja's heart skipped a beat. Her mind raced with the implications of Zade's words. Should they try to change their flights to leave that day?

"Thank you for letting me know," Aja told him. her voice steadier than she felt inside.

Zade gave her a sympathetic nod before rushing off. Aja watched him go, a sense of urgency taking hold of her. She turned back to the stairs, but the thought of leaving without resolving things with Del weighed heavily on her heart.

Taking a deep breath, she sprinted up the remaining stairs and arrived at Del's door, her knuckles rapping sharply against the wood. Silence greeted her. She knocked again, this time with more force.

"Del?" she called out, but there was no response.

~

A few days after she and Nezzie returned from their trip, Aja took a deep breath as she walked into her office, trying her best to get back into work mode.

She'd also been thinking about Del. If she was being honest, longing was a better description of her current state. Aja shook her head to clear those thoughts. She was back in Atlanta and back at work, and she needed to focus.

She reached the outer door of Exposé and keyed in the code, trying not to spill her travel mug of coffee as she entered.

Had it been only two weeks since she'd last been in the office? That day she'd come stomping into her cousin London's office late, with her glasses, crap, she still needed to get a new pair with her current prescription, and Del was sitting there.

The office was still cramped as ever but for some reason, it wasn't as stifling as it had been before she left. Her heart wasn't racing with anxiety about moving to a bigger space and all the details that entailed.

She sighed. She was back in her world.

As soon as Aja opened the door, she was greeted by a barrage of colorful balloons, floating cheerfully around the empty receptionist desk. A box of Krispy Kreme donuts lay on the counter. Aja peeked into the box and nabbed a raised donut with pink icing and sprinkles.

"Welcome back!" Zaria burst into the reception area, pulling her into a tight embrace, "We missed you!"

"Glad to be back. Looks like the office is in one piece still so that's good," Aja joked.

She turned to see Lavender standing beside her with a matching grin on her face. "Hey Boss! Welcome back!"

Aja gestured at the balloons and donuts. "What's all this?"

"We wanted to give you a proper return to work," Lavender said, grabbing a napkin and selecting a donut. "And we're dying to hear about your trip. How was Barbados, aside from the hurricane and all?"

She felt tears prick the back of her eyes at the gesture. She loved these women so much.

How could she summarize her trip in a few words? She'd faced some hard truths about her life and her relationships, gotten to know more about the woman that gave birth to her, and taken some actual time to relax.

And she might have slipped up and fallen in love.

That thought slammed into her gut like a wrecking ball.

Oh God. She pictured one of those memes where a woman slid down a wall in despair.

No time to dwell on that right now.

She gave Lavender what she hoped was a grateful smile. "For the most part, It was good. The weather was wonderful and warm, at least while we were there. Nezzie and I made it out right before the airport closed."

"We'll have to do lunch so I can get all of the dirty details. How's Ms. Nezzie?" Zaria asked.

Aja nodded. "She's fine. She met someone and I think he's planning to visit her this summer."

"What? Ms. Nezzie got her groove back? With some Bajan Casanova?"

"Honestly, I don't know that my grandmother has ever lost her groove." Aja rolled her eyes. "But no, he's from Miami."

"Wow. I knew I should have gone with you. Where's London by the way? She coming in today?"

"No, she's stuck in Miami, but hopefully she can get out today." Aja bit into her donut, savoring the sugar.

"I don't know how you manage the contractors...I've had to whip them into shape to get them to do basic things. They're great when it comes to technical stuff but getting them to submit their timesheets on time and accurately is like herding goats and drunk cats." Lavender said.

Smirking, Aja agreed. "Welcome to my world."

Zaria took a donut. "I don't need this but I'm starving.

"Nothing much happened while you were out. The real estate agent keeps calling to see when you want to look at office space. I told her to stand down."

"Yeah, I'll call her when I get settled." she looked around the office. "We've had a good run here but I do think it's time for more space. Don't you agree?"

Zaria and Lavender stared at her.

Zaria recovered first. "Well, yeah, we've been saying that for a while now but I got the impression you weren't ready for that."

Shrugging, Aja popped the last bite of donut in her mouth and wiped her fingers on a napkin near the box. "You know, I realized while I was gone that on some level, I've been afraid to expand, afraid to take on more risk, but when I think about the worst that could happen, it's not the end of the world. It's time, don't you think?"

Zaria and Lavender eyed each other as if she'd sprouted a second head.

"I guess the time off was productive for you," Lavender said slowly. "Or you did what we told you to do and got some island peen."

Zaria's eyes narrowed. "I don't know why I didn't see it before. You trollop! You look all relaxed and brown, you're like glistening. Ugh," Zaria mock rolled her eyes. "Start talking...how was it?"

Zaria was the opposite of Aja in so many ways, she often wondered how they had managed to become friends. But she couldn't imagine her life without the tall, outspoken sales manager.

Bringing Zaria on had been one of the best decisions Aja had made during her tenure at Exposé. Zaria had built a team of business development reps that worked remotely and brought in leads hand over fist for the company.

She had been hesitant to mix business with pleasure, wondering if she and Zaria could remain friends while they worked together but thus far, things had been good.

Del had given her lots to think about. One was making sure

she prepared her staff to take on larger roles in the company and that's what she intended to talk to Zaria about. Zaria, she knew, would make an excellent VP of Sales or she might want to run the sales department for the app Aja wanted to build for the new dating platform.

There she went again, thinking of Del.

CHAPTER 19

Del

Del pulled his luggage toward him as he surveyed the neon lights of the mojito bar in front of him. The place was full of weary travelers and there were no seats at the bar. He huffed a sigh and debated on whether he was going to wait for someone to leave or make the journey to another restaurant. Not that it mattered; he was stuck in the Miami airport for the foreseeable future.

Out of the corner of his eye, he saw a couple at a table tucked in a corner gather their luggage. He swung his bag around and strode toward the table.

"Del?"

He turned sharply, his heart pounding. The voice sounded like Aja's but that couldn't be right. She should be back in Atlanta.

"Del?" the voice called again, closer this time, and Del breathed a small sigh of regret mixed with relief. He watched as London waved at him.

"What are you doing here?" Del asked, pulling his luggage out of the way of oncoming foot traffic. "I thought you'd be home by now."

She shook her head, resting her elbow on the handle of a

bright red suitcase. "I wasn't able to get on the same flight as Aja and my grandmother since I flew standby coming in. I've been here since this morning trying to get a flight to Atlanta. Everyone is trying to get out of the path of the hurricane."

She regarded him. "What about you?"

Del watched as a man in a suit snagged free table. "I was planning to stay and ride out the hurricane just to make sure my aunt was okay but she insisted I head home," Del said. His headstrong aunt had practically thrown him out of her house. "We did manage to get her house prepped. She's got plenty of water stocked in the freezer and non-perishable food plus necessities like a first aid kit and plywood for the windows."

He ran a hand over his head. "I might as well have stayed, the flight was delayed and now I missed the last flight to Atlanta for the night."

"I tried to go standby on that one but it was oversold. There were a bunch of us hoping to get on that one." She looked around. "Let's go sit at the bar. I could use a drink."

Del rubbed his chin. "Sure, I was going to see if the hotel attached to this airport had any rooms available."

London shook her head. "I checked. It and every other hotel nearby is sold out."

"Alright, not my choice to spend the night in the Miami airport, but," Del said, trying to muster some semblance of optimism. "we can figure something out."

They made their way to the bar and managed to get two seats at the end of the bar.

After ordering mojitos and empanadas, the two settled into their seats, the hum of conversations around them filling the air.

Del drummed his fingers on the table, wanting to ask about Aja.

The bartender dropped off their drinks and London took her first sip. "Yep, that's what I needed."

Del stirred his mojito and took a tentative sip. He'd never had one before but he liked lime and mint.

London rested her elbow on the bar. "I feel like you want to ask me about my cousin."

Del leaned back in his chair. "She and Ms. Nezzie got home okay?"

"Yep, they got back yesterday," London said, then paused. "She was worried about you though."

Del felt a warmth swell in his chest. He wanted to drill London for all the details. Instead, he took another sip of his mojito, the tangy lime and refreshing mint wasn't bad but he preferred Bajan rum. "Oh?"

London nodded. "She went up to your room looking for you before the safety briefing but you weren't there."

He groaned. "No, I went to my aunt's early to help out with the hurricane prep."

How many times had he started to go to her room after their confrontation? Each time, he talked himself out of going, afraid she'd reject him again.

Now, sitting at the bar with London, he wondered if his pride was going to cause him to lose her forever.

"I don't want to get into your business...I'll just say this," London's eyes searched his face. "Aja isn't the best at saying what she feels, but it's clear she's got feelings for you. She was worried sick."

The bartender placed hot plates of empanadas in front of them.

Steam wafted up from the empanadas, their golden-brown crusts crisp and inviting. Del tore one open, the aroma of spiced meat and vegetables filling his senses. He took a bite, savoring the flavors that, for a moment, pulled him away from his inner turmoil. He had half a mind to call Aja right then, but they needed to have their talk in person.

London chewed thoughtfully on her empanada before continuing. "Anyway, let's talk about something else before I say too much. Aja would have a small stroke if she knew I was telling you any of this."

Del chuckled, though his mind still lingered on Aja. He was relieved she'd made it home safely but he wasn't quite ready to let go of the topic. "Alright," he said, "How's Jewel's case going?"

She put up a finger, indicating she wanted to finish chewing. "That profile picture of Malik is a fake. It belongs to a man, probably Malik's age or close to it, who died a couple of years ago."

"How'd you figure that out?" Del didn't count himself as tech savvy. He knew enough to get things done efficiently but it wasn't something that normally interested him. However, he found himself intrigued by what Aja and her team did.

London's eyes lit up. "Great question," she said, taking another bite before continuing. "Aja taught me how to spot inconsistencies in digital profiles. I ran a reverse image search and found the original photo on an obituary page."

London finished her last empanada. "Want to see what I mean?" Not waiting for an answer, she said, "Let me pull up his picture and I'll show you."

Del stacked their empty plates to make room for London's laptop.

She tapped the keys then the touchscreen. When the picture popped up, Del peered closer. He'd seen that man recently. "Cheese on bread!" He said suddenly. "That's him?"

London jumped. "What?" then, "What does cheese on bread have to do with anything?"

"It's a Bajan expression...I'll explain it later," He pulled his phone from his pocket then scrolled through the pictures, looking for a specific image.

He found it, enlarged it and passed it to London.

She scrutinized the picture. "Yeah," she said, holding the phone up to her laptop. "Looks like it could be the same person. Where did you get this?"

"Diana was your aunt, right?" London nodded. "She did a lot of her sketches on this electronic device, like a kind of sketch pad, using a drawing app, I guess, but she sketched that image."

"What's that he's holding?" She pointed at the orb in the man's hands.

"I think it's one of Diana's creations."

London nodded absently, her attention drawn back to the image on Del's phone.

The bartender cleared their plates and silverware then dropped off their bill.

"Where is that device, do you know?" London asked, pulling a card from her wallet. "This is my treat, by the way. I think you've given us a clue."

Del rubbed his hands together, grinning at her. "Thanks, it's in my bag. I meant to give it to Aja after I charged it but..." he shrugged. "Anyway, let's go see if we can find seats near chargers."

Once they were seated, Del retrieved Diana's device from his bag and showed London the sketch.

She used her fingers to enlarge the image. "See that?" She pointed at the background. "I'm pretty sure that's the Atlanta skyline."

He gestured at the image. "I was right! I thought that looked like downtown Atlanta in her sketch. This is a drawing of this man's profile pic. Which means," he started.

"Aunt Diana knew him too," London finished, grabbing her phone. "I'm calling Aja."

London tapped the speaker icon as they waited for Aja to answer. "Hey London, did you get a flight out?" she asked, her voice muffled by what sounded like wind in the background.

"No, I'm stuck in Miami for the night. And Del's here," London said quickly, "I think we might have a lead on Malik. Del found a sketch your mom did of him."

"Del?" Aja said.

Del held his breath, waiting for Aja's reaction. The pause on the other end of the line felt like an eternity.

"Hey Aja," Del said, trying to keep his tone neutral, "London figured out that his profile pic isn't him. And remember that electronic device I found in her house?" He paused then rushed on, "once I was able to charge it, I reviewed her recent sketches and the background is definitely the Atlanta skyline. Diana drew a sketch of the exact same guy, holding one of her glass orbs and standing in front of the same skyline."

Del and London stared at the phone, waiting for Aja's verdict. "You're thinking my mother knew the guy Jewel is seeing," Aja said finally. "That's interesting. Can you send me the sketch and the fake profile pic?"

"Already on it," London said, typing quickly on her laptop. "We're thinking maybe Diana was seeing him at some point. Maybe she even made the orb he's holding."

"Okay, now that you mention it, I saw a glass piece in Jewel's house when she had us over for lunch. You should ask her where she got it"

"I'll check with her after we hang up." London looked at her laptop then shot a look at Del. Abruptly, she pushed her phone toward him. "Here, talk to Aja for a sec, I need to run to the ladies room."

Del narrowed his eyes at her convenient excuse. She wasn't fooling anyone with that explanation. She wanted to give Del time to talk to Aja alone.

Del took Aja off speaker phone. "London said she'll be back," he said before realizing she'd heard London just as he had. He held the phone, wanting to ask her a million questions. Did she miss him as much as he missed her?

"How's Ms. Nezzie?"

Aja sighed. "She's fine. She's been asking about you. She'll be happy to hear you're okay."

He grinned. He could see the older woman saying that. "You back at work?"

"Yep, I'm in my office right now," she said, and he detected a wistfulness in her voice. "I miss the beach already."

He noticed she didn't mention missing him.

"Yeah, same here. But mostly, I miss..." Del hesitated, unsure if he should complete the sentence. He decided to keep it light. "I miss my own bed."

Aja didn't say anything for a beat and Del tried to gather his thoughts. "So, what do you think of the lead we found?"

"Sounds promising," Aja said. "I don't want to get too excited until we have more information. But I've found that most times the most logical answer is the correct one," she paused, then, "Thank you for your help."

Del's heart pounded at the genuine gratitude in Aja's voice. He had been eager to help London with this case to occupy his mind with something other than Aja, but it wasn't until that moment that he realized how much he wanted to figure out who Malik really was and what connection he had to his former client.

Del nodded. "You're welcome. We'll check out that glass orb."

Del held the phone as neither of them said anything.

"Del," she said suddenly, "please be careful."

Was that concern he heard in her voice? "Don't worry about me. I can handle myself."

"I don't doubt that," Aja said. "but it doesn't hurt to be cautious. Let me know what you all find out. Tell London I'll call her later."

"Okay. Stay safe," Del said before ending the call.

He sat there for a moment, staring at London's phone, thinking about Aja. He missed her more than he thought he would.

London returned. "Much better," she said, opening her laptop once more.

He handed her phone back to her and she scrolled through it. "Let me call Jewel."

Del checked his own phone. "I'm going to hit the men's room myself. You gonna be here?"

"Yep," she said, her thumbs sliding over her phone.

Del wandered through the airport, his thoughts alternating between the case and Aja. Memories of their time together in Barbados assaulted him. Everything from the sweetness of the first time their lips met all the way to the pain that had sliced through him like a laser the last time he let her walk away.

The restroom was empty, giving Del a moment of solitude. As he splashed water on his face, he caught his reflection in the mirror. For a split second, he didn't recognize the man staring back at him—eyes shadowed with fatigue, face drawn tight with unresolved longing. He rubbed his hands over his face, willing himself back to the present.

When he finally exited the restroom, he felt marginally more composed. He took a deep breath and made his way back to where London was seated.

He sat down beside her just as she ended the call with Jewel. "What did you find out?"

London put her phone on her lap. "She showed me the piece and said she bought it from Malik's online store. She wanted to support him since he's just starting out."

Her phone beeped and she pulled up the pictures. "I didn't get to see Aunt Diana's studio, what do you think?"

Del took the phone and enlarged the image. The orb was clear with what looked like colorful ribbons flowing through it. It reminded him of streamers and confetti at a party. The piece was joyful and looked like the piece Aja had selected to take home.

"This is one hundred percent Diana's work," he held the phone so she could see. "This image here is the bottom and those are her initials."

"It's beautiful," London said, scrolling through the images again. "Jewel looked at her search history and she said the name of the site was glassworksbyMalik.com, which I'll pull up in a minute."

Opening her laptop, Del watched as she pulled up the e-commerce site. As she scrolled through the images, Del scowled. "This is all of Diana's art. All of these pieces are in her studio," Marveling at the audacity of the man calling himself Malik, Del pointed at the screen. "He didn't even bother to rename them."

London tapped the "About Us" page and the same picture of

Malik she'd shown Del earlier was now grinning at them. Del read the one-line description aloud. "As a self-taught glassblower, I strive to create pieces that capture and preserve moments of beauty and wonder."

He and London stared at each other.

"Son of a bitch," he muttered.

CHAPTER 20

Aja

Ending the call, Aja rested her forehead on her palms, unsure of what to feel. She wanted to be furious with him for not calling, not caring enough to come after her but when she'd heard his deep accented voice on London's phone, she'd been giddy with relief that Del had made it out before the hurricane hit.

They needed to talk, she knew, but not while he was stranded in the Miami airport with London hovering.

She'd have to wait until he was home and they could meet face-to-face.

Aja walked into the kitchen and grabbed a bottle of wine from the fridge, pouring herself a glass as she tried to clear her mind. She took a sip and closed her eyes, relishing the slight spiciness of the chardonnay.

God, she missed him. But she knew what the issue was. Fear.

When she'd seen him dancing with that woman, all of her insecurities and fears leapt to the forefront, planting tiny seeds of doubt. Fear of rejection. Fear of being vulnerable. Fear that his feelings might not mirror hers. Fear that once she expressed them, her feelings would become real, tangible things that could be used against her like weapons to destroy her.

Aja was terrified he'd want her to stifle her dreams to be with him.

She took another sip of wine, feeling the warmth spread through her body. Maybe she should just call him back and tell him how she really felt. "Hey, Del, I just wanted to say I love you but I can't afford to give you my heart."

She snorted. She hadn't had nearly enough wine for that conversation.

But what if he was still stuck on the whole American woman thing and didn't see her as more than a casual hook up?

What would happen when he met The One, Miss Not American Princess of Zamunda or wherever and married her?

Oh God. The mere thought made her blood run cold.

Aja shook her head, trying to clear her thoughts. Now she was just being hateful. She needed to focus on something else. When in doubt, there was always work to distract her. Aja strode into her home office and sat at her desk, one leg tucked under her body. She did her deep thinking in this space and she desperately needed a distraction now.

Polishing off the last swallow of wine, Aja set the glass on the desk.

Her phone buzzed in the other room and she hopped up to retrieve it, hoping the message was from Del.

But no. London had sent her a text.

London: Looks like we can both get out on the first flight to ATL

Aja: Good. Fingers crossed. Be safe and let me know when you land tomorrow.

Aja put her phone down and leaned back in her chair. Her thoughts drifted back to the case they were working on.

Closing her eyes, she took a deep breath, trying to clear her mind. But her thoughts kept wandering back to Del. He sounded exhausted and his words had been laced with an emotion she couldn't quite place. Was it regret?

She wished she could reach out and soothe him, even if just with words. But she felt like she was standing on the edge of a cliff, needing to jump but terrified to actually do it.

Enough. She sat up, pushed the thoughts of Del aside and decided to focus on her work. She needed to think through some things.

There was a large white board on the wall facing Aja's desk and she grabbed a dry erase marker, uncapping it with her teeth. She drew three squares, and wrote a name in each one: Diana, Malik, Jewel.

She connected Malik and Jewel with a double-sided arrow then placed a question mark between the Diana and Malik boxes.

Malik had her mother's art work on sale on his website. Del had given her the URL and Aja pulled it up on her phone. She scrolled through, looking for a customer service number.

Surely it wouldn't be that easy.

There was no number and his domain registration was set to private so that yielded no clues. All she had was a generic info email address that bounced when she attempted to send an email to it.

She made note of it as she continued to look at the site. Picking up the marker again, she wrote

Found out Mailk was selling her art under his name?

under her mother's box.

"Dating Malik?"
"How did she meet M?"
"M sent flowers?"

Under Malik, she wrote:

"How did M fulfill orders?"

Aja capped the marker, then tapped it against her chin.

She stared at the board, the pieces of the puzzle swirling in her mind but she couldn't make them fit.

And now the wine was kicking in, making her thoughts fuzzy and nonsensical.

What was she missing? Her mother was the first name she'd written but Diana seemed to be at the center of everything.

Maybe it was time she learned more about her mother.

Aja yawned and decided she was done for the evening. She'd read somewhere that if you went to sleep thinking about open questions, the subconscious worked on providing answers. She was going to try the theory out tonight.

As she tied her hair up in a satin scarf, she ran all her questions through her mind.

She'd see what her subconscious had up its sleeve.

And it was time to have a long overdue conversation.

The next day after work, Aja found herself heading out of midtown Atlanta and into the suburbs where she'd grown up.

Her father lived in the Cascade area of Atlanta, a predominantly African-American affluent area located southwest of downtown.

Aja and London had grown up in the area, London and her dad still lived in a subdivision up the road.

Aja let herself into her dad's house. The familiar scent of sandalwood and aged leather greeted her as she stepped into the foyer.

The house, a large mid-century ranch with a basement, was one of her dad's renovation projects. He'd completely gutted the house, adding a screened in porch and a three car garage. He liked to boast that he'd created an environment fit for a king. The house was decidedly male with lots of dark wood and leather pieces.

Aja locked the door behind her, glancing around the house. "Dad?"

She figured her father was probably in his home office. She'd gotten her workaholic ways from him and she was sure he was still logged in to his work even though it was nearly eight in the evening.

She knocked on the partially open door, sticking her head in.

Edwin Lewis looked up from his computer, his reading glasses perched on the edge of his nose. He was an imposing figure, even seated. His hair was salt and peppered, cut short and neat, framing a deep brown face that wore a perpetual scowl. His broad shoulders filled out the tailored dress shirt he wore, sleeves rolled up to his elbows, revealing a muscular frame that still managed to turn heads.

"Aja," he said, in the rich baritone that had always commanded respect both at home and in his office. "To what do I owe the pleasure?"

"Hey Dad, I just thought I'd stop by and see how you're doing." She walked in and flopped on a leather loveseat across from her father's desk as she'd done since she was a teenager. "You busy?"

"Nah, I was actually looking at some new golf gear your uncle told me he bought. Like it's gonna help his game," he chuckled. He and London's dad were twin brothers and golf rivals.

Aja rolled her eyes, wondering if they'd ever get tired of trying to one up each other on the golf course. "When's your next golf trip? Next month, right?" Aja asked.

"Yeah, first weekend in April. You and London should come with us. It's high time you girls learned how to play. More deals happen on the golf course than you can imagine, Aja."

She shook her head. "I have zero desire to learn golf. London and I would be better off hanging at the beach. And besides, I just got back."

His tone flattened. "Right. I told you to have the lawyers handle everything."

Aja sighed. Her father would never get tired of saying 'I told you so', she assumed.

Taking a deep breath, Aja tried to steady her nerves. This was a conversation that she had put off for far too long, but she knew it was time for answers.

"Dad, why exactly did my mother leave us?"

He took off his glasses and rubbed them with a cloth on the desk. Aja knew this was a stalling tactic of his. "I don't know what you want me to say. She left. I wasn't begging her to come back."

"I want to know the truth. You've never told me, I think I deserve to know. Nezzie says I should ask you and that I'm old enough to hear it."

Her father placed his glasses back on and stared at her over the tops of them. "Ma told you to ask me. Your grandmother acts like Diana was a saint now but she never cared for her before she took off."

Aja continued to stare at her father, waiting.

"When we had you, I was over the moon. I'll admit, I was thinking we'd have a boy...but when I first laid eyes on you," he shook his head. "You were perfect."

He sighed. "But Diana wasn't herself. Now it's clear she was suffering from postpartum depression but back then, she just seemed off."

Aja leaned in. "What did you do?"

"Your grandmother and I stepped in and that seemed to help. Then after a while, your mom seemed to be okay. She opted to stop working until you were old enough for school and she took you everywhere. When you were about three, I asked her about having another child. I wanted a house full of kids and I figured you should have a sibling. Plus Gene and your aunt had just had

London...I wanted you all to grow up with cousins and all of that like we did."

He got up. "You want something to drink? Eat?"

Aja shook her head, impatiently waiting for him to finish the story. "No, Dad, please, I want to know more about her."

Her father reluctantly sat back down.

"Well, your mother hemmed and hawed and said we could talk about it," he said, tenting his fingers. "Then I found out she'd gotten her tubes tied."

Aja's jaw dropped. "What? She didn't discuss it with you?"

He ran his hand over his head. The gesture reminded her of Del. "No. And when I confronted her about it, she told me it was her body, not mine."

"I was hurt and angry," he said. "Of course I don't know what it's like to birth another human and I know it's her body but I felt betrayed."

A surge of anger toward her mother seized Aja. She couldn't imagine making such a decision without involving her husband.

"We argued about it for weeks," he sighed. "Finally, I was tired of talking about it. I told her that if she didn't want to be a mother, she should just leave. I told her I would take care of my daughter by myself, told her she could go for all I cared."

He looked down at his hands. "And that's exactly what she did," he finished softly.

Aja's heart ached as she processed her father's words. Edwin Lewis had always been a man of few emotions, yet here he was, vulnerable and exposed. She wanted to be angry at him for driving her mother away, for not trying harder to understand Diana's pain. But more than that, she felt a deep sadness for everyone involved.

"I didn't mean it," he said, shaking his head.

"I never thought she would actually go. I thought—no, I hoped—that it would scare her into finding a way to reconcile. But Diana...I guess that was the opening she needed," Edwin said, his voice cracking slightly.

Aja felt tears prickling. Her father looked older than he had when she'd arrived.

Gone was the powerful man she'd grown up with that expected perfection from her. The man sitting at her father's desk was a broken old man full of regrets. She saw her father's wounds as clearly as she now saw her own.

She got up from the loveseat and walked around the desk to hug him. He was hesitant at first then he held onto her tightly.

"I'm sorry, baby girl...should have told you the truth long ago but I didn't want you to hate me," he said, his voice gruff with emotion.

"I don't hate you," she said, her own voice choked with tears. "I'm glad you told me."

They stood like that for a few minutes before her father pulled back, wiping his eyes.

"We all have regrets, Aja. I regret saying those words. I regret not taking her pain seriously. And most of all, I regret not fighting harder for our family."

Aja nodded, understanding now that regret was a universal burden. Turning her thoughts inward, she reflected on her own choices. She had broken up with Del with the same kind of rash certainty her father had displayed. Now, with every passing moment, she realized how much she missed him.

"I know, Dad," she whispered. "I have regrets too."

Her father gave her a pained smile. "We all do, but if there's a chance you can make them right, you should do it."

Aja nodded, his words working their way into her heart and mind.

"So, how was Barbados?" he asked, changing the subject. "Your grandmother certainly enjoyed it, even with the looming hurricane. I'm glad you all got out before the storm hit."

Aja wanted to know more, had a million questions but decided she'd let things go for tonight.

She smiled through her tears. "Did she tell you about her vacation beau?"

He rolled his eyes, holding up a hand. "No. I don't even want to know."

"I'm glad I went," Aja said. "I think that trip helped me make peace with my mother."

Her father nodded. "Ma said you had to cancel your mother's funeral service because of the hurricane?"

"Yeah. I'll reschedule at some point." And she'd include Del in the planning. Assuming he still wanted to be involved.

Aja reflected on all she'd learned but she had to know. "Dad, how did you move on after she left?" Aja asked.

He took his glasses off, gave her a half smile. "As for moving on, a certain five-year-old boss-in-training kept me too busy to think about much else."

Aja smiled in return, glad for her father's attempt at levity. "Well, I'm glad I could keep you on your toes."

He chuckled. "You definitely did that. Still do if I'm being honest," he sat back in his chair, his arms folded. "But seriously, Aja, I didn't move on for a long time. I was bitter and hurt and I didn't trust anyone. Eventually, I realized that holding onto that pain wasn't doing me any good. You know your uncle was a big part of that. We were both raising little girls, had no idea what we were doing and while I hoped maybe one day your mother would come back, Gene's wife was gone forever and he needed me. I focused on my family, on building my business, and on living my life. And slowly but surely, things got better."

Taking in her father's words, Aja nodded

"When I met your former stepmother," Edwin picked up a pen and tapped it against the desk. "I thought that I was ready to close that chapter on Diana and accept that she wasn't coming back but I think a small part of me always hoped she would. It's good you got some closure."

They sat in comfortable silence for a few moments then her father sat up, studying her.

Aja tensed. She knew that look. He was about to ask her something that she didn't want to answer.

"Now, when do I get to meet this Del I keep hearing about?"

~

As Aja drove home, replaying her conversation with her dad, her phone rang, startling her. Immediately her pulse raced.

It could be Del, calling from somewhere else. The display showed unknown caller. She answered with a breathless hello.

"Hi...is this Aja?" The voice pronounced her name "Asia".

"This is Aja Lewis," Aja said, emphasizing her first name.

"Oh, I'm sorry, she sent me a text and I just assumed it was pronounced...anyway, Jewel Forrester sent me your name and said you could maybe help me."

The woman spoke slowly like she assumed Aja was taking copious notes.

Before Aja could ask, the woman launched into a rambling story that bounced from thought to thought and Aja rubbed her temple, trying to make sense out of all the words being thrown at her.

"Ma'am, I didn't catch your name?" Aja cut in.

"Oh, I'm Nikki. Sorry, Nikki Compton. Jewel said she'd tell you I'd be calling?"

Aja hadn't heard from Jewel since she'd left Barbados. Jewel was reaching out to London directly now. "No, she didn't. She might have told my cousin, I'm thinking."

"Oh, I think she did! Anyway, I realize your work day is over, but Jewel assured me I could still call now?"

Aja realized they were setting bad practices by being available after working hours; this was one of the reasons she worked all the time. She didn't set any boundaries with her clients.

"How can I help you, Ms. Compton?"

Next time she vowed to let the call roll to voicemail.

"Well," the woman exhaled. "I've been married about six months now and I'm afraid I made a huge mistake."

Aja blinked. She hadn't seen that coming. Rule one of

investigations: keep the client talking. "Okay, why do you say that?"

She heard Nikki Compton sigh deeply. "Let me give you some background. I'm gonna be fifty this year. And I've never been married. So I was watching some videos on manifestation, you know, where you visualize what you want in your life? You picture having whatever it is you want?"

Aja smirked, thinking of Del. He'd love that this woman was into manifestation. "Yep, I'm familiar with the concept."

"Okay, anyway, I have been envisioning my future husband for a few years now and I finally met him.

We dated for about a year, mostly long distance, and he moved here to Atlanta. We got married last year."

"Congratulations," Aja said automatically, then wished she hadn't. Clearly something in this story had gone south and it wasn't the fairy tale the caller envisioned.

"Thanks." Another heavy sigh. "Anyway, I thought everything was great but he's up to something. Probably cheating, if I had to guess."

The woman was now releasing information in shorter bursts and Aja found herself wishing she would just spit the story out already. "You think he's cheating?"

Nikki Compton didn't answer immediately.

"Ms. Compton? Are you still there?"

"Oh, call me Nikki, please. Maybe. I don't know but something is off."

She paused again. "Here's an example. We honeymooned in Barbados and he didn't do any research before the trip. We just went and stayed at my friend's house...Jewel's, as a matter of fact...and it was lovely, but we didn't do much...it was a lazy vacation. We hung out on the beaches, hit the rum bars, that sort of thing."

Aja's heart started pounding so loud she couldn't hear Nikki. Whatever Nikki was going to say wasn't good, she knew. This was too many coincidences to be normal. She broke in. "You vacationed in Barbados and stayed at Jewel's house?"

"Yes, Jewel told me we could use her house since she was going to be cruising. Since she retired, Jewel's become quite the jet setter. Anyway, we stayed at her house and didn't do much, he didn't research. But he went to Vegas with his boys about a month ago, and since then, he's been looking at stuff about Barbados," she paused, took a breath. "I hinted around, wondering if he was thinking of taking me back for our one year anniversary or something but he clammed up and got snippy, told me to stop snooping."

Aja had pulled into a gas station parking lot and was taking notes on her phone. "Okay, let's go back to your honeymoon. You said you didn't see Jewel while you were there?"

"No, we got married in June and she was on an Alaskan cruise the whole time. I was hoping we'd get to see each other...I haven't seen her since she moved to the island and she hasn't met Everett, but we couldn't make the dates work."

Nikki still sounded disappointed.

"Okay, you're thinking he didn't go to Vegas like he said?" Aja asked.

"I don't know. I mean, I guess he did." Nikki sounded less certain now. "And I can't check any credit card receipts, he mainly uses cash. He said his friend Ron bought the tickets so they could all be on the same flight, sitting together, whatever, so they reimbursed Ron for their flights."

Aja nodded. The man had covered his bases, but she'd find something if there was evidence to be found.

He might be good but Exposé was better.

"Ms. Compton, We normally hand these kinds of things off to a private investigator since they're better equipped to handle physical surveillance and stuff like that. Is that what you're looking for? Someone to document your husband's activities?"

Nikki paused then said, "I think I want someone to check out what he's doing online. He spends a lot of hours late at night on his laptop and it's locked down tight when he leaves it here. I'm pretty sure he's up to no good."

Aja tapped her nails on the steering wheel, thinking about Nikki's case. "Okay, I need to wrap up Jewel's case. Once we do that, we can take yours on if you still want to move forward. Will that work?"

"Oh yes." Nikki's relief was palpable. "Thank you, Aja, Jewel said she was sure you all would be able to help me."

"You're welcome. I'll be in touch soon."

Ending the call, Aja leaned back in her seat. Something strange was going on with Barbados at the heart of it.

CHAPTER 21

Del

Del arrived at his office and cursed the cold. While he'd been grateful to sleep in his own bed again after spending the previous night in the airport, he longed for the warm Bajan sun. The Atlanta weather forecasters were predicting an icy mix of rain, possibly snow, and advising Atlanta residents to stay home if possible. Del wondered why he had even bothered to come in that day.

He rubbed his hands together, the chill of his office seeping into his bones. He should be catching up with the work he'd let lapse while he was gone, but his mind kept drifting to the Caribbean, to the small island where he'd grown up and where his family still lived. Every time he checked his phone, desperate for an update, there was nothing new. Hurricane Juno was predicted to hit Barbados later that day and he prayed his aunt and cousins would be safe.

They lived in a small house on the island's southern coast, right in the path of the storm.

Del checked another website dedicated to hurricane tracking and watched the animated radar swirl of dark reds and ominous purples moving steadily toward Barbados. Before he left, he'd done as much as he could to help his aunt prepare for the storm, but he worried they hadn't done enough. His Aunt Felicity now had her son and his small children living with her. Would they have enough non-perishable food to sustain them?

Closing his eyes, Del took a moment to breathe. Worrying and overthinking wasn't productive. He sent his aunt a text asking her to check in when she could.

After a few calming breaths, he opened his eyes and turned on the space heater. His office tended to be drafty and Del had broken down and bought a small space heater that he kept near his desk. He'd get a few hours of work done and head home before the roads got bad.

The hum of the space heater was a small comfort as Del edited a video he'd use to promote his business on social media. He frowned as he listened to his voice. Had his accent gotten thicker? He debated re-recording the video but thought better of it. He always drilled into his clients to be their authentic selves and he should follow his own advice.

As he uploaded the final edit, his phone buzzed with a text and he immediately opened his texting app.

> Aunt Fe: OK for now. Wind picking up, but we're safe inside. Will keep you updated.
> Love you.

He exhaled, relief coursing through him. As he was typing out a response, another text came through and Del's heart raced once again.

> Aja: Hey, London told me you're back home.

He finished the response to his aunt, then focused on Aja's text.

> Del: Yep, got in yesterday morning

Aja: You heard from your family yet? Any updates?

Del: Just heard from them. So far, so good.

Aja: Glad to hear that. It's been on my mind too.

Del: Thanks for asking

He stared at the phone, mesmerized by the moving dots indicating she was typing. But then they stopped.

Del put the phone down, tried to regain his focus.

The phone beeped and he snatched it up.

Aja: Need to talk, can you come by my place after work?

Need to talk.

He read the words again. Those three words could mean a thousand things, none of them simple. Del sighed, stroking his beard, and glanced at the time on his laptop. It was almost noon. He picked up his phone and stared at the message, then before he could talk himself out of it, pressed the call button.

"Hey," Aja's voice came through, soft but slightly tense.

"Hey," Del replied, rubbing the back of his neck. "I saw that last text. What's up?"

There was silence on the other end.

Then Aja spoke. "I, um, wanted to talk to you more about Jewel's case, get your observations."

Del hesitated, refusing to let himself hope. Drumming his fingers on the desk, he asked, "Do I really need to brave the weather for that? I can just tell you what you need to know now."

Aja sighed audibly. "It's not just about Jewel's case, Del. There are some things I need to say in person, things that can't be conveyed over the phone."

Del's heart beat a little faster. "Alright. After work then."

"Thank you. I'll send you my address. I'm closing the office at one due to the weather so I'll be home any time after two," she said softly.

Del stared at his phone, then slipped it into his pocket.

He hadn't meant to be so brusque with her but he needed to know where her mind was. If this were just about the case, he could do the call from home instead of torturing himself by seeing her again when she didn't want anything to do with him.

The rest of his workday passed in a blur of barely-there focus and stolen glances at the clock. Del's mind vacillated between the work he needed to do and anticipation of seeing Aja again. He had to admit, he did want to talk about her case and see what she had come up with since he and London had shared the images they found.

Checking his phone before packing his belongings, Del saw that she'd sent her address promptly after their call. Now it was time to face whatever awaited him.

Del braved the freezing rain, his breath visible in short puffs as he made his way to his car. The drive to Aja's in Midtown Atlanta felt longer than it was, traffic crawled along as the rain pelted the streets, making Del wonder why the hell he was doing this.

Because he was in too deep. He longed to see her again, even if she only wanted help with her case. He also wanted to explain about the dance with Lydia.

After pulling into a parking spot, Del glanced again at the text Aja had sent with her address, wondering if he was in the right place. He got out and followed the GPS on his phone until he found himself in the center of a courtyard, looking for her unit. The brick building was older, possibly mid-century if he had to guess, and looked as if older people resided there. Not what he imagined for Aja. He pictured her in some swanky high rise with a concierge and state-of-the-art fitness center. This was quaint, peaceful with an amazing view of the Atlanta skyline and he'd noted Piedmont Park was within walking distance. As was Aja's office, so the location made sense, but he had no idea which unit was hers.

There were two two-story buildings parallel to each other, connected to a third building, forming a U shape.

He read each of the unit numbers on the doors nearest him and deduced that she must be on the upper level. As he was climbing the stairs to the top floor, a door opened and Aja stood there, her arms crossed close to her chest.

She wore a thick sweater and jeans. Del paused at the top step, taking in the sight of her. Her eyes met his, and for a moment, neither of them spoke.

"You made it," she said finally, her voice cutting through the tension.

"Yeah, the roads are getting bad," Del replied. "But here I am."

Aja stepped aside to let him in. "Come in before you freeze."

He stepped in Aja's home, taking a look around. This looked more like Aja: minimal with bold design.

Del admired the sleek and sophisticated decor of Aja's condo. The open-floor plan showcased a modern living room with a plush granite colored sofa, a white shag rug, and a unique black and white abstract painting hanging above a crackling fireplace.

He stood awkwardly near the entrance, not quite sure what to do with his hands. "Nice place," he murmured.

"Thanks," Aja replied, closing the door behind him. "Let me take your coat."

"Sure." Del shrugged out of his damp coat and handed it to her. Their hands brushed, sending a jolt through his body. Aja's eyes met his as she hung his coat on a rack by the door, next to her own.

Resisting the powerful urge to touch her again, Del broke eye contact. "Something smells good," he said, sniffing the air.

"Yes, thank Nezzie for that," Aja motioned him toward the kitchen. "She loves to cook and she made me a chicken pot pie which I'm heating up now. I loved them as a kid."

Del followed Aja as he took in her space. The kitchen boasted stainless steel appliances, white cabinets with black handles, and a black granite countertop. The dining area had a round glass table surrounded by black chairs with white cushions. The whole place had a minimalist feel, yet it was still warm and inviting.

"Do you want some wine? Food should be ready in another ten minutes," Aja said.

Del regarded her. She was fidgeting with a pendant around her neck and he could tell she was nervous. Her vulnerability prompted him to step closer, closing the distance between them.

"Before you do that. I need you to know something," he started. "I was all set to tell you that dancing with Lydia, the woman with the locs, meant nothing, but since I've had time to think and consider things from another perspective, I've realized that wasn't entirely true."

Aja's shoulders slumped and she took a slight step back. "Oh," she said softly.

Del quickly reached out and grasped her hand. "Wait, Aja, let me finish." He paused to collect his thoughts, trying to find the right words. "I realized just because I didn't think it meant anything to me, that doesn't make it right. It meant something to *you*."

Aja nodded slightly, her thumb brushing against his knuckles. "Thank you for acknowledging that."

Del sighed, a weight lifting from his chest as he felt the tension between them diminish. The soft glow of the kitchen lights cast a warm halo around Aja, and he marveled at how beautiful she looked even in this casual setting.

They were still touching, Aja's thumb brushing rhythmically against his skin and Del felt himself falling deeper.

He cleared his throat, needing to regain his composure. "Wine sounds good," Del said, hoping his voice sounded steadier than he felt.

Aja blinked, releasing his hand. "Oh, yeah, I was getting wine for us."

He watched as Aja fetched two glasses from a cabinet and pulled a bottle of red wine from a wrought-iron rack by the refrigerator.

"Technically we should be having a white wine since we'll be eating chicken but I really like this one," she held up the bottle as she spoke. "It's a Black-owned brand and I met the owners at a networking event I attended."

She opened the bottle with a complicated contraption then poured their glasses and handed him one.

"Thanks," he said, holding up the glass. "Tell me the latest on Jewel's case."

Aja perked up. "Oh, let me show you what I've come up with."

She sounded relieved and his hopes sank.

He followed her into a hallway that led to her second bedroom which she'd transformed into a home office. She pointed at her white board.

Del looked at the board, took a sip of wine. "This is pretty impressive," he said, turning to face Aja. "What does it all mean?"

Aja nodded. "Okay, here's Jewel, retired and living in Barbados," she pointed at the arrow between Jewel and Malik. "And here's the man she met online who is somehow connected to my mother," she moved her finger over to Diana's name. "Excuse my artwork, I've never been good at drawing anything."

Del peered closer. "Is that supposed to be your mother's orb that Jewel has or is that the island? Or a pirate ship?"

She rolled her eyes. "Yes, that's the orb, smart ass."

"Yeah, maybe stick to technology," he added with a smirk.

"Anyway...focus. My mother and Malik are connected but what about Jewel and my mother? And how did she meet Malik?"

Del walked closer to the screen. "When London talked to her,

Jewel said she didn't know your mother and had never been to her shop. I don't think there's a connection."

He pointed at a name on the opposite side of the board. "What's this? Who is Nikki Compton?"

Aja drew an arrow from Nikki to Jewel. "She got my name from Jewel. She just got married and she thinks her husband's up to something."

Del nodded. "Is she in Barbados too?"

"No, actually she lives east of Atlanta, in Lithonia, But she honeymooned in Barbados. Jewel offered them the use of her place since she was going to be on a cruise." Aja said.

"And she thinks the husband is cheating?" Del asked.

"She said he might be but she also thinks he's gotten into something shady. I told her we could take her case after I wrap up Jewel's. That one should be straightforward. We'd monitor the husband's online activity and see what shakes out."

Del nodded, fascinated. "Did you find anything on your mom's computer?"

"Sure did. A couple of things that I need to add to the board," she said, adding a square. "There was a shipping label for the art piece addressed to Malik. He's here in Atlanta. But it's a P.O. box so that's not as helpful."

"Okay, Diana shipped him the piece and he sold it to Jewel."

"Yep. She'd also drafted a note to him in Word. Basically saying she thought he'd like it and it was a gift."

"Yeah, he liked it enough to sell it as his own work," Del scoffed. "I'm guessing he saw her as a mark so he turns on the charm. He sent her those flowers and she did a sketch of him. I'd say there was something romantic going on, at least on Diana's side." He stroked his beard. "But she never mentioned anything to me."

"I really wish she had. We don't have anything concrete on him. Nothing illegal about selling a piece of art you received as a gift but I'm pretty sure he was planning to do something illegal with my mother's art," Aja capped the marker and tapped it against her chin. "If I pursue this, It will be his word against mine. He can always just say he was doing a prototype of the website she wanted him to build."

She pulled two drink coasters from her desk drawer and handed him one.

"I need a break in this case...I feel like I'm missing something," Aja said, setting her wine glass and coaster on the desk.

Del watched her, intrigued. She was deep in thought and he could practically see the wheels turning in her head. He enjoyed hearing how they worked their cases and seeing Aja in her element.

"You need to flush him out, force his hand somehow." he said, turning back to the screen.

"Exactly...but I haven't figured out how," she trailed off. "Wait!" She snapped her fingers. "I could just act like a buyer. Contact him on social media and make him an offer on his artwork."

Del frowned. "What if he knows who you are? Diana might have told him about you. He's going to smell a trap if that's the case."

The more he thought about it, the less he liked the idea of Aja putting herself in the man's path.

She sighed. "True. I need a cover."

Inspiration hit him like a punch to the head. "What about our resident reality star? Mia could reach out, say she needs artwork for the set and she's well known enough. I'll bet he's probably heard of her."

Aja drummed her fingernails on the desk. "That could work. You think she'd do it?"

Del shrugged. "Let's see," he pulled out his phone and called his client.

"What's up, Mia? You got a minute?"

"I always have time for my coach, what's up?"

Del laid the phone on Aja's desk and tapped the speaker icon. "I'm here with Aja. We need a favor."

Aja leaned toward the phone and explained what she wanted Mia to do.

"Ooo...I'm part of some intrigue! Aja, you got Del working for you now? I love it. How do I contact him?"

Aja recited the website and Malik's handle on social media.

"I'll have my assistant reach out to him...makes people think I'm more important, and, Del, I'll let you know when he responds, cool?"

"That works. Thanks, Mia."

Del ended the call and gazed at Aja. "Now what?"

She glanced toward the kitchen. "I think the food is hot, are you hungry?"

The scent of the potpie filled the condo and his mouth watered. He hadn't had anything to eat since his toast and coffee that morning. "Yep, thought you'd never ask."

"What kind of hostess would I be if I didn't feed you?" She led the way back toward the kitchen. "Don't answer that. I think it's a good day to sit in front of the fireplace and eat, don't you?"

"Works for me. As long as there's food." She could have said they were sitting on the floor over newspaper and he'd agree.

"Have a seat on the couch and I'll bring you a plate."

Del sank into the plush couch, appreciating how it enveloped him in its warmth.

Opening a hall closet, Aja pulled out two television trays. Del took them and set them up in front of the blazing fire.

Aja placed a steaming plate in front of him then settled into the couch.

Del took a bite of the potpie and savored the tender chicken and vegetables. He closed his eyes briefly, enjoying the warmth and comfort of the fireplace, the delicious food, and Aja's company.

"Mmm, this is amazing," he said between bites. "Tell Ms. Nezzie I'm available if she wants to adopt another grandson."

"I'll pass that along," Aja said, taking her own bite. "How did you meet Mia and become her life coach?"

Del paused from taking another forkful of chicken. "She was a referral from another client. It took a while for her to develop her trust in me, but it's been good so far. Were you two friends growing up?"

"Nope. We fought once when we were younger," Aja said suddenly.

Del's head snapped up. "What? Ms. Polished Professional fighting at school? I don't believe it."

"Oh yeah. We were waiting in line to get on the bus and London stepped on her shoe or something and Mia went off, calling her a fat, clumsy, motherless cow."

Del's mouth dropped.

Aja nodded. "London and I both grew up without our mothers and I didn't play that. Nobody messes with my family so I told her she needed to apologize," Aja said. "She didn't, got in my face and said something to the effect of 'make me, you short bitch' so I did."

Del blinked, unsure he'd heard her correctly. But Aja's matter-of-fact facial expression spoke volumes. "What did you do?"

"I used to play a lot of tetherball back in the day," Aja smirked. "I acted like her head was a white ball and I power punched her."

Del snorted, envisioning Aja's younger self taking down the taller woman. "Damn, you punched a reality star? I should call you Creed," he smirked, shaking his head. "What happened after you clocked her? You two seem okay now."

"She learned her lesson," Aja grinned. "You have to stand up to bullies and she saw I wasn't afraid of her. Long story short, we both got grounded. Her dad made her apologize to London and my dad made me apologize for starting it. I wonder if she even remembers that fight."

"She might not, but I'll bet she knows not to mess with your family."

Aja shrugged nonchalantly. "My family is everything to me."

Del admired Aja's loyalty. He felt the same way about his

family. It was one of the many things he found attractive about her.

His phone rang as they were clearing the dishes. "Mia, what's good?" He took a seat on the couch.

"Well, your man responded immediately. He said he needs to get back to his office and wants to talk tomorrow to discuss pricing." Mia said. "Do you and Aja want to be there when I talk to him? You can stop by the house and I'll call him."

Del looked up at Aja as she folded up the trays. She gave him a thumbs up. "Yeah, we can do that. What time are you talking to him?"

"I told him I'd call him around seven. That work for you all?"

Again Aja nodded. "Cool, see you then. Thanks, again, Mia." Ending the call, Del turned his attention back to Aja. "Sounds like you've got a plan in motion."

"Yeah, we'll see what he says." Aja said, taking a seat next to him and tucking her legs under her. She rested her head on her fist and glanced at him with a mixture of anticipation and vulnerability. Del could see the flicker of uncertainty in her eyes.

"When I first started my business, I was seeing this senior broker at my dad's firm. Everyone thought we looked great together, my dad liked him and he was gunning to be my dad's right hand," Aja's voice trailed off, her eyes distant as if she were peering into a memory. Del shifted slightly closer, sensing she was on the verge of revealing something deeply personal. He remained silent, letting her tell her story in her own time.

"He was supportive at first, but as I started putting in more and more time building Exposé, he started to resent the time I was spending on it," she said, her voice tinged with bitterness.

"He accused me of being too ambitious, of prioritizing my work over our relationship. He couldn't understand that Exposé was my passion, my dream," Aja continued, her voice growing softer. Del noticed the slight tremble in her hands as she spoke. "Everything came to a head when I got chosen for that Forty under Forty list. There's another list that Georgia Trend runs for both men and women and he didn't make it."

Aja paused, taking a deep breath. Del could see the hurt in her eyes, though she tried to mask it with a steely resolve.

"I was nothing but a spoiled princess who had her daddy give her anything she wanted, he'd said. He spread rumors that the only reason I made the list is because my dad pulled strings," she said, her voice dripping with sarcasm on the last part.

Del clenched his jaw. He had seen men like that before—intimidated by a strong woman's ambition. It infuriated him to think of someone trying to dim Aja's light. "And what did you do?" he asked quietly, feeling a fierce protectiveness surge within him.

Aja stared straight ahead into the crackling fire. "I ended it. I wasn't going to let anyone, especially someone who claimed to love me, hold me back." She shrugged lightly, as if shaking off the weight of the memory.

"My father found out and fired him, he tried to sue the firm, it was a mess but nothing came of it and last I heard, he moved to DC," she sat up. "I tried to put all of that behind me but sometimes I hear his voice telling me no man wants to be with a woman who puts her work before him and I'm terrified he might be right."

Del's chest tightened at Aja's admission. Their fears were like the opposite sides of a coin: his centered on not being enough, hers on being too much. He reached out and took her hand, feeling the warmth and strength in her grip.

The crackling fire cast warm shadows on her face, and he could see the vulnerability she rarely showed. He reached out and took her trembling hands in his.

"Aja," he said softly, "that man was a fool. Anyone who can't see how incredible you are, who can't support your dreams and ambitions, doesn't deserve you."

"I've been gun shy since then and I've not met anyone that made me want to take that risk again." Aja's gaze met his. "Also, I need to apologize again for not including you in the planning for my mother's service. I've been so caught up in how I feel about my mother that I forget that you suffered a huge loss as well."

Del felt a lump form in his throat at her words. He squeezed her hand in silent reassurance. "Aja, you don't owe me an apology for that. Grief is messy and we all handle it differently."

She gave him a small smile. "If you want, we can plan the rescheduled service together."

He moved closer to her. "I'd like that."

Aja

Aja's gaze drifted down to their clasped hands. She'd never articulated her fears out loud before. She felt like she'd just taken a leap into a massive canyon and was now freefalling, waiting to see if Del would catch her or let her plummet.

"I could use more wine," she said, trying to keep her voice steady. She let go of Del's hand and moved quickly toward the kitchen. With her back to him, she took several deep breaths to calm herself while she poured the remainder of the bottle she'd opened earlier into her glass.

Aja heard the floor creak as Del made his way into the kitchen but she didn't turn around immediately; she needed just a moment longer to collect herself. Grasping her glass, Aja took a quick gulp. When she finally did face him, she found his eyes fixed on her with an intensity that made her heart skip a beat.

"Hey," he began, his voice low.

She turned her head to look at him and he cupped her chin with his fingers, lifting it up until she met his gaze.

"I get you, Aja. And I'm not like most men, if that's what you're worried about. I love that you're successful. It's one of the things that drew me to you in the first place. If I can help you be even more successful, that's what I'll do. I have no problem with you being successful and honestly, I admire it." He eased the wine glass from her tight grip and placed it back on the counter. "And I'm not going anywhere. I messed around and fell hard for you while we were in Barbados, so you're pretty much stuck with me now."

He smiled, that lopsided grin that always made her stomach flip.

There was a tiny voice inside that wouldn't fully accept Del's words and she had to know. "But what about your rule? No American women?"

He frowned. "What are you talking about?"

She crossed her arms. "I heard you don't date American women."

Del grunted, a low rumble in his chest that sent warmth spreading through Aja. "That's never been a rule...where'd you hear that? From Mia?"

He took a sip from his glass. "I guess I could see where people might think that. Andre has been my plus one lately and her parents are from Kenya, but we've never dated."

"It wasn't from Mia," Aja said, thinking back to her conversation with Zaria.

"I'll admit, it's been a while, but that's never been intentional." He took a step closer and Aja felt herself being drawn toward the heat of his body. "You think I'd let a little thing like your being an American stop me from falling for you?" Del's voice softened, his eyes locking with hers.

She hadn't realized how much she needed to hear those words until Del spoke them. She squeezed his hands, feeling a warmth spread through her chest. "When you put it like that, I admit it may sound a little ridiculous," she said with a small chuckle. Her chest felt lighter, as if some invisible weight had lifted.

Del tsked, the sound deep and comforting. "Considering I dropped everything and ran out in this ice storm," he teased, "it's very ridiculous."

His hands slid around her back, pulling her closer, and Aja

couldn't say who made the first move when their lips met in a slow, soulful kiss. Icy rain pelted the window and Aja could feel Del's heart beating against her, each steady thump soothing her own pounding heart.

She could kiss him like this for the rest of her days. His lips, soft and velvety, tasted faintly of the wine. She snaked her arms around his neck, needing to be closer. As if sensing her wishes, Del hugged her tighter.

Slowly, reluctantly, they pulled apart. Del rested his forehead against hers.

"Welcome back," she breathed. "I missed you."

Del's thumb traced her cheek, sending sparks of electricity through her skin. "I missed you too, Aja. More than you know."

Her phone lit up, chiming like a dinner bell. Aja groaned, pulling away. "I almost forgot I have a conference call in a few minutes. Technically, my work day isn't over just yet."

"Mine isn't either. I should probably try to get back home before dark," he glanced at his watch. "I know the temperature's going to drop and the roads are going to get worse."

Aja placed a hand on his arm. "Why don't you stay? You can use my office to work. I'll do my call at the dinner table." Her voice softened. "Please, Del. The roads are already terrible and I'd rather you be stuck here than risk driving in this mess."

She left out the part where she'd fantasized about cuddling with him in front of the fireplace.

"I guess if you insist." He gave her a half smirk. "I need to get my laptop bag out of my car."

Aja rubbed her hands together. "It's almost four, you want to get a couple of hours of work in and meet in front of the fireplace at," she checked her phone. "Let's say six?"

Del nodded, a glint of excitement flickering in his eyes. "Sounds like a plan. I'll be quick."

As he shrugged into his coat and hat, Aja watched him, anticipation coursing through her. The thought of Del staying the evening, cozying up by the fireplace with her, filled her with an unexpected joy she hadn't felt in months. She couldn't imagine a better way to spend a cold, stormy night.

～

Later that night, after she had completed her work tasks and changed into a pair of lounge pants and a t-shirt, Aja surveyed the living room. The ice storm outside raged on, battering the windows with icy pellets. She arranged a couple more pillows on the floor and shifted the blankets so they formed a cozy nest in front of the fireplace.

Del was still in her office working; she could hear the rhythmic tapping on his laptop and she debated sitting on the couch to wait for him. She jumped up to grab a couple of scented candles to light.

As Aja lit the candles, their warm glow filled the room with a soft, flickering light that danced on the walls. The scent of vanilla and cinnamon soon mingled with the smoky aroma from the fireplace, creating an inviting atmosphere. As she stood in the middle of the room, taking it all in, she couldn't recall the last time she'd gone through this much effort for a man. Was she trying too hard to impress him?

Del appeared in the doorway, laptop bag slung over his shoulder, a tired but satisfied smile on his face. "All done," he announced, setting the bag down beside the door. His eyes roamed around the transformed living room. "Okay, you keep this up and it's going to be hard to leave when the storm is over."

"Maybe that's the idea," she teased, motioning for him to join her on the plush array of pillows and blankets she'd laid out. She handed him a steaming mug of hot chocolate.

As he settled beside her, he took her hand. "This is perfect," he murmured, brushing his lips over her knuckles. "Much better than what I'd planned at my house."

"Oh yeah? What would you be doing if you were home right now?" Aja watched him as she sipped from her mug.

Del grimaced slightly. "I'm going to admit something…"

She rolled her eyes. "Don't tell me you'd be playing the sappy Publix commercials on a continuous loop."

"No…and they aren't sappy."

"Hmm…you say so. Anyway, what would you be doing?" Aja couldn't help the grin spreading across her face.

Del sighed. "Honestly, I hate to say it, but I'd probably be working. It's a good night to make videos."

Aja side-eyed him. "Ah…all that talk about work-life balance and streamlining your processes…the coach doesn't practice what he preaches?"

He shrugged. "I'd be home alone…might as well get some work done." He rested a hand on her leg. "What would you be doing if I wasn't here?"

"You know…a month ago, I would have said I'd be working with no hesitation but now…" she lifted her shoulder. "I might find a movie to watch. I am so behind on everything, there's plenty for me to choose from."

Del rubbed her leg. "See, I told you I add value to your life."

She couldn't argue with him. Aja felt a warmth spread through her that had nothing to do with the fire or hot chocolate. "You do," she said softly, leaning into his touch. "I think I forgot how to relax somewhere along the way."

She turned to face him. "I had no idea my grandmother is a Sidney Poitier fan and I will admit, I've never seen any of his movies. I figured since you love them, we could watch one tonight?"

Del's mouth fell open in mock horror. "You're serious? You've never seen any Sidney Poitier movies? Not one?"

Aja dropped her head. "Nope."

He clasped his hands together. "We're going to fix that right now. How about we start with 'In the Heat of the Night'? It's a classic."

Aja nodded, her curiosity piqued. "I've heard of it, but never watched it. Let's do it."

She fetched the remote and navigated through the streaming service until she found the movie. Hitting the play button, Aja settled into Del's chest as she pulled a fluffy throw over them. "This came out in 1967 and it's set in rural Mississippi," Del explained in a low voice.

She turned to look at Del. "He's not going to die, is he? Am I going to be pissed off at the racism in this?"

"No...he doesn't die and yes, there's blatant racism, but you'll have to trust me...it's excellent."

"Okay then," Aja relaxed against him. "I guess we'll see."

As Aja watched the suspenseful scenes unfold, she found herself captivated by Sidney Poitier's commanding presence. Every line delivered, every expression he wore resonated deeply, and she could see why the actor had such profound effect on Del. In him, Del saw a fellow Caribbean immigrant that had overcome enormous odds to find success in America.

"He was the first Black man to win an Academy Award for Best Actor, right?"

Del nodded, his eyes still on the screen. "Yep, for *Lilies in the Field*, which came out in 1963. It's a good movie too."

Aja turned her attention back to the movie, appreciating it for its history as well as its story.

When the movie was over, Aja turned to Del. "I don't think I would have ever watched that movie if you hadn't been here. I hate to admit it, but you were right."

He smirked. "I should probably record you saying that so I can play it back whenever there's doubt."

Aja lightly punched Del's arm. "Don't get used to it." She reached for the mug of now-lukewarm hot chocolate, taking a sip before setting it aside.

When she looked up, she found Del regarding her with a smile that didn't reach his eyes.

Immediately Aja tensed. Del had something on his mind, she could tell. "What's wrong?"

Del stood abruptly. His shadow stretched across the room,

cast long and thin by the flickering firelight. He turned his back to her and took a deep breath, as if summoning the courage to speak.

"Now that we're back home," he started, "and assuming there's no ice storm keeping you inside." Del turned to face her. "Where do we go from here?"

Aja's heart skipped and her pulse raced as she processed Del's question. The only light in the room was from the candles, which were now burning low, and the fireplace. She tried to read his face while taking a moment to gather her thoughts, choosing her words carefully.

Aja stood. "You're talking about...us?" She didn't want to assume anything right then.

"Yes," Del replied, his voice gentle but firm. "Us." He took a step closer, his eyes searching hers. "I want to know if this was just a vacation thing for you."

Aja felt the weight of his words settle over her. A million responses raced through her mind, each one more frantic than the last. Initially, she'd thought it best to keep him at arm's length but as she looked into Del's eyes, she understood that was the fear speaking and she wasn't going to let it win.

"No," she said, almost too quickly. She cleared her throat and tried again. "No, it wasn't just a vacation thing for me."

He exhaled slowly and his shoulders relaxed. "I figured you were going to fight me on that."

"I'll admit, I tried to fight it, but these last few days, I've had to ask myself why I'm fighting so hard. Of course, there's a chance I'll get my heart broken but there's also a chance that I won't. And I'd rather take that leap of faith than let fear dictate my life."

Del reached out to take her hands in his. "I've been thinking the same thing," he confessed. "Life is too short to let fear dictate our choices."

"To answer your original question, I want us to take things slow. I would love more nights like this," she motioned at the fireplace. "But I'm not used to making time for myself and as you've pointed out, I might be a bit of a workaholic."

Del cocked an eyebrow. "Now that has to be the understatement of the year."

Aja held her hands up. "I know, I know. Seriously, I want to make this work but we both have businesses to run and demands on our time," she moved closer to him, placing her hands on both sides of his face. "I don't ever want you to feel neglected or like you're playing second fiddle to my business. Because you're important to me, Del."

He leaned into her touch, closing his eyes for a moment as if savoring the feeling of her hands on his skin. When he opened them again, they were filled with an intense tenderness that made her knees weak. "I don't want to be a distraction or an afterthought in your life either," Del said quietly. "I love you and I want to be a part of it—fully."

"I love you too, Del," she whispered. The words slipped out before she could reel them in and filter them but she realized in that moment they were true.

CHAPTER 23

Del

Del and Aja pulled up to the gates leading to Mia Germaine's lavish estate and Del pressed the call button for entry. The iron gates swung open as if presenting the snow covered landscape to them as they drove toward the entrance.

"I still can't believe this is Mia's world now," Aja mused. "When we were growing up, she'd always boast to anyone that would listen that she was going to be rich and famous one day. Only in Atlanta..."

Del glanced over at Aja, a small smile tugging at the corner of his mouth. "She made it happen," he said, steering the car through the winding driveway.

Parking in front of the four car garage, Del strode around to open Aja's door.

As they approached a massive wood front door, Mia's current wife, Charlene, or Charlie to friends and family, stood in the doorway, rubbing her arms. "Come on in...man, It's miserable out there."

The tall, slender woman embraced them after taking their coats. "Mia said she'd be a few minutes, she's wrapping up a meeting."

"Thanks, Charlie." Del smiled at the younger woman who

gave him a frosty half smile in return. Del sighed. He'd never been anything but nice to Charlie but the chill in her demeanor was as constant as the winter air outside.

Charlie led them to a sitting room off the large foyer. "Have a seat, I just mixed up some chocolate peppermint martinis," her hazel eyes slid towards Del. "Would you like one, or do you want your usual?"

Del shook his head. "Not today, Charlie. Just a coffee, black."

Did he visit Mia's house so often that Charlie knew what he liked to drink? He shrugged. Maybe so. They normally met every other week for their coaching sessions and more often than not, Mia invited him to her house.

Charlie led them to a large sitting room done in shades of olive green and muted gold.

"I'll take one of those martinis," Aja said, sinking into a plush armchair.

Nodding, Charlie strode out of the room, leaving Aja and Del alone.

"God, I hope Malik comes through today," Aja muttered. "We need to wrap this case up."

Del nodded, his fingers drumming on the armrest of the emerald green chair. His gaze swept across the room, taking in the framed art and polished wood.

"He seems like the greedy type. He'll take the bait," Del said, the confidence in his voice masking the doubt gnawing at his gut. "People like Malik always do."

"I hope you're right," Aja started to say something else but went silent as Charlie returned holding a tray with three martinis and a coffee mug. She placed the tray on a glass coffee table and took her drink to the arm chair across from them.

Charlie glanced toward the stairs then took a sip of her martini. "Aja, how are you? Business is good, I'm hearing?"

Aja sipped her drink and immediately placed it on the tray. "It's going well, thanks. Online dating is still on the rise which means our jobs are secure."

Del watched the exchange between the two women with interest. Aja was in full corporate mode, her back erect and her shoulders near her ears.

"You know, no offense," Charlie crossed her legs. "but if people would just be decent, your company wouldn't be needed. I think it's sad that people seek to deceive others."

Aja's eyes narrowed ever so slightly. "Yes, but we help people find the truth, and that's the most important thing, don't you agree?" She didn't wait for an answer. "I heard you recently got your real estate license. How's the real estate business going?"

Charlie hunched her shoulders. "Inventory is still too low...we need more houses on the market." Her eyes lit up. "You have a condo in Midtown, right? Would you be willing to put it on the market? The area is still red hot."

Del watched Aja give the fake smile again and knew before Aja answered that she'd turn Charlie down. "Ah, no," she said sweetly, "I love my place."

Just then, Mia sauntered in, wearing a vibrant printed silk duster that billowed as she walked, giving the illusion she was walking into the wind. Her cropped tank top and leggings displayed an impressively toned curvy body.

"Sorry to keep y'all waiting," Mia said, her eyes meeting Del's. She grabbed him into a bear hug that nearly knocked the wind out of him.

She squeezed him one last time before releasing him and turned to Aja with equal warmth, giving her a quick hug and a kiss on each cheek.

Mia had her back to them and Aja raised an eyebrow at him. He lifted his shoulders in response. Mia was being her usual flirty self.

"I see Charlie has taken care of you both," Mia said, glancing at the martinis and then over to Charlie who gave a slight nod before excusing herself from the room.

Mia glanced at her phone. "We're talking at seven and it's about five minutes till, so let's get this party started." She tapped the phone and laid it on the coffee table in between the three of them. The phone rang twice before a smooth deep voice answered.

"Ms. Germaine, good to hear from you."

Del rolled his eyes. He could tell the man was deepening his voice intentionally, trying to sound sexy.

Aja leaned in.

"I'm glad you were able to take my call. I'm sure you're a busy man." Mia made a face as she said this.

"I can always make time for a beautiful business woman such as yourself. Now, what can I do for you, Ms. Germaine?"

Mia's tone was light and airy like a soufflé that could collapse with the slightest disturbance. "I'd like to place an order. I saw that Jardin collection on your site and it's exactly what I want to display in the house. Those are exclusive pieces, right?"

Del watched Aja's eyes narrow almost imperceptibly; she was focused on every spoken undercurrent. Del felt a tingle of anticipation in his chest. Malik didn't know he was now in deep, shark infested waters.

"Of course, that's a one-of-a-kind collection." Malik's voice slithered through the speaker. "How soon do you need them?"

"As soon as you can get them to me," Mia said, deliberately vague. "But I'll need some sort of letter of authenticity and certification that they are one of a kind. I want them to be the envy of the other women on the show and for that, they must be unique and not available anywhere else."

"I can certainly provide whatever documentation you require. But the exclusivity aspect means I'll need to charge a bit more for them."

Mia looked up from the phone, meeting Aja's eyes. She held up her hands as if to ask how Aja wanted her to respond.

Aja nodded and motioned with her hand for Mia to keep talking.

"I assumed you were giving me a break on the price as I'm

buying the whole collection, is that not the case? How much are we talking?" Mia's tone indicated that of a shrewd negotiator.

"Tell you what, I'll throw in a couple of bonus pieces. I will need a week or so to get everything together and get your documents prepared. Will that work?"

Del had to admit, the man was smooth, but weren't most con artists?

Mia looked up again before responding. Aja gave her a thumbs up.

"That should be fine...I need them as soon as you can get them to me." She sat back. "If you can send me the documents, I'll have my office wire a deposit once everything looks to be in order."

"Absolutely, Ms. Germaine. I'll send those over first thing tomorrow morning," Malik's voice oozed confidence, the sound of a man who closed lucrative deals all the time.

Mia gave a satisfied nod. "I look forward to it."

Ending the call, Mia set the phone down and turned to Aja and Del. Her expression was filled with triumph. "How was that? Did you get what you needed?"

Aja stood. "Yes, that was perfect. We know he doesn't have the pieces so he'll have to travel to Barbados to get them or make arrangements to have them shipped but unless he's working with a team, I don't see him letting someone else handle such a big order."

"What's his game? You said he's stealing this art?" Mia asked.

"Yes, that art you saw on his website is actually my mother's work. We think he was stealing it and selling it and now I'm pretty sure he's catfishing another woman on the island." Aja said.

"No shit? I hope you nail him then. What will you do next? Or what do you want me to do when he sends everything?"

Before Aja could answer, her phone rang.

She pulled the phone from her purse and looked at the display. "It's Jewel," she turned to Del. "That was fast."

"Hey Jewel, how are you?"

Del couldn't hear the other side of the conversation.

"Oh, he did? And what did he say?"

Aja nodded, a knowing smirk directed at Del on her face.

Aja stood up and started pacing the room as she talked to Jewel.

"Here's what we're going to do. When you call him back, tell him you'll pick him up from the airport, he can stay with you and you'd like to talk about investing in his company when he gets to town."

Del marveled at how fast things were moving now. Aja had wanted to force Malik's hand and he seemed to be playing right into the trap they'd laid.

"No, you won't have to do any of that. We'll be there," she stopped in front of Del, her eyebrows raised in question.

He nodded. There was no way he was letting Aja do this alone. if that meant they hopped a flight back to Holetown, then so be it. He was in.

"Yes, see if he can come in Friday or Saturday. That'll give me a couple of days to get there and get set up. Let me know when he's made his flight arrangements. Yes, good night. See you soon!"

Aja ended the call. "Malik just called her and left a voicemail saying he wants them to meet in person."

She tapped the phone on her chin and Del could tell she was deep in thought, piecing together the logistics of her ensnarement plan.

Del rubbed his hands together. "When are we leaving?" he asked. He knew he sounded like an eager little boy but he couldn't help it.

"I'm aiming for tomorrow but I need to see when he's planning to arrive. We'll need time to get things in place," Aja said. "It's short notice, so if you can't-"

"I'm coming too." Del cut her off.

Aja's eyes flicked to him. He saw the uncertainty there but after a beat, she reached over and gave his hand a quick squeeze. "Okay," she said, her shoulders relaxing.

Out of the corner of his eye, he saw Mia watching their exchange with a curious smile.

"First thing," Aja continued, releasing Del's hand to tap her chin thoughtfully with her phone again. "I need to make some calls—law enforcement in Barbados, maybe even here. If we can catch him in the act, they can pick him up."

Del nodded in agreement as he watched Aja dial a number on her phone. He could tell she was in full strategist mode now, meticulously planning their next move. He couldn't help but admire the way she took control of the situation, her cool and collected demeanor never faltering.

After a few minutes on the phone, Aja hung up and turned to Del, determination in her eyes. "I didn't get to speak to anyone in charge since it's after hours. I think this will best be handled in person. I'll see about making our travel arrangements."

Mia interjected, "Oh, hey, Aja, I've got an endorsement deal with a local charter, I'll ask my assistant to see what we can arrange. It'll be about what you'd pay for commercial if they're already heading that way. You'll need to post on social media though."

Aja's eyes lit up at the offer. "Thanks, Mia. That could save us some precious time, and I don't mind a bit of social media promotion if it speeds things up."

"Great, I'll handle it," Mia said, already tapping away on her phone.

The morning sun was just starting to warm the Atlanta skyline when Aja and Del found themselves at a small, private airfield on the edge of the city. Mia's connections had come through more smoothly than either of them could have expected. They stood now, watching as ground crew made final preparations to the sleek silver charter plane that would whisk them away to Barbados.

As Aja stood near, talking on her phone, he took a moment to reflect on the past few months. This time last year, his coaching practice had taken off and he was getting into the groove of working with his clients, thinking that he'd like to take time off but unable to commit to doing so. If anyone had told him he'd be boarding a charter flight to his home country in pursuit of an art-thieving catfish, he'd have scoffed, told them they were insane.

But then his favorite client and friend died, leaving him in charge of her estate.

And he met her daughter.

After hefting their small bags into the belly of the aircraft, he waited as Aja motioned to him.

Aja ended the call. Despite her otherwise calm façade, he could tell she was anxious about what lay ahead.

"What's up? Everything okay?" he asked, his voice soft but clear against the hum of activity around them.

Aja looked up at him and nodded. "I think so," she replied. "I keep feeling like I've forgotten something...or that I've let something slide through a crack."

"We can get anything you need once we get there. When does he arrive?" Del said, wanting to pull her in for a reassuring hug. She was in professional mode and he wasn't sure she'd respond well to a public display of affection.

"He told Jewel he was arriving tomorrow morning, so we should have time to get everything in place. Then we'll just see what he does."

Del reached out and placed his hand on Aja's shoulder, offering a silent form of support that wasn't as intense as a hug but still conveyed care. He felt her shoulders relax a fraction as she glanced at his hand.

"Just focus on one thing at a time," he reminded her, "We'll handle it together. Whatever you've missed, we'll figure it out."

Aja gave a small nod. "True. Let's do this."

In that moment, Del realized just how far they'd come in working together and trusting each other.

The pilot approached them, tipping his cap courteously. "Ms. Lewis, Mr. Parris, we're ready to take off whenever you are."

"Thank you," Aja smiled warmly at the older man before turning to Del. "Parris, you ready?"

He slid her laptop bag over his shoulder and nodded. "Yep, after you."

As they made their way onto the plane, Del whistled softly in awe. Mia had come through for them big time. The charter was more luxurious than anything Del had flown before; it was like stepping into a flying lounge. Del placed Aja's bag at her feet then settled into a seat next to her, taking in the details of the small aircraft. Deep leather seats, polished wood accents, and a stewardess offering them chilled bottles of sparkling water—a stark contrast to his last flight on a major commercial airline. He could get used to this.

"Does Mia travel like this all the time?" Aja wondered aloud.

"I'm not sure, but maybe we should get you a reality show," he joked.

"Normally, I'd say 'hell no' but..." she rubbed the soft leather seat, "if this is one of the perks, I could be persuaded."

She beamed at him and he decided there was no place he'd rather be in this moment.

"We're supposed to take some pictures and post," she reminded him.

They both took turns capturing images on their phones while they waited for takeoff.

A few snapshots and a glass of champagne later, Del found himself grinning as Aja's poses got more and more ridiculous.

She'd taken the scarf she had worn around her neck and pulled it up so it covered her hair and draped over her shoulders then added a pair of huge black sunglasses like a throwback movie star avoiding the paparazzi.

After posting and sharing the pictures with Mia, Del adjusted his seat belt and settled back in in his seat. "I could see you with a fleet of planes like this with your company's logo on them," he said, rubbing her arm.

She slid the shades off. "A whole fleet? I don't know. I'm still adjusting to the idea of larger office space and purchasing a building." Aja removed the scarf, placing it in her laptop bag.

"Exposé can be a billion dollar brand but you have to be able to see that and know it's possible." Del said, resisting the urge to jump into coaching mode.

"On some level, I believe that-no I know that-but deep down, I still have my doubts, I'm still waiting for society to accept me, a Black woman, owning a large, profitable tech company." Aja rested her chin on her fist. "I watched my dad and all the bullshit he dealt with as his company grew, how he had to prove himself each and every time, while others just walked in and were accepted as belonging."

She paused, studying the ceiling. "Sometimes, I don't want to be the trailblazer. It's a heavy burden."

Del covered her hand in his. "I know it is, but you don't have to carry it alone. You have a team and you have me."

Aja nodded then turned to gaze out of the window and Del could tell she wanted time to process her thoughts.

He shifted, settling back in his seat as the plane ascended and they laid out their plan for capturing a catfish.

CHAPTER 24

Aja

Aja studied the landscape as Del drove them toward her mother's studio. Hurricane Juno had weakened as it hit land but it left behind a trail of broken branches, scattered debris, and battered houses. The island's vibrant spirit, however, seemed unbroken. Brilliant blue sky and warm sun welcomed them while soca music blasted from a work site where a group of men were rebuilding a shattered rooftop.

Eager to feel the wind on her skin, Aja cracked her window as Del drove. They had checked in to the same resort, only the one room this time, and dropped their stuff off. Aja was happy to switch the jacket and scarf she'd worn on the plane for a tee shirt and light sweater.

"Once we're done setting up the cameras, we should go see your Aunt Felicity," Aja said. "I'd like to meet her."

"I was thinking the same thing. She told me everything was fine at her house, minimal damage from the hurricane, but I want to double check," Del glanced at her. "And she definitely wants to meet you. She's already suggested a couple of wedding venues for us."

Aja's head snapped toward him. "Wedding venues? I thought we were taking things slowly?"

"My aunt thinks my biological clock is ticking loudly," Del scoffed. "Don't pay her any mind."

Aja laughed lightly, but the sudden mention of weddings left a strange flutter in her chest. She shook it off and focused on the winding road ahead.

But the thought lingered in the back of her mind. She hadn't given marriage much consideration after her last relationship crashed and burned. She hadn't had time, but now she was more open to the possibility.

She reached for her laptop bag, shoving those thoughts to the back of her mind. She should make sure they were ready for Malik.

As they approached her mother's glassblowing studio, tension knotted into Aja's stomach. What if her plan didn't work and Malik, or whatever that man's real name was, stole her mother's art?

She pressed her lips together. No, they needed to catch him; put an end to his schemes.

"You ever think about leaving the U.S. and moving back here?" Aja asked.

"You coming with me if I do?" His tone was light but Aja could tell her answer mattered to him.

Aja turned her gaze to the sea, the horizon a perfect blend of cerulean blues. "Maybe," she said softly. "I've never lived anywhere other than Atlanta."

"Hmm...I was joking. I have no plans to move back here but that's good to know."

A year ago, Aja wouldn't have imagined herself living outside the U.S.. But her mother's death had changed things. Now Aja owned property in Barbados, thanks to her mother's will, which meant she could come here whenever she wanted and have a place to stay. As much as she loved Atlanta, there was something about this island that called to her.

As they approached the studio, the large For Sale sign in the window made Aja pause. She frowned. Why did seeing the sign hit her so hard? She'd contracted a real estate firm to handle managing the property and selling the studio the last time she'd been here.

She'd actually received a couple of low ball offers from investors which she had quickly rejected.

Seeing the sign made it all real. She was selling her mother's legacy. Suddenly Aja wasn't so sure that was the right move but now wasn't the time to second-guess herself.

"We don't have much time," Aja said, grabbing a case from the trunk that contained high-tech surveillance equipment. While Exposé normally did its surveillance online, Aja had invested in some equipment just in case they needed it. "I need to set up the cameras and make sure everything is running smoothly before Malik arrives."

Del nodded, his eyes lighting up as she pulled out the equipment. She chuckled softly, handing him a roll of duct tape. "You mind giving me a hand with all this?"

He rubbed his hands together like he was about to construct the pyramids. "I thought you'd never ask. What do we do first? And what's the plan for the duct tape? You going to kidnap someone?"

Aja chuckled, shaking her head. "No kidnapping today, Del. The duct tape is just a precaution in case we need to secure any wiring or equipment," she explained.

Del picked up a sleek, palm-sized gadget—a motion sensor camera encased in matte black. The device was designed to be discreet, with a wide-angle lens and night vision capability that could capture clear footage even in the dimmest light conditions. Del turned it over in his hands. "I can't believe this is a fully functional camera."

"Yep, that one has a wide angle lens and night vision capability which you can control with an app," Aja said.

"Alright," Aja clasped her hands together. "We need to place the cameras in strategic locations where they'll give us maximum coverage. Entry points, near any valuable pieces—basically anywhere Malik might snoop around."

They went to work, setting up several small cameras around the room: above the doorframe, tucked into a shelf that overlooked the display of her mother's most popular collection. The Jardin Paradiso. This was the collection Malik touted on his website as his own and the one Mia was "buying". He couldn't overlook the collection if he'd tried and when he got close to it, they'd have him on camera.

They were so close, Aja knew. According to what he'd told Jewel, Malik was scheduled to fly in the next day. They would be ready. Excitement and trepidation coursed through her. What if something went south? What if he didn't show?

Del seemed to pick up on her silent fears, casting her a reassuring look as he adjusted a camera. "We're ready for him. These cameras should pick up anything he thinks he wants to do."

Aja exhaled slowly, allowing herself to absorb Del's optimism. She glanced at the gleaming, colorful pieces of art scattered around the studio. As she'd studied the pieces, she felt like she'd gotten to know a bit more about her mother.

"We need to check the feeds," Aja said, once they finished placing all the cameras.

Del surveyed the room. "Why don't we take a quick break to eat first? I'm sure you're starving by now, I know I am."

Aja glanced at her smartwatch, ready to protest that they'd just eaten on the plane. But that was hours ago. The bright sun she'd basked in earlier was now starting to set.

"Okay, just give me a few minutes to tweak some things," she trailed off, intent on fixing one camera that wouldn't stay powered on.

Del was pacing when she looked up a few minutes later.

"It's been twenty minutes, what are you doing?"

She frowned, glancing again at her watch. There was no way twenty minutes had passed.

"I just want to check one more thing, and I got a message from Zaria that I need to respond to," she said.

Del huffed. "I'm going to get takeout...you okay with seafood?"

"Fine," she murmured, not looking up from her screen. He got crabby when he was hungry, she realized with a smile. Better to let him go handle that.

The door closed behind Del with a soft click, leaving Aja alone with the quiet hum of the studio's air conditioning, the faint scent of molten glass, and her mother's perfume that always seemed to linger in the corners of the room.

Absorbed in her task, Aja didn't notice the minutes slipping away, the studio turning darker as the sun fully set. Aja's head snapped up as she realized she was sitting in the dark and she rose to turn the studio lights on. The studio's interior lights cast long shadows across the floor, creating pockets of darkness where the cameras' red dots blinked discreetly.

She settled back into the seat at her mother's desk, intent on getting some work done while she waited for Del. Her stomach groaned with hunger. She should make sure he brought back some rice and peas, another dish she'd discovered while on the island. Where was her phone? She glanced around and sighed, certain she had left it on the display counter while she was testing the camera closest to the Jardin display. She'd get it in a second, she wanted to finish reviewing one of Zaria's proposals before it went to their client.

The soft glow of her laptop screen was reassuring, the familiar keys beneath her fingers grounding her fluttering nerves. She had just about settled into a rhythm, reviewing invoices and approving payroll, when the faintest sound prickled at the edges of her consciousness. It was a subtle shift in the ambient noise causing her to be immediately on high alert.

Aja froze, her fingers hovering over the keyboard. Had Del returned already? No, he'd have announced himself; besides, he couldn't have ordered food and gotten it back so quickly. She strained to listen, but there was nothing more—just the stillness and her own heightened breathing.

She tried to shake off the unease gnawing at her and returned to typing out her message.

Down the road, someone cranked up a speaker, blasting hip-hop, its rhythmic bass vibrating through the walls, providing an unintentional soundtrack to her solitude. She knew there was at least one rum bar on the block and Aja assumed the music was coming from them. Aja glanced at the door, wondering if the noise could have been her imagination playing tricks on her with the sound of the music. Del would be back any minute, she tried to reassure herself, they'd eat, test the cameras then head to the resort.

But just as she was about to focus on the screen again, a shadow darted across the room's periphery—a fleeting presence that had no business being in her mother's studio. Aja's heart rate spiked; her fingers went still. It was not paranoia.

Someone was here.

Why hadn't she gotten up to retrieve her phone?

She stilled her breathing, tried to focus. She needed a plan and panicking wasn't planning.

Turn the cameras on.

Find a weapon.

Don't panic.

Aja set each camera to active and muted the audio.

The cameras showed everything was as it should be. No figure skulking around the shop. She frowned. She wasn't alone, she could feel another presence in the space but where were they?

She tapped on the keys again.

One of the floorboards in the studio creaked and Aja's hair stood on end. She needed a weapon.

Her eyes swept her mother's desk, now clutter free, thanks to Aja's earlier cleaning efforts. Most of her mother's stuff was boxed away in a storage unit. All she had was her laptop, some additional power cords and cables in case the wireless cameras needed them. She guessed if they got close enough, Aja could strangle the intruder but that seemed highly improbable.

She stood, trying to stay calm, taking in each aspect of the office. Her heart sank. There was nothing left that could be used to defend herself.

Think, think, think.

"You must be the estranged daughter."

The man she'd come to know as Malik stepped into the office, pointing a large gun at her.

Aja's mind raced, her pulse hammering in her ears as she took in the man they'd been chasing for weeks now. The man calling himself Malik was brown skinned and shorter than she'd imagined, still taller than she, but not by much. Where he lacked in height he made up in weight. The man was stocky with thick muscular arms and legs. There was no mistaking the danger in the cold set of his dark brown eyes or the ominous way he held the gun, its barrel pointed straight at her.

He wouldn't go down easily, she knew.

"Who are you and why are you in my mother's studio?" Aja fought to keep the tremor out of her voice. "What do you want?"

Malik moved further into the room with an unsettling confidence, as if he owned the space. "I think you know what I want."

"Who are you?" She repeated.

Malik's lips curled into a contemptuous smirk, and his eyes bore into her with an intensity that belied his casual stance. "Aja, right? Let's not play dumb. You know exactly who I am and why I'm here." He waved the gun at her. 'Step away from the desk. I don't want you using that laptop to do anything foolish."

She took a step backward.

"Move over here where I can see your hands."

He reached into his jacket pocket with his left hand. "Good that you left this in the studio," he held her phone up then as she watched in horror, he dropped the phone, stomped on it then kicked it under the desk.

So much for calling Del.

Aja did as he asked, keeping her eyes locked on Malik. The gun glinted in the dim light, a lethal weight in the air between them.

"How did you know my mother?" Aja asked, hoping her voice sounded conversational and casual. She moved slowly, deliberately, each step measured to give her time to think.

"This is not a game, Aja! You're not going to distract me from what I came here for," his voice rose sharply and Aja could tell he was desperate.

"What you're gonna do is start wrapping up all those sculptures in the front," he stepped closer to her and Aja forced herself not to cower. "And you'll want to do it before your boyfriend gets back, otherwise he's getting a bullet to keep you motivated. I bought you some time...he won't be back for a while, I'm guessing."

Aja's eyes widened in shock. "Why? What did you do to him?"

"Calm down," Malik sneered. "He's going to find he has four flat tires and he'll need to call for roadside assistance. Which, given the hour, might take a while."

Aja's mind raced, the implications of Malik's actions crashing into her like relentless waves. This man had carefully orchestrated his intrusion and managed to outmaneuver them. Del was out there, delayed and unaware. She had to keep Malik talking, buy time for Del or anyone else to notice something was amiss.

She feigned resignation, her shoulders bowed. "Fine," she said, her voice steady despite the tremors that threatened to undermine her composure. "I'll wrap the sculptures." Her eyes darted toward the Jardin display, scheming silently.

As she moved toward the intricate glass flowers that were her mother's legacy, Aja carefully assessed each one. They were beautiful but heavy—too heavy to wield as weapons and he could fire the gun quicker than she could heft the glass piece and strike.

She'd have to figure something else out.

Aja could sense Malik's desperation under his calm demeanor. He kept looking beyond her shoulder as if he expected someone to emerge from the shadows at any moment.

Aja knew she had to push that fear, exploit whatever paranoia was bubbling beneath his skin. "You're nervous," she stated softly, more an observation than a question, as she took another step toward the sculptures. "Who are you expecting?" She hoped to add to his unease, make him slip up or reveal more.

Malik stiffened, and his grip on the gun tightened. "Shut up and do what I told you," he barked but Aja noted the flicker of uncertainty in his eyes. He wasn't just worried about Del; he was afraid of someone or something else.

"Were you seeing my mother?" She asked, her tone casual.

"You must be joking," he barked a laugh. "You think I want to sweet talk these old women? You think I like hanging out with them? It's a necessary evil, that's all."

"What do you get out of it?" Aja asked. "Are the women that desperate for companionship?"

Malik's jaw clenched, and an ugly sneer twisted his features. "Desperate for companionship?" he echoed, his tone laced with mockery. "I get information, opportunities, access to places like this." He gestured broadly with the gun, its movement causing Aja to flinch internally, though she didn't let it show on her face.

"I haven't worked a nine to five in years," he boasted. "You could say I'm an entrepreneur like you."

"Really? What do you do?" She made a big deal of wrapping a piece carefully in bubble wrap like she was intent on making sure the artwork was secure.

"I find lonely older women with money and I become whatever they need. Like your friend Jewel. Yeah, she confessed that she'd hired you to check me out. I've taken care of her though."

A chill skittered down her spine as Malik's words sunk in. These women, including her mother, had been a means to an end for him, a stepping stone in whatever grand scheme he had concocted. She wondered how much her mother had known about Malik's true nature, or if she'd been taken in by his charm like so many others seemingly had been.

Aja forced herself to focus even though she was seeing red. This man couldn't be allowed to get away with another scam.

She couldn't show him any emotion. "Did you hurt Jewel?" She asked calmly.

"Not physically," Malik's voice was a low growl, as though the idea of exerting force upon Jewel was beneath him. "But she won't be interfering any time soon. She became a liability."

He shifted his weight, and the gun momentarily pointed away from Aja.

For an instant, Aja's gaze landed on the large zip ties Del had slapped on the counter, she entertained the thought of lunging forward, but Malik's stare snapped back to her, as if he could sense her intentions.

He opened his mouth to speak, his face twisted in disgust.

Suddenly there was a loud crash as the glass door shattered. Aja ducked her head, instinctively shielding it with her hands. She raised her head cautiously.

Glass shards were everywhere, winking like stars on the floor. Malik whipped around, his cocky stance wavering as he aimed his gun in every direction.

Now or never.

With Malik distracted, Aja seized the glass hibiscus she'd started to wrap and swung it with all her might toward his head. She missed, hitting his arm and causing him to drop the gun. The blow sent ripples of pain up her arm as the gun clattered onto the floor tiles.

Aja's heart was pounding in her chest as she watched Malik stumble back from the blow, a pained howl leaving his lips. He lost his footing and fell back, his head hitting a display shelf.

The glass hibiscus had shattered on impact, but Aja barely noticed, her gaze fixed on Malik. He wasn't moving but she wasn't taking any chances. She grabbed the duct tape and made quick work of winding it around his wrists as tightly as she could. She paused for a beat, deciding she should do his ankles as well.

Hearing him moan, Aja lunged for the gun. But before she could reach it, a pair of high-topped pink Nike sneakers stomped over the glass and kicked the gun out of Aja's reach.

CHAPTER 25

Del

Del swore as he shifted the bags of take out from one hand to the other. Eyes narrowed, he scanned the parking lot for witnesses, but the lot was dark and quiet. His stomach growled in protest as he bent to examine the tires on the rental car they'd picked up at the airport. All four tires were flat.

His pulse quickened, a mixture of anger and anxiety blooming in his chest. Why would all of the tires be flat? The dim streetlights offered no answers, only casting shadows that seemed to mock his predicament.

He half expected someone to be propped against the nearest streetlight pole, smirking at him. But he was the only person around. There were a few people inside enjoying their food but no one had paid him any attention.

This was supposed to be a quick run: get the food, finish setting up the security system and wait for Malik to arrive. But now this? He crouched, running his fingers along the edge of one tire. He froze in disbelief.

it wasn't just flat—it had been punctured.

A quiet rage simmered within him as Del saw the telltale slashes. Someone had done this deliberately.

He pulled out his phone to call Aja but hesitated. There

wasn't much Aja could do and she was probably still staring at her laptop.

The phone felt heavy in his hand as he deliberated. Shoving it back into his pocket, he decided that calling for roadside assistance first was a better move. He opened the car, put the bags of food on the floor of the passenger side, and pulled the rental paperwork out of the glove compartment. As he entered the number for twenty-four hour assistance, a sudden, sharp sound broke the night's quiet. Del's instincts kicked in, and he pivoted, eyes narrowing as he scanned for the source. A cat darted from behind a dumpster, vanishing into the shadows.

An automated service answered and he followed the prompts to get a human on the line. The friendly recorded voice told him he was tenth in line, someone would be with him shortly. He groaned.

He took deep breaths to calm down as he listened to the drone of classic elevator music interspersed with reminders of his place in the queue. He cast another wary glance around the parking lot. Nothing had changed. No shady form appeared to claim credit for stranding him.

As Del paced in front of the car, he could smell the fragrant flying fish and grilled vegetables in the takeout containers. So much for a quiet dinner with Aja.

His thoughts were interrupted by a terse, "Roadside assistance, how can I help you?" from an operator who sounded as though she'd been answering calls without pause for hours without a break.

Del sighed, not wanting to take his frustrations out on her for his horrible night. He greeted her, asked how she was doing and after relaying his location and situation, she softened, told him she was sorry but it would be at least an hour before help arrived. Hanging up, he slid into the driver's seat. He should call Aja and let her know what was going on.

Her phone rang and rang then her voicemail prompted him

to leave a message. Del stared at the phone. Why wasn't she picking up?

He tapped out a quick text.

The message was marked 'delivered'. He waited for it to show as 'read'.

Nothing happened.

Del's unease transformed into a sharper concern as the minutes ticked by and Aja's status remained unchanged. The stubborn digital word 'delivered' on his screen felt like a taunt, a reminder of his helplessness. Del fought the urge to call again, not wanting to seem desperate, but the anxiety was gnawing at him.

He called again.

No answer.

He hung up before the voicemail prompt ended.

He tried to distract himself by sorting through the possible reasons for the flats.

It was almost as if someone wanted to delay him.

With a sigh that carried all of his pent-up frustration, Del leaned back against the headrest, running a hand over his head. He couldn't shake the worry for Aja or the feeling of being watched. He scanned the perimeter of the parking lot again. Something was going on, his gut warned him. Aja should have answered or called him back by now.

Del slammed his fist against the steering wheel. He couldn't just sit there and wait for help.

He decided to call his aunt. She'd be in bed already, he knew, but he was desperate.

She answered on the first ring. "You back in town I heard and you just now callin' me?" she asked in greeting.

"Auntie, this is a quick trip, I got in earlier today. But I need a favor. Can you come get me? I'm near Bridgetown at Barry's. My rental has a flat," he didn't want to go into full detail over the phone. She'd have a ton of questions before she left the house.

Del heard his aunt shifting in the old creaky recliner she loved.

"I'll get your cousin to come. Not like he's got a job to go to," she muttered. "Rashad! Rashad!"

Del pulled his earbud out, muffling his aunt's bellows.

She told him to hold on and he heard shuffling and more muted yelling.

Rubbing his beard, he sighed. Maybe he should have tried the bus.

"Rashad's coming," His aunt was back on the line, huffing like she was out of breath. "You said Barry's, right? Over off Beckles?"

He nodded. "Yep, that's it. I need a ride back to the studio."

"You all find a buyer for it yet?" His aunt asked. "That why you here?"

"No, I'll tell you about it later, Auntie. It's a long story."

"Too busy for your family, I know," she grunted. "When you bringing your new lady friend by so I can meet her?"

"Soon, I promise. Is Rashad on his way? It's urgent."

"He just grabbed my keys, he's on the way," she said. "You tell him to come straight back in my car when he's done."

"Yes, ma'am," Del stifled a chuckle. His cousin was only three years younger than him yet his aunt acted like they were still teens.

"Alright then. You sit tight. And Del? Be safe," his aunt's voice softened with a maternal concern that made Del's chest tighten.

"Thanks, Auntie. I'll be fine," he reassured her, but as he disconnected the call, he wasn't sure he believed his own words.

The minutes stretched out, each one making Del more aware of the humid night air pressing down on him. He checked his phone again, praying for a response from Aja. But the screen remained blank. Leaning forward, he rested his forehead on the steering wheel, trying to focus on anything but the fear clawing at him. If anything happened to Aja-he stopped. He couldn't think like that. She was resourceful and smart.

He texted her again and stared at the phone, willing her to respond.

Finally, Rashad pulled up in his aunt's catering minivan,

honking loudly. Del grabbed the food, locked up the crippled rental, and jogged over to meet his cousin.

Rashad was tall with a broad chest and arms that hinted at years of manual labor. His hair, worn in short, neat locs, framed a deep brown face dominated by sharp cheekbones and expressive dark eyes.

"Yo, D!" Rashad shouted as he leaned over to push open the van's passenger door. "What happened, man? All your tires flat?" He swiveled his head, scanning the rental car. "Big Man, who you piss off?"

Del shook his head as he climbed inside, the smell of grease and spices from countless delivered meals lingering in the vehicle. "No idea," he said, but realized that wasn't entirely true. The person they were here to track might want to sabotage their efforts. But that wasn't possible, was it? Malik wasn't scheduled to arrive on the island until the next day.

Rashad rubbed his chin as he continued to stare at the rental. "That's usually a woman's MO...Ma says you got a new chick, what'd you do to her?"

"Why are you assuming I did something?" Del regarded his cousin. They hadn't been close growing up, even though they were close in age. Del always had the sense that Rashad resented Del's close relationship with Aunt Felicity, and maybe even the occasional favoritism she showed him. But tonight, Del couldn't afford to think about old family dynamics.

"Cause you're the one with the flat tires," Rashad shot back.

Rashad pulled out of the lot and onto the road back toward Holetown.

"That leads me to conclude that you pissed somebody off," Rashad said. "You ain't gotta be Columbo to figure that out."

"Columbo?" Del let out a snort. "Man, how old are you? Anyway, it's not Aja. I was picking up dinner for her when I came out to find the tires like that."

"Shit, I loved that show," Rashad grinned at him.

Del couldn't suppress a smile, despite the gnawing tension in his gut. He stared out the window. "I think those flat tires have something to do with a case Aja is working on," Del said, turning back to his cousin. "She's investigating a man that may be catfishing women here on the island."

Rashad glanced over at him, eyebrow raised. "What, so you all are like Columbo now?" He chuckled but soon realized Del wasn't joining in. "Oh shit, you're serious."

"Yeah, I'm serious," Del confirmed, his voice low. What if Malik was behind this? That meant Aja was in danger.

Del had to do something. He pulled his phone out. Jewel might be able to confirm that Malik was in town but he didn't have her number.

He let his head roll back against the seat. How could he get in touch with Jewel? Running a hand over his head, he pondered his options.

London! They'd exchanged numbers while they'd been stranded at the Miami airport. He scrolled to find her and initiated a call.

"Hey London, it's Del. You heard from Aja lately?" He kept his tone casual, not wanting to worry her just yet.

"Umm, not since she texted saying y'all landed. Why? Did you lose her?"

Technically she wasn't lost. "No, I was just curious. Hey, can you send me Jewel's number?"

"Yep, I'll send it in a sec," London said. "You sure everything's okay?"

"Yeah, yeah, everything's fine, just tying up some loose ends," Del said, hoping he sounded more confident than he felt. "Thanks, London."

"I hear you. Be careful," London advised before hanging up.

Rashad glanced at him again, his eyes narrowing as he navigated the darkened streets. "Man, you never could lie worth a damn," Rashad said with a chuckle. "But don't worry, we're family. If this is some big deal thing, I got your back."

Del managed a half-hearted smile in response, grateful for the support but preoccupied with the weight of the situation.

Praying she'd pick up, Del called Jewel.

Jewel's voicemail came on immediately and Del's stomach dropped.

The voicemail beep sounded like a marker of doom in the silence of the van. Del clenched his jaw, forcing himself to speak with a calm he didn't feel. Now he knew something was wrong. "Jewel, it's Del. Call me back as soon as you get this, no matter how late."

He ended the call, sliding the phone into his pocket and staring out into the night. The road seemed endless, each stretch more deserted than the last.

They reached a stop sign and Rashad put the minivan in park, facing him. "What's going on?"

Del gave his cousin a quick rundown of Aja's case and his fears that Malik had turned the tables on them, squashing the element of surprise they'd planned for him.

Rashad resumed driving. "You think this Malik dude is here already?" His tone was serious now, all traces of the smirk gone.

Del shrugged half-heartedly. "I don't know. But it feels like someone's playing chess and we're just pieces."

The van slid through the warm night, town lights flickering past as Rashad wove through Holetown's quiet streets toward the art studio. It had been a place of creativity and solace for Diana, but now it loomed in Del's mind as a potential crime scene.

About a block away from the studio, Del turned to Rashad. "Pull over here and let me out. I don't know what I'm gonna find but I don't want the car lights giving us away."

"Shit, I'm not letting you go in by yourself, Ma would kill me if something happened to her favorite nephew," Rashad sighed then pulled the minivan into an empty lot.

Nodding, Del was out of the van before Rashad cut the engine. He rushed around the corner to the studio, not waiting for his cousin.

"Del!" Rashad hissed. "Can we come up with a plan before we just rush in?"

Del paused, catching his breath and trying to calm his racing heart. Rashad was right, they needed a plan. But all Del could think about was getting to Aja and making sure she was safe.

"Okay, okay," Del said, rubbing his temples in frustration. "We need to figure out if Malik is already here. I don't want to walk into a trap."

Rashad leaned against the van, running a hand over his head as he thought.

Del pulled out his phone and dialed Jewel's number once more.

Once again, straight to voicemail.

Del wanted to slam the phone to the ground. He called Aja's number again.

No answer. He sent up a quick prayer. Please let her be safe.

Rashad's voice cut through the tension. "How about I go around back and you go in from the front? We'll have both exits covered."

Del nodded, the idea sound enough in theory but he scowled at the thought of splitting up. "Stay on your phone. If anything seems off, we call the police immediately," Del commanded, his tone leaving no room for argument.

Rashad agreed with a somber nod. "You got it, D."

They split up, Rashad disappearing into the shadows as Del approached the front entry of the art studio with caution.

The first thing Del saw was that all the lights in the studio were on.

And what was left of the glass door was wide open.

He approached with caution, his head swiveling to make sure no one could sneak up on him.

As he got closer to the entrance, he could see the door had been breached by a large rock. Tiny shards of glass glittered on the hardwood floor of the studio.

His pulse raced as he glanced beyond the studio floor.

There was a large box on the counter and half wrapped glass pieces next to it.

Someone had been in the process of wrapping the pieces and boxing them up.

He stepped into the studio, careful not to touch anything or step on the glass shards.

The space was deserted, he could tell.

But it was the silence that was most unnerving; a heavy, expectant silence, as if the air itself were holding its breath.

He moved forward, each step deliberate as he scanned for any sign of Aja or an intruder. His heart thundered in his chest, each beat echoing like a drum in his ears.

He reached for his phone again, punching in Rashad's number with hands that trembled slightly despite his best efforts. "Anything?" he whispered, not wanting to disturb the eerie silence that enveloped him.

"Nothing out here," Rashad's voice came back low and tense. "All quiet—too quiet."

Del hurried to the back door and motioned his cousin inside. "She's gone but something went down."

They cautiously made their way back to the front of the store.

"Looks like somebody threw a rock in here to break the glass then let themselves in," Rashad looked around. "They didn't trash the place," he bent down, peering at the floor. "But there's blood over here."

Del

Blood.

Del's own blood chilled and his pulse raced. What had happened while he was gone? Where was Aja?

He rushed around the studio, checking the workspace first and sticking his head in the office. He knew there was no one in the space but Rashad and him. Approaching the front of the studio with dread, he had to know.

"How much blood?" He forced himself to sound calm.

Rashad looked up, his face a mix of worry and concentration. "Enough to know there's been trouble, but not enough to think the worst, not yet." He pointed to the smeared tracks leading out the door. "Lots of footprints so she wasn't alone," he added. "And there's a broken glass sculpture over here with blood on it."

Del nodded, his mind racing as he tried to piece together the scant evidence before them. A small print with the words "Beautiful Day" in script lay on the ground. As much as he wanted to examine everything, Del had seen enough police procedurals to know they shouldn't touch anything.

His heart was pounding a vicious rhythm against his ribs, each beat screaming Aja's name. This was all his fault. He shouldn't have left her alone. He should have insisted she take a break and come with him to the restaurant. He ran a shaky hand over his beard. If anything happened to her, Del would never forgive himself.

He straightened his spine and looked around, avoiding the blood pool near the front door. The steady red camera light he'd installed earlier caught his eye. "Let's check the security footage. Maybe it caught something that can help us figure out what the hell happened here."

Rashad nodded and they made their way to the small office tucked in the back where Aja's laptop was set up. Del fumbled with the mouse, pulling up the video feed. They both leaned forward, eyes glued to the grainy images as they started to rewind through the recent footage.

The first image captured was of a man in his early to mid-forties dressed in black from head to toe peering around the shop, a gun in hand. Del frowned, peering closer. He'd seen that distinctive gait before but where? As he studied the face, Del knew he was indeed the man in Diana's sketch. Malik. He ran a hand over his face, trying not to explode. How had he gotten in? How had he known they were laying a trap for him?

Malik moved stealthily, making his way to the Jardin collection and they watched as he nodded his head while he picked up the pieces, like he was confirming he had the right set. He wore gloves, Del noted, so dusting for fingerprints wouldn't help. But the camera footage should suffice. Del squinted at the screen as Malik placed the piece he was holding, a glass replica of a single hibiscus flower, back on the counter abruptly then picked up a cell phone. Malik glanced to his left then right and slipped the phone into his pocket.

"He took Aja's phone," Del said aloud, leaning back. "I saw that phone sitting there earlier and I meant to give it to her when we left to eat but I got impatient."

Rashad shrugged. "You couldn't have known this fool would break in right after you left. Didn't you say you thought he was coming in tomorrow?"

"Yeah, we figured he was going to try and steal the pieces once he got to town...that's why we were setting up security cameras tonight. Son of a bitch got the jump on us," Del frowned, rubbing his tired eyes. "What happened? Where did he go?"

Del had taken his eyes off the screen for only a second but now the footage showed an empty room.

"You said you left Aja in the office, right?" Rashad stroked his chin.

"Yeah, she was in here when I left, working on her laptop." He pointed at the chair Rashad occupied. "Sitting there."

"You got cameras in here?" Rashad looked around the small office.

"No, we didn't put any in here. Aja was debating on it but decided not to." Del said with regret in his voice.

"I'm thinking he probably heard her in here and confronted her."

Nodding, Del rose from his seat. "Yeah, makes sense...then I saw that someone had been wrapping the pieces out there," he said more to himself. He motioned toward the laptop. "Fast forward some. They had to go back to the front to wrap up the sculptures."

"How did I get to be in charge of the footage? Like I'm your assistant," Rashad muttered.

A noise at the front drew Del's attention. Footsteps crushing glass. His head swung, looking for a weapon.

Rashad held a finger to his lips, signaling silence. Del nodded, both men listening intently as the footsteps grew louder. Each crunch of glass echoed through the otherwise quiet studio. He couldn't explain how he knew, but he could imagine Aja in this exact same position before Malik appeared, pointing his gun at her.

The thought of Malik hurting her, even implying that he would hurt her, had him seeing red. The fierce need to protect what was his, and he'd finally come to terms with the fact that he was hers and she was his, gripped him like a vise.

Seconds stretched like taffy as they waited for the intruder to reveal themselves. Del could feel the tension building in his shoulders, his instincts telling him to charge, but his mind urging caution. Finally, the figure stepped into view.

~

Jewel Forrester stood in the doorway, wringing her hands together.

"Hey, Del," she said quietly.

"Jewel! What happened here?" Del's eyes narrowed as he took in Jewel's disheveled appearance. Her sundress was wrinkled and there was a wildness in her eyes that spoke of panic and fear.

She sat gingerly in the seat across from the desk. "Malik showed up at my door earlier today, and we went to dinner. He kept asking me all these questions about the studio and then he left for a couple of hours," she exhaled.

She chewed on her lip, her eyes downcast.

Del waited for her to continue, sensing she was about to confess something he wouldn't like.

She took another deep breath, her eyes darting away from Del's intense gaze. "I thought he was into me, you know? He took me to dinner and I had a couple of glasses of wine." She looked away. "I think he put something in my drink."

Del shook his head, swearing. "Jewel, why didn't you call Aja the minute you suspected something?"

Rage boiled in Del's veins, but he fought it down. He needed to hear what Jewel had to say.

"I thought I could handle it. I didn't realize until it was too late." Her eyes filled with tears she quickly wiped away. "When I woke up, I was handcuffed to my bed and Malik was gone. I keep a gun in my nightstand and when I checked, that was gone too."

Del's jaw clenched, his mind racing with the implications of Jewel's story. "How did you get here?" he managed to ask, struggling to keep his voice calm and steady.

"One of my friends from the U.S., Nikki Compton, came to the house. She knows where I keep my spare key because she and her husband stayed at my house before. She was here to confront me about sleeping with her husband...turns out Malik's name is really Everett Compton and he's married to one of my best friends."

Del frowned, holding up a hand. "Wait a minute...that name, Nikki, sounds familiar. Aja might have mentioned something," he said, trying to coax the details from his memory.

"Yeah," Jewel nodded, "Nikki told me she wanted to get her husband checked out and I gave her Aja's contact info."

Malik was Nikki's husband?

He had a dozen questions, but Jewel continued before he could gather his thoughts.

"Nikki finds me handcuffed to the bed and I told her everything I knew. I swore to her I had no idea her husband was the man I'd met online."

Jewel's voice broke on the last sentence, as tears streamed down her face. Del reached out, his hand instinctively going to her shoulder in a gesture meant to be comforting. "Did he target you because you knew his wife?"

She nodded. "We talked, after she got me out of the handcuffs, and we think he might have gone through my files and computer while they were staying in my house. I knew I was going to be traveling so I gave them the use of my house for their honeymoon as a wedding gift."

Del crossed his arms, trying to piece together this chaotic puzzle. "Okay, let's straighten this out. You're saying the man we know as Malik is actually Everett Compton, Nikki's husband, and he's been catfishing you?"

Jewel nodded, her eyes wide and her voice barely above a whisper. "Yes. And when I told Nikki that he was probably planning to break into Aja's studio, she told me to stay put and call the police if I didn't hear from her by a certain time. So that's what I did."

"And Nikki," Del asked. "Where is she now?"

"I don't know," Jewel admitted, her voice shaking. "She said she would handle Everett, that she needed to confront him—but that was hours ago."

A moment of heavy silence hung between them, Del digesting the twist of events. Then, the tension was broken by the buzzing of his cell phone in his pocket.

Del glanced at the screen. Unknown Number.

"Is that her?" Jewel asked anxiously, following Del's gaze to the phone.

Del held up a finger and answered the phone. "Del Parris."

A gruff voice responded, "Mr. Parris, this is Inspector Ramsey. We need you to come to Saint James station immediately. It concerns Everett Compton and Aja Lewis."

CHAPTER 27

Aja

"Everett Harvey Compton! What the fuck is going on?" A female voice called out.

She knew that voice. Aja, crouched down so she could examine her duct tape work, raised her head at the sound of the feminine voice. She frowned. She knew she'd heard the woman recently.

Her mind scanned her recent interactions, clicking when it came to a match. She'd spoken to the woman on the phone but she hadn't seen her face-to-face until now.

"Mrs. Compton?" Aja scrambled to her feet, putting weight on her trembling legs.

Nikki Compton, Jewel's friend and Aja's newest client, stood with her arms fisted on slender hips, waiting for an answer.

She looked to be in her early forties, average height and build, with light brown eyes narrowed at the man on the floor. She wore a sleek black hoodie and matching joggers. If Aja didn't know better, she'd think the woman was on her way to the gym.

Judging by appearances, Aja assumed Malik was younger than Nikki, maybe in his late thirties.

Aja dusted shards of glass from her clothing. "This is your husband, Everett Compton?" Aja asked, incredulous.

Nikki turned toward Aja then, seeming to realize what she'd done and where she was. "You're Aja Lewis...we talked on the phone," Nikki glanced around at the door she'd just broken into, "Shit...sorry about the door. I'll replace it...but yeah, this is the man I hired you to investigate."

She made a face as she glanced at Everett. "Is he dead?"

As if on cue, Everett moaned in response.

Curious, Aja asked, "How did you know he was here? I didn't expect him until tomorrow."

"I had no idea if it would work but," Nikki smirked, "I put one of those luggage tracking devices in his wallet."

Aja nodded, impressed.

"Wait, you were tracking me?" Everett slurred, raising his head. Then he held up his bound hands. "Nik, I can explain, but I'm hurt, need medical attention-"

Abruptly, Nikki ran over to the gun and grabbed it, aiming at Everett's forehead. "You're damn right you're going to explain," she snapped. "You're supposed to be in New York."

Everett's mouth opened but nothing came out.

Aja turned to his wife, her hands held up in surrender. "Okay, everyone stay calm."

"I'm perfectly calm." Nikki cut in. "I need my husband to start talking or I start shooting."

When it was clear Everett had nothing more to say, Aja glared at him then broke in. "Nikki, this is, was, my mother's studio. She created all of the glass pieces in this store and your husband here was catfishing her so that he could steal her artwork," Aja's eyes slid to Malik, or Everett, who looked like he'd rather be anywhere else. "And," she continued, "he was catfishing your friend Jewel as well."

Everett scowled, not meeting Nikki's eyes. "It's...not like that."

Nikki, keeping the gun pointed at him, turned toward Aja. "I knew he was too good to be true. You okay?" she asked.

"Why are you asking her if she's okay? I'm the one bleeding over here! That bitch assaulted me," he whined.

Nikki's gaze snapped back to Malik, her eyes aflame. "Assaulted...right," she said with a snort. "You're lucky she didn't do worse."

Aja kept her eyes on the gun in Nikki's hand. "I'm fine, just a little shaken up," Aja admitted, her voice wobbling more than she liked. She straightened up. "I would love to know what's going on though."

"Well, Everett told me he needed to go meet with a client in New York for a couple of days, which I'm guessing he chose because he knew I wouldn't want to go...too cold for me this time of year," Nikki waved the gun like it was a child's toy and Aja winced.

"But he was acting a little too squirrely and talking a little too much, telling me he was going to have drinks with his boss and hopefully get a promotion," Another wave of the gun. "And I was stupid enough to fall for his bullshit."

Aja kept her eyes on the other woman, extending her hand, palm up. "Nikki, please hand me the gun."

Nikki's eyes slid toward Aja, then back to Everett. Her grip on the gun tightened momentarily. "Sorry, yeah, you better take this," she slowly lowered it and handed it over.

Aja sighed in relief, carefully placing the gun in a drawer beneath the point of sale terminal. "Thank you," she said, her voice steadier now.

"Anyway, where was I? Oh yes," her voice took on a cadence as if she were unraveling a mystery for Aja alone. "He left for his trip two days earlier than he initially mentioned. Said there'd been a change of plans and he had to prep for that big meeting with his boss. But something told me to dig a little deeper, check things out, right? I look in his suitcase and what did I see? Linen pants and tee shirts, sunscreen...he's very into his skin, you know. He spends more on facial products than I do and I'm older than him."

Aja gave Everett a sidelong glance, taking in the freshly cut hair and neatly trimmed beard. She had to admit, the man did have incredibly smooth cocoa skin.

"Yeah, clearly not packing for typical New York winter weather. I check his email and, boom! Emails from my friend Jewel saying she can't wait to see 'Malik' and a round trip ticket to Bridgetown."

Nikki's eyes narrowed at Everett. "I was coming here to catch them in the act but Jewel had no idea the man she knew as Malik was my husband."

Surprised, Aja pursed her lips. "She didn't attend your wedding? She hadn't met Everett?"

Nikki shook her head. "No, she wasn't able to come to my wedding. I hadn't seen Jewel in forever...well, since she moved here a few years ago. She'd never met him. And she doesn't really do social media. I'm willing to bet she didn't see any of my wedding posts."

"But you stayed at her house for your honeymoon here?" Aja asked.

"Yep, she was on that cruise so she offered her place as a wedding gift," she sighed and Aja heard the wistfulness in that exhale. "It was perfect."

She stepped closer to Everett. "And less than a year later, here I am, back in Barbados to watch my new husband get carted off to jail."

"Nik, baby," Everett began to protest, but Nikki cut him off with a look cold enough to freeze the waves outside hitting the shore. "Shut up, Everett. The only talking I want from you is in front of a lawyer."

"You called the police?" Aja asked, her voice still shaky from the confrontation.

"I didn't," Nikki said, not taking her eyes off Everett. "I told Jewel to give me thirty minutes and then call them so I'd have enough time to find him. I was livid...ready to lay hands on him but he's not worth jail time."

The reality of his situation seemed to hit Everett then and he shook his head slowly, wincing. "Shit, Nikki! I can't go to jail," he flexed his arms, pushing at his restraints. "Baby, please," he lowered his voice. "Nik! Don't do me like this...I did this all for you, for us." Everett writhed on the floor, trying to free himself from the tape as Aja watched.

Aja heard the sound of distant sirens beginning to filter through the evening air. With a jolt, she realized Del still hadn't returned. She had no idea where he was or if he was still stranded at the restaurant. Her heart stuttered. What if he was in trouble? Out of habit, she started to grab her tote, where she normally kept her phone and stopped short when she remembered that Everett had destroyed her phone.

Before she could ask Nikki for hers, the Bajan police swarmed in, guns cocked, shouting orders. The police officers quickly surrounded the group, their guns trained on Everett and Aja. Aja slowly raised her hands. Nikki stepped forward, holding up her hands in surrender as well.

"Officers, this man assaulted my friend. I have a witness who can attest to that," she said calmly.

"That's not true! She attacked me first!" Everett protested, gesturing at Aja.

One of the officers motioned for two others to come forward and remove the duct tape from his wrists and ankles. They then handcuffed Everett. "All of you are coming with us. We'll sort this out at the station," he said firmly.

Despite his pleas of innocence, Everett was led outside to a waiting patrol car.

A slender female officer approached Aja. "Are you Miss Lewis?" Aja nodded.

"And you are in charge of this property?

"Yes," Aja confirmed. "This was my mother's studio. She passed recently and I'm the sole heir."

The officer regarded Aja then said in a firm voice, "I need you to come with us too. For your statement and for your own protection."

The woman's voice was soft with that melodic Bajan cadence Aja heard around the island that she'd come to love but she could tell by her clenched jaw that the officer meant business.

"Of course," Aja replied. "Do you mind if I call my..." her voice trailed off. She supposed Del was her boyfriend now, but "my boyfriend" sounded so juvenile. When was the last time she'd uttered that phrase?

"Partner?" She finished and winced. That somehow sounded worse to her ears.

The officer nodded brusquely. "You can call them from the station once we're done."

Aja exhaled, taking in the chaos of the studio: shattered door and broken glass, Everett's blood on the hardwood floors, the sculpture she'd used to disarm him now in fractured pieces. She would call Del as soon as she could, let him know she was okay and that they'd done what they set out to do.

As they were ushered into separate police cars, Aja struggled to process the chain of events. Her two cases had converged into one, with Everett Compton at the center.

She recalled that when she'd met her, she'd assured Jewel and Nezzie that she could look into the case and figure out what was going on with Jewel's new man quickly. Aja sat in the back of the police vehicle, her head spinning. She couldn't believe how rapidly things had escalated. What had started as a simple investigation into a man Jewel met online had turned into a dangerous encounter where she'd been held at gunpoint. But despite the chaos, Aja couldn't deny a sense of satisfaction. They had successfully exposed Everett's crimes and preserved her mother's artwork. Now Everett would face the consequences of his actions. And even though she was still shaken by the events, Aja was grateful for Del's support throughout it all.

Aja marveled at all the changes in her life since she'd first met Del a few weeks ago. She'd been adamant about not wanting anything to do with her mother or her estate and now she was thinking she should reconsider selling her mother's assets. She'd come to Barbados seeking closure for her mother's death, but instead she had found danger, adventure, and she'd fallen in love with the country. And most importantly, she'd fallen in love with Del.

The more she'd gotten to know Del, who'd been cheering her on each step of the way, the more she worked with him, the more she knew she wanted him by her side. They made a good team. Her heart pounded at the thought of Del arriving back at the studio to find her gone. She was worried about him. What if he was stranded somewhere? What if something happened to him? She needed to hear his voice and make sure he was okay. She couldn't wait to see him again, tell him everything that had happened.

When they arrived at the station, she was led into a room that smelled faintly of stale coffee and sweat. The walls bore witness to countless interrogations, their off-white paint job long overdue for a refresh. Aja sat down at the metal table bolted to the floor, hands folded in front of her, trying to project an image of calm she didn't feel.

The door opened, revealing a stoic officer with his hat tucked under his arm. "Miss Lewis," he said in a tone that suggested he was about to do something he didn't enjoy. "I'm Inspector Ramsey. I'll be taking your statement."

Later that night, as they finally settled into their luxurious suite at Sapphire Cove, Aja allowed herself to relax and sink into the soft cushions of the sofa. She could still feel the rush of adrenaline from earlier, and she couldn't calm her mind from all the what ifs running through her head.

Del had ordered a fruit and cheese tray, insisting she eat

something, but Aja could do nothing more than push the fruit around her plate.

She glanced at Del, who was standing by the window, his silhouette framed by the moonlight, watching her with worry in his eyes.

"Hey," he said softly, settling in beside her. "You sure you're alright?"

Aja nodded, though it felt like a lie. "I will be," she said, attempting a smile.

He ran his hands over his face before locking eyes with hers. "Seeing that footage of Malik, or Everett, whatever his name is, in the shop...knowing he was right there with you. It got to me." Del paused then exhaled like he needed to collect his thoughts. "And then rushing to the station, not sure what I'd find when I got there. I needed to see for myself that you were okay, that nothing had happened to you."

He took her hand in his and let out another deep breath. "I shouldn't have left you alone."

Aja put her other hand over his. "Del, I was scared, sure. But I also knew that he wasn't going to get away. We got him. Nikki and Jewel know the truth and whatever they do with that is up to them, but we exposed Everett for the crook he is."

Del squeezed her hand, a half-smile playing at the edges of his lips. "You did more than that, Aja. You were brave. You cracked both of your cases and now Everett will have to pay for what he's done."

"Oh, I didn't tell you," Aja sat up. "Everett is apparently wanted for embezzling money from his ex-wife's company as well. He's going away for a long time. I doubt he'll be able to keep up his fancy skin regimen in prison."

When Del raised a puzzled brow at her, Aja relayed what Nikki said about Everett's flawless skin.

Del frowned.

"What's wrong?" Aja asked.

"That's where I saw him." Del shook a finger at her. "He was lurking near Diana's studio that first day we visited. And now that I think about it, when you rushed out, I'm pretty sure I didn't lock the studio. He could have slipped in then and figured out a way to break in."

Aja's eyes widened as the pieces clicked into place. "Everett had been watching us from the beginning," she said, raising a hand to her mouth. "I'm glad he's in custody."

Del pulled her into his arms. "Yep. All thanks to you."

"We make a good team, you know?" She murmured against his chest.

"We do," he agreed, kissing the top of her head.

Aja closed her eyes, letting herself enjoy this moment. She could hear the ocean waves rolling in and Del's steady heartbeat aligned with her own.

"I've made some decisions," Aja said, opening her eyes and sitting up so she was facing Del. "I want to take the house off the market," she said softly. "I can use it as a vacation home. And I'll come here when I need to unplug."

Del leaned back, looking thoughtfully at Aja. "But you still want to sell the studio, right?"

"I do. For a moment, when we drove up and I saw the For Sale sign in the window, I considered keeping it as well, but I know nothing about glass blowing," she said as she examined her hands, tried to still the slight tremor in them. "and I don't know if I can erase the memory of what happened. There aren't any good memories in the studio for me."

Del's thumb rubbed her palm and she knew he understood the weight of her decision. "Makes sense. The house can be your sanctuary, your place to recharge. Plus if you ever decide to learn glass blowing, you can find another studio, one without the emotional baggage."

"Exactly." Aja sat up and took a forkful of pineapple. Speaking her decision out loud lifted a huge weight off her shoulders she hadn't realized she'd been carrying.

Aja bit into the pineapple. "It's time to create new memories," she said, savoring the sentiment as much as the fruit.

She held a chunk of pineapple to his lips. "Try this. It's maybe the sweetest pineapple I've ever had."

"That's supposed to be my thing, feeding people," he said in mock protest between bites.

Aja smiled. "Well, consider this a role reversal. Tonight, I take care of you."

Her eyes darkened as she said this.

"I'm all yours," he said, using the tip of his tongue to lick the pineapple juice from her bottom lip.

Epilogue

THREE MONTHS LATER

Aja strode into the conference room at Exposé, feeling confident as all get out in her new red bottoms and a cherry red power suit.

Her leadership team sat around the small functional conference table, looking expectantly at her. The air buzzed with energy and anticipation. The women had worked hard, putting in late nights and early mornings to keep on top of the new clients and projects coming in from every direction.

Aja cleared her throat, bringing the room to a respectful silence. "Good morning, everyone." She nodded at each woman in the room and felt a surge of almost overwhelming love for her team. They had shown her time and time again that they had her back; now it was her turn to show them her appreciation.

"We have a lot to celebrate," Aja continued, using her clicker to start the presentation streaming from her laptop. "But before we dive into the numbers, I want to take a moment to reflect on what we've accomplished."

She clicked to the next slide. "We have had double digit growth for the past two years but this year we did exceptionally well, despite my being out of the office for nearly a month and I appreciate you all stepping up while I was gone."

"You needed the time off," Zaria said, shrugging, "and if I'm being honest, you were practically glowing when you came back. I guess the island sun was good for you," she had a knowing smirk on her face and Aja knew she was about to say something wildly inappropriate. "Or maybe it was a certain smooth talking Bajan."

Aja breathed a small sigh of relief as the other women laughed, effectively diverting the attention from her.

"Alright, alright," Aja said, waving her hands to get everyone back on track. "Yes, the sun was fantastic, and the company..." She let her words trail off with a shy shrug. "But let's focus on why we're really glowing—our incredible performance this past fiscal year."

She clicked through the slides, showcasing the impressive graphics that depicted their growth: hiring more full-time help, upticks in client engagement and referral business and finally, the revenue charts that had everyone in the room nodding with satisfaction.

"As much as this is about numbers," Aja turned from the screen to face each woman directly, "it's really about the people behind them. You are the heart and soul of Exposé. Without your dedication and creativity, none of this would be possible."

She paused, letting her gaze linger on each of them with pride. "In recognition of our success and your hard work, I have a couple of surprises for you."

Murmurs of curiosity filled the room as Aja clicked to the next slide, revealing a photo of a luxurious beach resort and a frozen drink properly topped with a beach umbrella and cherry.

"We're going on our first corporate retreat," she announced with a flourish. "I fell in love with Barbados and made plenty of contacts there. I've decided we will go for a week, all expenses paid, for fun, sun and a teeny, tiny bit of work," she held her thumb and index finger up for emphasis, "to keep the IRS happy."

"Oh, a whole week? That's amazing!" Lavender said, rubbing her hands together.

"Yes, and before we get into logistics and dates, please take these as a token of my gratitude for your hard work," she handed each woman a colorful greeting card sized envelope. "These are thank you cards and your bonus statements. The money should hit your bank accounts before the end of the day."

The room swelled with a collective gasp, followed by the rustle of envelopes being eagerly torn open. London was the first to get her envelope open. Her eyes widened as she scanned the contents of her bonus statement, and she let out a yelp. "Aja, this is...I mean...thank you!"

One after another, expressions of shock and delight painted the faces of her team as they processed the numbers before them. Zaria stared at the statement. "Well, shit, we need to get you laid more often," she cracked.

"Let's stay focused on the presentation." Aja rolled her eyes. Speaking of which, Del was due at her place later on. She and Del had managed to carve out a routine where they worked remotely together either at his house or her condo then wrapped the day with a home cooked meal—Del was in charge of cooking--and falling asleep wrapped in each other's arms.

Lavender stood up impulsively and wrapped Aja in an impromptu hug. "So. Fucking. Brilliant! You're the best boss ever," she exclaimed, and the sentiment was echoed around the room as one by one the other women joined in for a group embrace.

As they eventually settled back into their seats, chatter turned toward beachwear for the retreat, suggestions for team-building activities, and plans for sunbathing on the island's beaches.

Everyone's reactions warmed Aja's heart. She'd made strides in giving each of them more autonomy in how they ran their respective teams, a move that had initially frightened her. But with Del's guidance, she had learned to relinquish control, and it was paying off in ways she hadn't foreseen.

"We'll have some workshops and training sessions of course," Aja mentioned casually, reclaiming her seat at the head of the table. "And I'm also planning to have a memorial service for my mother there since we had to cancel due to the hurricane. But you all don't have to attend if you don't want to."

"I think we'd all like to be there," Lavender said gently, and the others nodded in agreement. "We want to support you."

Aja found her throat tightening at the sincere declaration. She nodded, blinking back tears before they could spill over her lashes. "Thank you," she cleared her throat, needing to get back to business. "We can do a catamaran cruise as well."

"Will there be booze on the boat? Cause I'm gonna need to sample all the rum I can in a week," Zaria said.

Aja grinned at her, thinking of the sunset cruise she'd done with Del. "Yes, I know of a perfect sunset booze cruise you're going to love."

"There's more," Aja interjected when there was a lull in the conversation. "We're building a dating platform so we can help our clients in their quest to find love."

The announcement hung in the air. London tilted her head, her brows knitting together in curiosity. "A dating platform? Isn't that counterintuitive to what we do?"

"Actually it isn't," Aja said. "But it's a natural extension of what we currently do—we are already vetting and screening people. This way, if you find out the person you've been seeing online isn't who they say, you can use our new app to find someone who has been cleared by us. Also, our app will be geared more toward professionals, not people looking for hookups."

Lavender, who had a penchant for technology and innovation, leaned forward, her eyes alight with possibilities. "We could incorporate AI to help with compatibility matching, and even use augmented reality so people can get a feel for their dates before they meet in person. This could be huge."

Zaria chuckled. "And maybe avoid some of those disastrous

first dates." Shared laughter rippled across the room, everyone recalling anecdotes of romantic encounters gone wrong.

Aja's phone sounded and she glanced down at the screen then attempted to hide her smile. Del. She'd take the call in her office. "Okay, you all have your bonuses and dates for the retreat. Please let me know who you're bringing as your plus one and we'll start getting tickets booked."

Zaria's head snapped up. "What? You would say this while I'm in between situationships," she crossed her arms. "I'm good and single right now."

"Don't worry, Zaria," Aja replied with a chuckle. "There'll be plenty of local charm to entertain you. Plus, you never know what can happen when you're away from home, relaxed and just enjoying life."

Zaria feigned a pout but the twinkle in her eye betrayed her excitement. "You did say Del's got a cousin, maybe I can get my groove back too."

Aja stood up, feeling a shift in the energy of the room—a mix of elation and anticipation. "Alright, team. Let's wrap this up for now. Please get back to me by Monday with your plus ones."

Aja had opted to do a luxury resort on the south side of the island in the St. Lawrence Gap area so everyone could take advantage of the nightlife nearby. She hadn't planned on going out but Zaria had talked her into it, dragging her and the rest of the women to a night club for a girls' night.

She was still feeling the effects the next morning as they sat on the beach in rented lounge chairs. Aja had dozed off when she felt a nudge. She turned to find London standing over her, a concerned look on her face. "Where are Del and Donovan? They've been gone for a while."

Aja sat up, resting on her elbows. When had she last seen Del? He'd gotten up and left a tray of fruit and juice on the table beside the bed then kissed her goodbye, but she hadn't heard from him since then.

"He left with Donovan? Where did they go?" She realized after the words slipped from her mouth that she'd just asked London the same question she'd already posed to Aja.

"He didn't tell me...just said they were going to 'bond' or something," London shrugged. "I was kind of out of it when Del knocked on our door. Remind me not to drink with Zaria again," she groaned.

"Yeah same. I forgot Zaria has the tolerance of a sailor." She looked around. The beach was bustling but not overcrowded.

Her grandmother, sunglasses and sun hat in tact, turned to them. "They went to the jewelry store on some street. I don't recall which one."

She went back to her book.

Aja frowned. "Why were they going to a jewelry store? And how do you know?"

Nezzie lowered her book, peering over the rim of her sunglasses with a knowing smile. "Oh, men don't just wander into jewelry stores for no reason, baby girl," she said cryptically. "Especially not when they're on vacation with their women."

A shiver of excitement tingled down Aja's spine, but she didn't want to get ahead of herself. Del could have a million reasons to visit a jewelry store that didn't involve her. Maybe he was getting a watch fixed?

"Maybe they're just browsing," London offered half-heartedly, though her expression mirrored the hope flickering in Aja's eyes. "They can't be buying what I think, right?"

Aja shook her head, trying to cast away budding thoughts of diamond rings and heartfelt proposals. "I seriously doubt Del is proposing so if they are, I'm sure he's there helping Donovan." She laid back. "Or we're about to get our hopes up for nothing and they're buying themselves jewelry."

"Nothing my foot," Nezzie muttered, turning back to her book. "You girls want to make a bet?"

"Umm...Nezzie, last time we bet you during what was supposed to be a friendly game of Uno, you took all the pennies we had. Ma'am, no thank you," London shook her head.

Nezzie's brow went up. "No faith in your man, huh?" She lowered her glasses, peering at Aja over the top of them. "What about you? Del could be buying you a ring."

Aja felt the weight of her grandmother's words settle in the air, as tangible as the salty breeze that wafted over the beach. She let out a laugh, a sound that was more anxious than amused. "Nezzie," she began, trying to maintain a level tone, "Del isn't proposing. We've only been together a few months. We're just enjoying the ride."

Nezzie smirked, a gleam in her eye that suggested she knew more than she was letting on. "Enjoying the ride can sometimes take you to unexpected destinations," she murmured before returning her focus to the novel in her hands.

London adjusted her sunglasses and turned to Aja. "You wouldn't say no though, would you? If he actually was...you know, getting a ring."

Aja's heart thudded in her chest as she considered London's question. "I...don't know," she said finally. "What about you? If Donovan got down on one knee tonight, what would you say?"

London fell silent, her gaze drifting out to the endless blue ocean. The question hung heavily in the air between them. "I would say yes. No hesitation." She turned to Aja, her eyes bright. "I actually believe in love again thanks to him."

Aja smiled at her cousin, touched by the sincerity in her voice. "That's wonderful, London. I love that for you."

London nodded, looking down as she brushed some invisible sand off her knee. "Thanks, Aja." She looked up again, regarding Aja with a serious expression.

"But It's scary, isn't it? To imagine your life changing like that. I mean, I've been through a lot of change the last couple of years. Some good, some not so much," London said. "But Donovan has been the best change. She grinned. "Yeah, if he asks, I'm all in."

Aja linked her fingers with London's. "Well you deserve all the happiness in the world and if you need a bridesmaid," she said, squeezing her cousin's hand. "You know where to find me."

London laughed, a soft, happy sound that blended with the seagulls shrieking above them. "Girl, please! I would have never met the man if it wasn't for you so you're my maid of honor, whether you like it or not."

They sat in silence for a few moments, each lost in their own thoughts until Nezzie's voice cut through their reverie.

"Well, if those boys are proposing today, they had better hurry up. We've got dinner reservations tonight and I refuse to be late because of youthful indecision," Nezzie said firmly, marking her place in her book with a finger.

Aja chuckled at Nezzie's practicality. "We'll make sure to remind them of your schedule if they pop up with rings," she joked, but the flutter in her stomach betrayed her lighthearted tone.

The sun climbed higher in the sky, casting a golden glow over the beach and warming Aja's skin. She closed her eyes again, though this time sleep eluded her.

London nudged her gently, breaking her train of thought. "Look," she whispered, pointing down the beach where two familiar figures were making their way back toward them.

Del and Donovan walked side by side, laughter reaching the women before the men did. Both held onto small bags, their contents a mystery that caused Aja's pulse to quicken. When Del caught sight of Aja, his smile broadened, eyes twinkling with a secret she desperately wanted to uncover. Donovan, too, seemed unusually chipper, brushing sand from his shorts as they approached.

"Hey, beautiful," Del greeted Aja as he bent down to kiss her forehead. The warmth from his lips lingered, sending a rush of heat through her. "Miss me?"

"Depends on what you were up to," Aja replied playfully, but her gaze was locked on the small bag in his hand.

London eyed Donovan with equal curiosity, crossing her arms over her chest. "What's with the secretive boys' trip?"

Del and Donovan exchanged a look, their smiles growing into matched grins that somehow filled Aja with simultaneous dread and excitement.

"It was nothing much," Donovan said casually, sitting beside London and pulling her close. "Just wanted to check out some of the local craftsmanship."

"Yeah," Del chimed in, taking a seat next to Aja. "What are we doing for dinner tonight? I'm starving."

"Nezzie says we've got reservations," Aja replied, her voice steady despite the thundering of her heart. She glanced at London, who seemed just as eager to maintain a nonchalant front, even though the suspense was killing them.

"Well then, we better get ready soon," Del said. He seemed to be avoiding any further conversation about their mysterious outing, and his eyes kept darting to the bag in his hand.

Aja decided to push a little. "You know you can't keep secrets from me for long," she teased, hoping her playful tone would coax more information out of him.

Del leaned in, his breath tickling her ear. "Who says it's a secret?" he whispered with a mischievous glint in his eye. "Maybe it's just a surprise."

Donovan chuckled at Del's response, clearly enjoying the situation. "Yeah, and surprises are best served at the right moment," he added cryptically.

~

THE END

Want to know who got down on one knee and proposed? Download the bonus epilogue using the link OR the QR code below:

Acknowledgments

I first visited Barbados during a cruise stop in the pre-pandemic days. I loved the vibe of the place, from the rum shops to the colorful houses and I knew I wanted to come back for a longer stay. We returned to Barbados in May 2023 and had a wonderful visit. Our hotel, The Club Barbados Resort & Spa, is in Hometown and where I based most of the scenes in Barbados.

The staff at the resort was warm and welcoming and I want to thank them for making our stay memorable.

During my research, I joined a few Facebook groups for travelers to the island and I met a wonderful woman in one of the groups. She tirelessly answered my questions about her home and we eventually met up while I was in Barbados. She's one of the few people I've encountered in my life where we just clicked immediately. Such a beautiful soul! Thank you, Pamela, for all your help!

I also want to thank my critique partners, Audrey and Arneida, for their support and encouragement. I look forward to our weekly meetups where were hash out plot ideas, cheer each other on and share bookish events.

Saving the best for last, my mother has been my biggest supporter and ride-or-die. She insists on paying for my books, but she reads them fast and points out any typos I may have missed.

I am so grateful for everyone that has helped me get this book in the hands of readers. Thank you!

Joi Jackson

Silver Santa

A single dad with a newly empty nest.

A strait-laced guidance counselor with one birthday wish.

This Christmas, a steamy second chance romance twenty years in the making is about to ignite.

Gia and Winston's friendship is tested when Gia discovers Dre, her one-night stand from Nashville, has moved to Kissing Springs. With both men vying for her heart, will Gia choose her best friend or take a chance with a younger man?

Lovie, a go-getter publicist, eyes a game-changing book tour for a social media sensation. Only snag? Saxon, owner of a bookstore/bourbon bar, won't endorse his ex-wife's juicy tell-all.

Tara, a driven 911 operator, has always kept her feelings for Levi, her older brother's best friend, hidden. But when a string of suspicious fires erupts across town, Tara finds herself working closely with Levi, the town's new arson inspector.

Levi is engaged, but haunted by doubts and growing feelings for Tara, the one woman he's supposed protect, not pursue. As the fires intensify and secrets come to light, Tara and Levi must navigate a web of deceit and danger, risking everything to expose the truth. In the end, they'll have to decide if they're willing to cross the line from friends to lovers.